HELLSPAWN AFTERMATH
BY
RICKY FLEET

OPTIMUS MAXIMUS
PUBLISHING

Hellspawn Aftermath
by Ricky Fleet

© 2020 Ricky Fleet
Published by Optimus Maximus Publishing, LLC in association with Dark Fleet Productions
Edited by Christina Hargis Smith
Cover art by Jeffrey Kosh Graphics

ISBN 13: 978-1-944732-50-9

DEDICATION

To my amazing wife, Carla, who faces down her troubles with the same grit and determination as any of the heroes in the Hellspawn world.

ACKNOWLEDGEMENT

To all of my readers, friends, family, thank you for your support. To the best beta reader team ever, thank you for all your hard work in helping me publish the best books possible.

CHAPTER 1

Jason Rechtman opened his eyes to stare up at the beautifully clear sky. Not one square inch of the serene, pale blue heavens were marred by clouds. Even the usual criss-cross pattern of aircraft trails was absent. *How lovely,* he mused. *I've got to show Clarissa and Sally.* Trying to move, he found it impossible. His body felt strange, awkward, so he lay still and returned his attention skyward. *I'll tell them shortly. Where are they, anyway? They must be in the pool.* It was their favourite place to spend time to get away from the heat of the Mauritian afternoon. *Perhaps I should join them?* A dip in the cool water would be just the remedy for his sluggishness. *What on earth was I drinking last night, anyway?* There was a local Mauritian rum that the bartender had recommended, he remembered that at least. Memories were foggy and disappeared as soon as he tried to focus on them. Whatever it was, it must have been bloody good. Ordinarily, the hangovers came with a splitting headache and sensitivity to light. This was something entirely different. He couldn't feel anything. At all. Couldn't hear anything either come to think of it. *I'll stick to lager tonight,* he promised himself. *Now get your ass up and in the pool. It'll do you the world of good.*

"Just as soon as I can get up from the sun lounger," he whispered.

Attempting to sit, he felt beyond weak. Tensed abdominals only managed to arch his back slightly before he gave up again with a frustrated snort. *Jesus, is this some kind of alcohol poisoning?* Guilt twisted in his stomach at the thought of his reckless behaviour wrecking their summer vacation. *I'll make it up to them.*

"Get up!" he muttered, gritting his teeth.

It was hopeless.

A mild tingling sensation started to creep into his toes. The slow advance of feeling rose through his calves and into the knees. Pins and needles followed, the imagined warmth giving way to the painful bite of cold. *Cold? How can that be?* A floodgate burst, sending the discomforting chill through his entire body. The preternatural silence which Jason had been unaware of until that point gave way to a piercing whine deep within his ears. Someone was messing with a dial as the shriek grew and ebbed, like a hellish case of tinnitus.

"What the heck?"

Judging a swift roll sideways onto the pool patio area would be an easier, though painful, first step, Jason rocked himself to the left. In place of the five-star resort hotel with their generous balconies, were the three floors of B wing. The glass on every cell window was either shattered completely, or exhibited a crazed spiderweb pattern. The comfortable lounger he lay upon was the frost hardened ground of the prison yard. The deafening whine in his ears changed to the deafening wails of the dying. Fighting the pain that was now coursing through his entire body, Jason rolled in the opposite direction. As the vast sky slowly passed and the true scene came into view, he wished he hadn't. What had once been soaring, solid, Victorian brick walls, was now a smoke tinged view of the fields beyond. Hunks of shattered masonry lay all around, a large chunk buried in the hard ground only a foot away from his head. Forcing himself to his knees, Jason saw the ragged depression where the tunnel had been. He also saw the bodies.

"Dear God."

More than a dozen inmates who were unlucky enough to be close to the blast were little more than unrecognisable slabs of bloodied meat. A dozen more were like Jason, battered and bruised, but alive. They cradled themselves on the ground, or stumbled around in shock. Pushing through the dust and smoke came more people. For a brief moment, the events of the past few weeks had been erased by the concussive blow. Coming close to standing up and running to their aid, the poor, injured souls forging through into the prison revealed themselves. Jason's mind reeled as the memory of the apocalypse flooded back in. To a man they were all in a state of advanced decay. The liquids of rot were frozen solid on their peeling skin. Catching sunlight, frost glittered on the mouldering carcasses. A young boy stepped forward, a single brick deeply buried in his frail chest. Jason's soul ached at the inhumanity. The others had all suffered damage from the explosion, but it was the child that tore at him. A twist of fate stole the small creature from his vision as it tumbled into the gaping hole.

Clarissa? Was she dead too? *No, Matt took her away.* It all started to come back. The Gypsies. The warnings. Hombre escaping. Then Matt. Handing over Craig and Mike. The ultimatum to find the fugitives on pain of death. It looked like the Hamptons had chosen to do the deed themselves and cut out the middle man. Permanently.

"Rechtman, help me!" begged a voice.

Turning, Jason found Eddie Banks splayed out on the ground. Both legs were horribly shattered. The offending projectile of brickwork was sitting close by, a scrap of torn prison trousers caught on the mortar. Eddie's mocking laughter rang out in Jason's mind. The way he had urged Keeping on when the bastard regaled with tales of debauchery carried out on Jason's wife. Moving towards the crippled man, Jason took hold of the imploring arms.

"Thank you! Thank you so... Ouch! That fucking hurts!"

Pulling on the limbs, Jason began dragging Eddie across the frigid, frost rimed grass.

"Wait! What're you doing?"

Jason ignored the question and carried on shuffling backwards, inch by inch, step by step.

"Stop! Please!" Eddie begged.

Staring at the terrified face, Jason smiled.

"You can't do this!"

Hearing the vile sounds of tearing skin close by, Jason released his grip. Eddie tried desperately to cling on, but with a final yank, Jason pulled his hands clear and stepped away.

"Enjoy," he said, to the undead as well as the brutal prisoner who was now crying like a baby.

The freshly dead of the prison were already surrounded, their tenderised flesh disappearing into eager, festering mouths. Rotten peg teeth tore and ravaged the unfeeling meat. Hands dug deeply into torso cavities, pulling out the choice organs within. A group of zombies competing unsuccessfully for the dwindling food broke away at the sounds of snivelling. Horrified by his own actions, Jason still held Eddie's frantically pleading gaze as they fell on him. *Justice, at last,* he thought as sharp fingers peeled the face from Eddie's screaming skull. Spared from the further dismemberment by the crush of corpses, Jason turned away.

"You're a fucking nutter!" cried another prisoner as he staggered past, giving the zombie feeder a wide berth. All colour drained from the man's face as Jason took a single, menacing step in his direction. Issuing a choked yelp, he turned and ran, lest he be the next soul delivered to hell by the engineer.

Carnage raged all around. Prisoners fought hand to hand with the undead, and lost. No amount of prison boxing training could prevail against foes that couldn't feel the crushing blows. Crisp winter air carried the warm, coppery scents of blood and faeces. For the first time in months, Jason felt... nothing. No fear. No anxiety. Nothing. A corpse shuffled towards him, half her face cleaved off. The old wound caused her unsupported jaw to loll to the left, blackened drool pooling on her torn breast. The blade had opened the rest of her skull for inspection like an anatomy journal, without damaging the brain within. The same couldn't be said for her right arm. A clean cut went deeply through her shoulder and collar bone, leaving the limb dangling uselessly. Her one remaining eye studied him, inhuman hunger evidenced by a roaming, scabbed tongue.

In the old world, he'd shied away from the mere suggestion of watching horror films on date night. Sally would tease him mercilessly for his cowardice. Now, with a rotting, horrifically mutilated, half-naked corpse stumbling in his direction? Jason took her gently by the active, grasping limb and turned her back towards another prisoner who was gurgling frothy blood from an open throat. A further push sent her reeling onto the shuddering body.

Another corpse caught sight of him and approached. Old Jason would have run screaming, probably voiding his bowels in the process. Unbelievably, new Jason crouched down and picked up a brick. Swatting aside the fleshless left arm, he slammed the flat face of the stone into the creature's mottled grey forehead. Brittle skull crumpled inward, killing the thing instantly. Ramrod straight, it fell backwards at the feet of the next wave of horror advancing into the yard.

I need to find Sally. I need to get her out of here.

The terror induced psychosis of the past few months gave way to razor sharp focus. While everyone else lost their minds, Jason's was unburdened for the first time.

"I'm coming, love," he said, forging on through the slaughterhouse.

CHAPTER 2

Inside the Baron's Hall, the crowd had fallen silent at Kurt's insistence. The general consensus among the remainder of Jasmine's group was why risk going to the prison? Kurt dismissed their suggestion with a menacing glare and they slipped quietly away in shame. Several of the other, more dependable survivors, aired the same view.

"I know you want to save everyone, mate," Bob explained, "but even if you do manage to rescue them, it'll mean dozens more mouths to feed."

"At least ninety if you save them all," added Louise. The implication of her words hung in the smoke tinged air.

Kurt knew her for a warrior and softened his tone in respect. "What else are we supposed to do?" he pleaded. "I know we don't have enough food. I know we will probably starve by winter's end. What I also know for certainty is that the bad guys outnumber us by a shit ton. All that *the meek shall inherit the earth* talk has been shown up for the bullshit it is. The brutal have inherited the earth. The killers. The lunatics. Violence is the only way of life we have now. *I'm* a killer. I've been brutal at times, as well. Some might even call me a lunatic."

"Sweetheart..." Sarah tried to interject.

"No, it's true, I know that. But, do you know what?" he continued, turning back to the group. "I also like to think I've managed to keep hold of a tiny shred of who I was before. When we took this place and found you all, I felt a glimmer of hope for the future. Granted, certain parties have stretched that belief to the limit, but the flame's still just about flickering. Those people at the prison are *good* people! If I can help just a few of them, I'll be tilting the odds a little bit in our favour. Does that make sense or have I just spouted a bunch of horse shit?"

No one answered, lost in their own thoughts. Bob broke the silence with an imitation of a horse's neigh.

"Fuck you, Bob!" Kurt spluttered through the laughter that spread around the room.

"Thanks for the offer, but you're a bit too male for me, mate," replied the handyman with a wink.

"But seriously, do you get where I'm coming from? When this ends, and it will, I want to rebuild with people like you. The arseholes might still be alive too, but if we're strong enough we can keep them at arm's length to do their own thing. It's not like the world's going to be crowded any more, is it?"

"It's just a shame we had to be stranded here instead of a Caribbean island," Bob grumbled, inclining his head towards the world renowned grey of the British weather.

"I don't know, we normally get a couple of days of summer before jumping straight back to winter," Kurt replied. "That's something to look forward to."

"We can stop off in Florida when you help me sail back to the States," offered Denise.

The soldiers looked at one another with raised eyebrows, unaware of the pact made between the couple.

"Nah, the hurricanes are a bastard. I'll get you home and then head on back."

Matt hobbled into the room, interrupting the banter, supported between Peter and Jodi. Anja followed behind, hand on the handle of her trusty axe. She seemed at ease. The man was proving to be an ally, not a threat.

Kurt had taken Braiden to one side and asked if the Scotsman was known to him. In hindsight it seemed an extremely rude and generalised question. Braiden's family were criminals, so they must know each other. However, the teenager hadn't taken offence and answered in the negative. A further explanation from the young man revealed that the Scot was a good'un. It wasn't purely a judgement based upon the selfless act of saving the child at great personal risk. Braiden was raised by the underworld. He was a child of villainy. During his formative years, when most children spent their weekends in front of the TV, young Braiden sat in darkened, smoky rooms. Robberies, extortion, drug dealing, murder. These were his cartoons.

Kurt placed total faith in his assessment.

"Thanks for joining us, Mr Hay. I can see how uncomfortable this is for you," said Sarah.

He smiled through the pain as best he could. "It's nothing, lass. And call me Matt."

"Ok, Matt."

Holbeck looked to Kurt for permission, a sign of his respect for the incredible feats they had achieved on the open road. Kurt yielded the fireplace.

"Mr Hay," Holbeck began.

"Matt," he replied, grimacing as his guards lowered him onto an empty sofa.

Several of the wider group moved away from him. After the failed assault with the truck, Kurt couldn't blame them.

"Matt. I know you couldn't have missed the noise from about twenty minutes ago."

"Aye, I heard it," he replied. Leaning forwards, he closed his eyes and relished the radiant heat from the crackling log fire.

"Do you know what it was?"

Eyes snapping open, a haunted expression twisted his features. "If I were a betting man, I'd say the Gypsies have attacked the prison. They don't care about life, or anything. They're evil."

"I think you'd win that bet," replied Holbeck.

"Then why are we sitting here?" Matt gritted his teeth and stood up unaided. "I'm guessing you need a guide. I'm in."

"We wanted a few answers before we push out all gung ho."

"Ask as we walk, then," he groaned, limping towards the exit. Peter and Jodi tried to assist but he shooed them away with a meaty hand. Each agonising step was a small atonement towards his life of crime. Besides, out in the world he would need to move under his own steam.

Holbeck marched after him, troops in tow. Kurt followed behind with the core group, leaving the others to ponder the coming hours and what it meant for their ongoing survival.

CHAPTER 3

Meandering between the slow-moving corpses, Jason morbidly noted their injuries. Even in shock, he knew it was a dangerous way of detaching himself from the danger. Still, he was unable to fully draw himself back to sanity.

A stooped, elderly lady in a floral pattern dress. The rim of a posh hat had parted, gradually sliding down her head to embed itself deep within the grey brow. Two fingers on her left hand were missing, her only injury, indicating she was an early victim of the apocalypse.

Another lady in full fitness gear; remnants of tight grey leggings and a bright red halter top hanging on the devoured frame. The efforts to keep in shape had doomed her to a far more brutal death. Jason pictured her racing away from danger, the five morning a week cardio regime saving her life as hell consumed the slovenly. Watching others turn from a lone bite or scratch, the pursuit grew from ten, to a hundred, to a thousand. Finally, exhausted by the inexhaustibility of the dead, she had fallen. The zombies left little but the torn clothing. Scalpless, faceless,

11

breastless, skinless, fleshless. Only tendons and supernatural power kept her upright.

A young girl, long dead judging by the way her sallow flesh drooped from the bones. Red hair, now covered in grime and grease from digging herself from the ground. They'd tied them in pigtails, with yellow bows. A fraud, a trick, an attempt to deny the youthful life was gone from the soulless husk. Another form of life had taken its place, a blasphemous, hellspawned life.

In Jason's mind the word flashed again; Supernatural. What else could it be? Dodging past the open mouthed, slavering creature, he started to analyse the situation. Word among the guards at the start of the outbreak was an experiment gone awry. *No shit!* But if an experiment was the cause, why couldn't it be the solution? What was the place called? The Large Hadron Collider? Could the apocalypse be halted? He remembered a story in *The Times* about efforts to recreate a God Particle, or some such nonsense. By the look of the world, they'd only succeeded in creating the Devil Particle.

"Stop this," a voice whispered.

Spinning around, he looked for his wife. Her soft, gentle voice was unmistakeable.

"We need you."

Startled again, he turned in a full circle, frowning. It had come from so close, he could almost feel the warm breath on his neck.

"Daddy?"

"Clarissa?" Jason called, whirling in a maddening loop. She was supposed to be safe, far from the prison. Hay had promised.

A faint scent of her perfume washed away the taint of decomposition, bringing tears to Jason's eyes. "Rissy?" he muttered, using the nickname she hated.

"Come back," whispered his wife, growing fainter. It might just have been the winter wind.

The carefully erected wall of disengagement toppled, and he could see clearly again. His wife was below, in the segregation wing. The prison had fallen, and the open yard was rapidly filling with the ravenous dead. Zombies shuffled all around him, and here he was considering the implications of a mission to fucking Switzerland! *Idiot!*

A scuffle was breaking out around the tunnel to the north. Two prisoners were inside the failsafe car, revving the engine. Another was headfirst through the window, wrestling with the gear stick judging by the awful grinding coming from beneath the bonnet. The passenger was doing his best to punch the flailing man who was preventing their escape, but the awkward angle was making the task difficult. Jason could see a half dozen of the inmates flee through the makeshift gate and down the steps into the gloom.

"What're you doing? They're in the tunnel!" the kicking man screamed from inside the vehicle.

A heavyset zombie stumbled over to the fracas, his suit and shirt hanging open, as well as the hollowed gut which flapped like an open mouth. Lunging forward, he bit deeply into the calf. The heroic prisoner screamed in pain from within the car. Taking advantage of the distraction, the driver shifted into first and gunned it. Simultaneously, the doomed hero fell in a twisted heap with his feasting murderer, while the heavy chains looped around the towing eye snapped taut. A cloud of dust followed the short-lived screams of terror from below. As the car accelerated away, the links ripped the twisted frame of the gate from the dark tunnel. Blood saturated the metal, shed from the men who it had cut to pieces on its way to the light.

"Wait for me!" yelled a prisoner from the open doorway of the gym hall, before sprinting towards the car.

The others inside sealed the door and began barricading it up. Watching the vehicle as it fishtailed across the frost hardened ground, the prisoner realized they couldn't hear him. Rushing back to the entrance, he started to beat on the wire reinforced glass of the gymnasium. Three rotters pulled him down before he could even curse the names of the faces that peered out in abject horror.

13

Without knowing how, Jason had closed the distance between himself and D wing. Most of the cadavers milling around were lured away by the crazed efforts of the driver who was careening towards the opening in the wall. Zombies bounced from the hood, splitting apart in their rot weakened state.

"Wipers," Jason said, still partly in thrall to shock and madness.

Unable to hear the words, the driver complied regardless, smearing the windscreen with clotted green blood. Jason was unsure if they were just blinded, or if in their panic they would have attempted the manoeuvre anyway. Crashing through the thicker mass of corpses at the shattered wall, the car nosedived into the crater, ejecting the occupants through the coated glass like bullets.

Losing sight of the twisted bodies as the zombies closed in to feed, he shook his head. "Morons."

As he neared the security door, Jason still felt devoid of fear. Once he would have shied away from the thugs fighting each other at the door in their desperation to get to safety. Walking up behind them, he patiently waited while they clawed and punched. Glancing back to the yard, the one-sided battle was over. Everything living was now either turned or on its way into cold, dead stomachs.

"Are you coming, or not?" begged Perry, a young prisoner serving two years for burglary. Blood soaked his prison shirt from a broken nose.

"Thank you," Jason replied, stepping over the concrete threshold as the youngster slammed the steel door.

The self-locking mechanism clacked into place, sealing them inside. Jason paused for a few moments, letting the other inmates disperse to whatever course of action they had planned. Dull thuds carried through the thick metal barrier as the new warders took over.

Looking at Perry, Jason said, "I'm going to get my wife now." He walked into the gloom, towards the admin block and the passages that would take him below.

14

"Can I come with you?" Perry mumbled through a tilted head and pinched nose.

Jason ignored the plea. He had one mission, and nothing was going to stop him.

CHAPTER 4

Christina approached the procession of resolute faces. The soldiers followed Matt, their strides disciplined. Kurt and the others trailed behind, lost in conversation.

Blocking their way, the doctor motioned for Matt to give his hand.

"What's that?" he asked, seeing the syringe with its clear liquid.

"It'll take the edge off and keep you mobile for the next few hours," was all she would say.

Sliding the needle into his arm, she pressed the plunger. Matt felt the chill of the drugs, swiftly accompanied by a warm glow that spread throughout his body.

"This won't slow me down, will it, lass?"

"No more than that leg wound," Christina replied.

"It's feeling a bit better," said Matt, stretching the muscle.

"You'll pay for it later, but I think needs must at the moment. Good luck."

"Thanks, Doc. I've got to make it back first."

"You will," she said with a certainty he didn't share.

Moving off, Holbeck joined his side. "If you're going to be a liability to us, now's the time to tell me."

"I won't slow you down. If it comes to it, just leave me behind," stated Matt.

"We need you to guide us to the prisoners. I just wanted to be sure you were capable."

"I walked miles carrying that wee girl with blood streaming from my leg. I think I can manage a few stairs and a trek across the exercise yard."

"Ok. Thanks."

Matt grunted and fought on.

Dropping back, the sergeant joined Kurt's party at the rear. "You really don't need to risk yourselves. We can handle this."

"Once you get inside the walls it's going to be hand to hand. Do you have much experience of that?"

"Well, not much," admitted Holbeck. The insanity of the farm attack came flooding back. How close they'd come to being killed. The night in the tree. "We'll manage."

"No. We're going with you."

"I'd feel a lot happier if I didn't have to watch your arses. This is a job for the army."

"No disrespect, Sergeant, but you guys haven't been doing too well of late, have you?" Kurt replied.

"Well, no, but we're trying to make amends. Baxter's taint will follow us long after this shit is over."

"That's if it ever will be over," replied Kurt.

"Let's hope so. I don't want to do this for the rest of my days."

Kurt scanned the faces and noticed the missing. "Babe, where are the boys?"

She shrugged. "I figured they were getting ready after seeing the soldiers."

"They weren't there when they arrived. So much was going on I didn't even give it a second thought. Has anyone seen the boys?"

17

Blank faces looked back.

Christina stepped forward. "I might have a hunch. I'm sorry that I didn't connect the dots sooner."

"What're you talking about, Doc?"

"They came to me yesterday, asking questions about my parents."

"So?" he couldn't see the connection.

"I fear they may have ignored my advice and snuck out to find them," she said, lowering her eyes. "I'm so sorry."

"Why didn't you say anything?" Kurt demanded.

DB stepped between them to calm the situation. "She just did. You know how headstrong they are, Kurt."

"But they're out there!" Kurt waved at the window. "Alone!"

Honey got between them all, growling low in her throat in warning. She didn't know who to protect, so turned her attention to both parties, barking once at Kurt, then a second time at DB.

"Ok, girl, easy," said Kurt, stepping back.

"You know she doesn't like it when we fight," said Sarah, scratching behind her ears.

"No fighting. What do we do?" demanded Kurt.

Jonesy spoke up. "I'll take the big man here and go and find the boys. You take Matt and the others to the prison. By the time we both get back, it'll be late afternoon I would guess?"

"My parent's home is only six miles away," offered Christina. "I'll show you on a map."

"We can be there in less than an hour," said Jonesy.

"Ok, mate, do it. Christina, I'm sorry for sounding off at you."

"I shouldn't have given them so much to go on. I'm really sorry, Kurt."

He gave her a quick *no hard feelings* hug and she left to pass along the location to the soldiers.

"What time is it now?"

DB checked his watch. "Just after eight. We can probably have them home by lunch."

"That's if they're ok," Kurt fretted.

"Mate, they're fighters. And on top of that, they're smart. They know how to play the game better than most. I know they'll be ok."

Kurt seemed to take the praise on board, but his face hardened. "Don't go easy on them. I want you to give them the bollocking of a lifetime. And tell them I'll be delivering round two of that bollocking when they get back."

"You got it." Jonesy grinned, heading away with DB in tow.

"Why can't things be fucking simple?" Kurt muttered, rubbing at his face.

"It's the apocalypse, babe. Things are never simple," replied Sarah.

"Sergeant, wait for us at the walls. We'll be along in a few minutes once we've geared up."

"Gotcha. We'll be ready."

The troops marched away, led by Gloria.

"Fucking kids!" Kurt snapped.

Sarah laughed and pushed him. "They're yours, not mine!"

"I think you had something to do with it."

"Nope. I deny all knowledge."

"What were they thinking?" Kurt said, dumbfounded.

"They were thinking they could help. You forget we've adopted a couple of ragged orphans."

"And?"

"Imagine how tempting it must've been for them to help reunite a family. They had an opportunity to un-orphan someone they love."

Kurt pulled her close as they walked the hallway. "Un-orphan, is that even a word?"

"It is now. I'm going to make my own dictionary."

Kurt kissed her neck. "I love you."

"Of course you do. I'm adorable."

"I'm still going to kill them."

19

"Three on one?" Sarah replied. "I don't fancy your chances."

"Our boys are growing up too fast," he grumbled.

"They are. And be grateful they can."

"Can't argue with that." He gave her a squeeze and they headed for the armoury.

CHAPTER 5

Inside the block, chaos reigned. Prisoners were fighting each other for any weapon they could find, only weakening their numbers further as the injured writhed on the grey floor. Jason shook his head in bewilderment at their stupidity.

"What?" asked Perry who had attached himself to Jason's hip.

"It doesn't matter. I need to get to my wife."

"I can help."

Jason ignored his offer and waded through the thickest of the hand to hand combat. A man fell at his feet, holding out a hand while the other tried, unsuccessfully, to hold his guts in. The prisoner who had stolen the knife rushed off, covered in blood. Jason simply stepped around the mortally wounded prisoner, leaving him to call out for help that wasn't coming.

"What're we going to do?" asked Perry, terror adding a shrill edge to his voice.

"I'm getting my wife, then I'm getting out of here."

"And if we can't get out? Those things are everywhere! This place is crawling!"

"Then at least we'll be together. I can spend a couple of days with her before dehydration does its work. I hear you dream towards the end."

Jason listened to himself and wondered where the new man had come from. One of his old teachers came to mind, a Mr Adams. He had been a squat, gruff, red headed Scot who instilled fear and discipline in equal measure. During one assembly he had recounted a phrase used by his grandfather during the First World War. *Forged through adversity,* or something along those lines. Was that what had happened? Had the beatings forged him like an ingot of steel? Had the wounds tempered him like a red-hot sword quenched in water? Perhaps. Inmates who had once jeered and struck him now gave a wide berth. Those that hadn't witnessed the calm execution in the yard could still see a glint in his eyes that made them wary of the engineer.

"Mr Rechtman?"

A crash to their rear caused Perry to flinch, but Jason marched on. The inmates had upended the pool table and were wrestling with the four thick legs. Those further down the infamy pecking order hovered in the periphery, waiting for the hardened cons to retrieve their prize. Moving in respectfully, they slipped several solid balls into socks. Against a human, they could be devastating. Against the undead? They would find out soon enough. Gavin, one of the slimiest prisoners Jason had come across took his chance. Swinging like a batter, the long cotton sock cracked against the face of Carl, a notorious bank robber. Roaring in pain, he dropped the club and tried to hold his shattered nose and cheekbones together.

"Now you've done it," Perry muttered.

Carl's crew circled the table, ready to murder the youngster. Seeing their old friend was blinded by the flowing blood, they weighed his value to their survival. Gavin backed away, eyeing them with bared teeth. With a single nod, he was pardoned, and they moved off as a foursome. So much for loyalty.

"Wait up!" called Perry.

Jason was almost out of sight at the end of the wing. A twin set of steel gates led through into the processing area and the individual wing segregation cells. Each block had ten repurposed cells, completely separate from the general population. Hearing a commotion coming, Jason stood aside as a group charged towards the kitchen area, hoping to secure some food. Water would have been a more sensible target, but the collection barrels were all outside. And outside now belonged to the dead. A handful of rice and beans would do nothing to fend off the lack of life sustaining liquid. Reality slipped in and for the first time he understood the likelihood of escaping the prison was near zero. One tunnel was blown up. The other had been collapsed by the morons in the car. The third, which had killed the two Gypsies, was back up and running. However, it would only be accessible by crossing a sizeable portion of the yard and communal garden. Dodging between the upright rotters wasn't difficult when they were focused on easier prey. Once the screaming meat had been turned or consumed, the zombies would besiege the wings themselves.

Suicide. It's got to be suicide, Jason decided. He would figure some way of ending it for himself and his beloved wife if they ended up trapped. Dying of thirst was slow and probably excruciating, despite the promise of pleasant hallucinations. They had both been through enough. Clarissa was safe. Hay had promised, and Jason trusted his word. At least his daughter would go on living.

"Shall I try and find the keys, Mr Rechtman?"

The dark opening that led down to the original segregation facility had been left open at all times to facilitate access to the females. Once the rota system had been brought in, the heavy steel door was still left open. Flaying alive was a natural deterrent to the darker whims of the brutal occupants of the prison. Families were isolated on one side, meaning the women and children. The men were kept in a completely separate part of D wing. The paedophiles were kept on the opposite side of seg, crammed eight to a cell. Until they were needed for entertainment, or... the other thing. Jason shuddered at the thought as he marched down into the gloom.

He'd been looking for a scrap of food about a month prior. Anything to quieten the painful growls of his deprived stomach after working forty-eight hours straight. Cupboards were bare and even the bins were empty. Deciding to risk a beating, he headed for the freezer. Pulling on the handle, defrosted water spilled from the walk-in appliance. Any ice from the previous night's sub-zero temperatures was collected and left inside to preserve the food as much as possible. If you could call human carcasses food. Connor was hanging from a pair of meat hooks, with an unknown molester to his side. Both had been hollowed out. Slowly shutting the door, Jason's appetite had mysteriously disappeared. He'd never set foot in the kitchen since.

"Wait, I can't see!" cried Perry as he followed.

Jason paused at the bottom of the stone steps. Probing out with his hands, he brushed up against the table he was searching for. Slowly feeling his way across the top, the flashlight was stood upright. Taking hold of the steel casing, he pressed the button. The corridor was short, the cells themselves tiny to ensure a suitably uncomfortable stay for the unfortunate occupants. A set of keys hung from a hook set in the wall which he knew would be there. If anything, his mute silence had yielded an incredible amount of overheard conversations. Being of little importance, the prisoners seemed unaware he was there. It was these titbits of information that helped him on the current course.

"Hey, you found them. Shall I go and lock the door?"

Jason held on to the bunch. If a fire should break out, they would die in darkness. It was the reason the dungeonesque wing had been mothballed until their new warden, Craig, took over in the aftermath of the apocalypse. Looping the largest key from the ring, Jason handed it to Perry. Sprinting back to the door, the dull boom of closing steel sounded loud in the subterranean confines.

"I've left the key in the lock so no one can open it from the other side."

"Ok," replied Jason. He didn't really care. What would be would be. They were in the hands of the gods now.

"What should we do? How do we get out of here?"

Jason had given their predicament some thought. "We can't get out. The prison is overrun. With the idiots running around up top, it won't take long before someone panics and tries to escape which will let the dead in."

"We're trapped?" Perry spluttered. "I don't know if I can stay down here."

"Then leave," said Jason, turning away.

He hadn't moved from the abandoned guard's table since picking up the torch. The beam was directed at one of the cell doors.

The cell door.

Sally's cell door.

"Is someone there?" called a male voice.

Jason scowled in the general direction of the paedophile and ignored him.

"Hello? What's going on? What was that huge bang?" asked another.

Jason stepped forward, the legs slow and unresponsive. What if this was just some cruel, psychosis induced dream? A nightmare within a nightmare. Would he open the door to find the cell empty? Or would Sally lunge out at him, already one of the undead in a cruel twist of fate?

"Who's there?" asked a female voice, filled with dread. A familiar voice.

Jason held his breath. Reaching for the door, he placed a palm on the frigid surface. All the other entreaties and complaints faded away to nothing. Nothing existed except for the sturdy door.

"Hello? Please answer me."

Letting the other keys drop as he found the correct number, he heard Sally hiss in fear and move away. Holding her cell key, Jason's fingers trembled so badly he nearly dropped the set.

"Go away! Leave me alone!"

Further voices mumbled from within, attempting to console one another. After three attempts, Jason managed to slot the key into the lock. Fear had developed into uncontrollable sobbing as the latch disengaged. Pulling at the handle, Jason expected to see Connor and the molester dangling from the thick hooks. Their empty abdomens. The buckets of viscera. It was all just a cruel joke to fracture the last traces of his sanity.

"Jason? Is that you?"

The cell was just a cell. No hooks. No stainless shelves. No dead bodies. Only the living.

"Sally?" Jason choked.

"Jason? Oh my God! Jason!" Her sobs changed from fear of sexual brutalisation to half choking gasps of relief. Rushing forward, Sally's stench hit Jason before her all-consuming embrace.

"Sally," he whispered.

"What's going on? How're you here?" she asked, wracked by her own tremors of emotion.

"We're safe," he replied, drowning in her unwashed musk. "I'm never letting you go again."

CHAPTER 6

Holbeck surveyed the now surrounded Warthogs. Hundreds of the undead had been drawn around the perimeter wall by the throaty engines. White eyes, prickled with frost, stared up at the soldiers. Killing them would undoubtedly draw more in, which would only weaken their ammunition supplies further. If the numbers at the prison were to be believed, they were going to need every shell.

"Sarge, shall we start picking them off?" asked Carpenter, sighting the threat from the crenulations. The stench of decay, weakened by the chill, flowed up and into her nose. It was enough, and she turned back to the castle to draw clean air into her lungs. Summer was going to be hell. If they made it that far.

"Sarge?" added Dougal, looking for confirmation.

"No, hold fire until Kurt and the others arrive."

"Aye, Sarge."

As the minutes passed, Holbeck took time to reflect on what the small group had achieved. The blackened ground of the funeral pyre lay to the north, a forest of charred bones. Perhaps Kurt's insistence that he and some of their group should tag along wasn't so crazy after all. The one time his team had left the safety of their APCs at the farm was nearly their last. Yet these folk had battled across rough terrain, at the onset of winter, with the dead harassing their every step. *Who're the real warriors?* he wondered. As if on cue, one of the heavy oak doors of the Duke's wing opened.

"Would you get a look at that," marvelled Eldridge.

The soldiers looked on in awe, some open mouthed, others grinning at the ingenuity. Sam's original armour design had been adopted once again from the findings within the castle. Kurt and the others were protected on all their limbs by thin layers of padded copper. Jonesy and DB were similarly clad, with swords in hand and rifles slung. None of the group were smiling, bearing instead a steely resolve that Holbeck recognised immediately. Kurt's war pick hung from one side of his belt, while the hammer that had served him so well as both a weapon, and talisman of good fortune, hung from the other. Marching out behind them came the students. Wielding the newly found bows, makeshift quivers held dozens of arrows across their backs.

"I think we're surplus to requirement, Sarge," said Harkiss.

"I think you might be right."

"Is that what I think it is?" Eldridge gasped as the warriors approached.

Held by the upper shaft, the long bladed claymore rose several feet above Peter's head.

"I cannae believe what my eyes are seeing," chuckled Matt. The Scots knew all about fighting. Tales of their bravery in the face of insurmountable odds at the hands of tyrants were passed down generation to generation. These brave souls, though English, were kindred spirits. At that moment, he knew he had done exactly the right thing in bringing Clarissa to them.

"I heard you're a sucker for a sword," Peter explained, handing it over. "You can use it in place of a crutch if you want."

"Thank you," Matt said, truly touched.

"Kurt, what do you need from us?" asked Holbeck.

Kurt barely looked up as he walked towards the upper bailey of the castle ground. "Keep out of our way for a bit while we clear the outside. The kids are going to need the walls. Could you keep a hold of them to stop them falling?"

Holbeck nodded, uncertainly. What was the man talking about?

Miss Lunsford emerged from the open doorway with other survivors in tow, all holding sturdy metal crates. The students broke away from the main group, running up the stone steps to join the soldiers. The earlier nerves at their arrival were gone as they made friendly small talk.

"How did you wind up here?" Eldridge asked Holly.

"We were on a field trip with our teacher," she replied, nodding towards Miss Lunsford. "She kept us safe and helped to seal us in the living quarters."

"You look pretty handy with those," said Carpenter, pointing at Pea's compound bow.

"We practiced a lot with the castle's show bows until we got these. It's how we helped your friends when they arrived."

Before Holbeck could probe further, the teacher and her entourage reached the wall. Dropping the boxes at each embrasure, they backed away and let the students climb atop them. Suddenly, Kurt's request became clear.

"Troops, get a tight hold of their belts or trousers. They need to lean forward at an awkward angle to fire."

Understanding passed through the soldiers and they all hurriedly took position. Unfazed by the smell that had caused Carpenter to retreat, the youngsters stared down at the waiting horde.

"What now?" asked the sergeant.

"They'll be along shortly," Pea said, as if that explained everything.

"Kurt, you mean?"

"Here they come now," she replied, pointing outside the wall.

Formed into a line, Kurt led them onward. Catching sight of a pitiful half zombie, his eyes blazed pure hatred and he broke formation. Slamming the spike down into the skull, the first blow stilled the corpse. For some reason, he withdrew the weapon and hammered it again and again until all that was left was a patchy mush. Peter pulled him gently away, but not before giving the body a final kick.

"Friend of yours?" joked Harkiss.

The withering stare from Sarah and Gloria who had now joined them shut him down instantly. Holbeck gave him an additional glare of reproach and he felt his cheeks start to glow.

"Kids, are you ready?" Kurt called. The outer row of undead were already breaking away from the crush around the vehicles.

"Ready, Mr Taylor!" they all replied.

"Gloria, if you'd be so kind?"

Slipping two fingers into her mouth, the teacher let out a piercing whistle. Startled by the noise, the zombies turned around to find the source of the disturbance. Seeing the line of fresh meat on offer, they disregarded the untouchable flesh above and shuffled forwards.

"There's too many," muttered Ewington.

Holbeck looked to Sarah who shrugged nonchalantly. If she wasn't worried, he needn't be, he surmised. It soon became clear why.

Facing off against the rotting monsters, the group didn't so much as wrinkle a solitary nose. Spreading out slightly to allow full range of movement, Kurt and the others started to pick their targets. Peter drew first blood with an overhead swing of his broadsword that cleaved the zombie in half down to the pelvis. Wrenching the blade free, the squelch had Harkiss's throat bobbing.

"Don't you dare!" Holbeck warned.

Swallowing hard, Harkiss nodded. His cheeks had gone from their earlier scarlet to winter white. A head shot was one thing. Seeing the black and green, putrid innards slop to the creature's feet was quite another.

Kurt was devastating, darting in and out, raining blows from the sharp and blunt end of the pick in equal measure. Jodi moved further away, circling the pack of zombies. Those foolish enough to grasp for her had their arm batted aside, swiftly followed by a precise strike to the forehead or temple with the aluminium bat. Louise and Peter were having the time of their lives, rending limbs and heads with the freshly honed swords. The rapidly growing stack of bodies became an impediment to the pursuit of the zombies as Kurt knew it would. The eager dead struggled on, tripping over or stepping onto a severed appendage, only to slip on the blood moistened hazard. Before they could spit out their remaining broken teeth or the hard soil, blades and bludgeons scattered the festering brains onto the ground.

"Now!" called Holly, drawing back her bowstring.

The creak of stretched carbon fibre precipitated the sharp twang of the arrow's release. Burying deeply into the back of a skull, the creature toppled forward, adding its weight to the push. Cracks and whistling flights added their song to the swoosh and cleave. Peppered with the coloured arrows, the groaning rear guard fell by the dozen.

"Well I'll be damned," muttered Holbeck.

The attack was nearing its end, with the remaining cadavers largely immobilised by the piled corpses all around them.

"Kids, hold up now!" Kurt yelled.

The melee fighters hacked away for all they were worth, circling the pile and killing any within range. Before long, only the inner core of about eighty zombies remained, pinned in place by their fallen kin.

"Have at it!" Kurt ordered, drawing his own group well out of range of the snipers on the battlements.

31

Five more minutes saw all movement cease from the mound of oozing corruption. The APCs were clear, albeit a bit marred from the grave juice which slimed its way down the armour. A lone arm strained from between the stone and lead vehicle, the owner horrifically mangled but still somehow alive.

"Still think you don't need us?" asked Gloria.

"I'm starting to think it's you that don't need us, ma'am," Holbeck replied.

"Your guns and vehicles will help a little bit, I promise," Denise said with a wink.

"And if not, just keep out of my husband's way," added Sarah.

"I plan to," Holbeck replied.

CHAPTER 7

The clear up was complete, and the melee fighters were back on the wall washing the gore from their masks and armour, ready for the mission. The smoke in the distance had vanished completely, emphasising the ticking clock.

"Folks, we don't have space for you in the cabs. We'll need to dump the ammo from the transports for you to fit," explained Holbeck.

"Then let's do it," replied Kurt, hopping the wall. Scurrying down the rope, he hopped down onto the roof of the Warthog and jumped to the ground.

"We need to move, Sergeant," said Jodi, following Kurt.

Her promise to Jason burned fiercely in her heart. The circumstances of the rescue were less than optimal, but what choice did they have? Something had either gone catastrophically wrong, or it really was an attack by the Gypsies. She was inclined to believe the expertise of the soldiers. By days end, they may well have a new enemy to contend with. One with the smarts and ability to tear open

33

the castle itself. It didn't matter. Innocent people were dead or dying, and she had made a promise. Clarissa peered over the wall, her face a mask of worry. Giving her a smile, Jodi prayed she could bring the child good news.

"Jodi, just stack it against the wall," ordered Kurt, throwing open the rear door. "The others can collect it all while we head out."

Loitering away from the main group were the remnants of Jasmine's band. Kurt stared at Zack for a moment before returning to the task at hand. Fully laden boxes jangled from the loose contents within. The weight was comforting. Every ounce was survival incarnate.

"We'll get more ropes from the northern wall!" called Zack. "It'll make it easier to get the goods inside."

"At least some good's coming from this," said Jodi, noting their efforts to help.

"They've got a lot of making up to do, but it's a start," Kurt muttered.

They were joined by the soldiers and the other fighters. Forming a human chain, the cabs were emptied in less than five minutes. An impressive stack of coloured steel and wooden boxes lined the stone. Kurt was filled with hope. Their days of cowering, waiting for the next disaster, were over.

"The guns are still inside the Hogs. We'll use them as seats for now and then winch them up when we get back."

Matt was the last to descend. Unable to use his legs, the powerful arms did all the work from knot to knot. Clarissa carefully dropped his crutches over the parapet. Peter and Jodi gave him as much help as possible around the aluminium supports. Joan leaned from the Warthog, grabbing his arms to help pull him aboard. Catching his foot on the low step, Matt clamped his eyes shut while the explosion of pain passed. Christina's cocktail was working, but a solid blow still sent slivers of white hot agony through each pellet wound.

"Sorry," said Joan.

"Don't worry, lass. I should've lifted my damned leg."

34

Slumping into the low, awkward seat, he could tell this journey was going to be hell.

"Kurt?" Holbeck called.

"Yeah?"

"What do you know of the route? Anything we should be aware of?"

"All I can tell you is it's clear all the way to the prison. You'll want to head south through the fields at the edge of town, though. The main road takes you straight to the entrance and it was crawling with the dead the last time we were there."

"Numbers?"

"Thousands," said Jodi. "Too many to count."

"Ok. Carpenter, Ewington, you're driving. Eldridge, Petermann, you're on the guns. The rest of you, buckle up. Kurt, if you could get the rest of your people stowed and join me at the front?"

"No problem."

Seeing everyone aboard and seated, he couldn't fathom the slatted steel siding. "Sergeant, what do we do with the rear gate?" Kurt shouted.

The soldiers laughed at his innocent mistake.

"It's RPG armour, Kurt. Shut the door and close it," replied Holbeck, climbing into the lead vehicle.

"I love you. Stay safe!" called Sarah.

Kurt mouthed the words back to her and slammed the door, before climbing in the front cab. Matt was shuffling, trying to find a position that didn't hurt so much.

"Sorry, mate. Did you want to swap places?" asked Kurt.

"I'll be fine, lad. If we could steer clear of any potholes, that would be swell."

"This is Britain, Matt. As well as death and taxes, the other certainty is shit roads and potholes."

"And women drivers. Fuck a duck!" Matt groaned.

"You can always walk if you want," teased Carpenter, flooring it.

Holbeck grunted and turned to Kurt. "What do we know about the prison?"

"It's got four walls and two main entrances. They've reinforced the front entrance with steel welded to the cage of the admissions area. It's like a holding bay for the prison vans while they load or unload the inmates. The rear gate is the same, but doesn't have the reinforcement. I think they used it to move in and out as they herded the zombies around the front and sides."

Matt concurred with the assessment.

"What about the tunnels Jonesy was talking about?"

"There are three according to their engineer. We can check the tunnel at the farm shop to see if Jason left us a map. If it's not swarming with escaping cons that is."

"I think we should see the damage first and get an idea of what we're up against."

"Sounds good."

Kurt looked through the side window at the receding castle. The faces on the walls were too small to identify, but he was heartened to see a bustle of antlike activity around the new supplies. Sometimes the rumour of a brutal execution could work wonders on the attitude of the feckless. Not that he would ever carry out the slaying again. If justice was required, it would be done swiftly. The feelings surging through Kurt as Vincent was disembowelled scared him more than all the dead at the walls combined. He'd enjoyed it. What did that say about his suitability to lead?

Carpenter veered right, crushing through the same section of mangled bush the truck had passed through.

"You ok, mate?" asked Holbeck, seeing the look.

"Memories, that's all," Kurt replied as the huge fortress passed by. The last time they had been coming in the other direction, cruising up the River Arun towards the fateful battle in the upper bailey. Towards the death of John.

"Who'd have guessed how much could happen in such a short space of time? It's insane what we went through. And what we've got to do in the coming weeks."

"Just when we think things are on the up, another disaster hits us. I'd appreciate a break," Kurt muttered.

"Things always look darkest before the dawn," said Holbeck.

"Do you really believe that applies to the zombie apocalypse?"

Knowing what was coming their way, Holbeck fell silent. Their ordeal had only just begun.

The clear up was complete, and the melee fighters were back on the wall washing the gore from their masks and armour, ready for the mission. The smoke in the distance had vanished completely, emphasising the ticking clock.

"Folks, we don't have space for you in the cabs. We'll need to dump the ammo from the transports for you to fit," explained Holbeck.

"Then let's do it," replied Kurt, hopping the wall. Scurrying down the rope, he hopped down onto the roof of the Warthog and jumped to the ground.

"We need to move, Sergeant," said Jodi, following Kurt.

Her promise to Jason burned fiercely in her heart. The circumstances of the rescue were less than optimal, but what choice did they have? Something had either gone catastrophically wrong, or it really was an attack by the Gypsies. She was inclined to believe the expertise of the soldiers. By days end, they may well have a new enemy to contend with. One with the smarts and ability to tear open the castle itself. It didn't matter. Innocent people were dead or dying, and she had made a promise. Clarissa peered over the wall, her face a mask of worry. Giving her a smile, Jodi prayed she could bring the child good news.

"Jodi, just stack it against the wall," ordered Kurt, throwing open the rear door. "The others can collect it all while we head out."

Loitering away from the main group were the remnants of Jasmine's band. Kurt stared at Zack for a moment before returning to the task at hand. Fully laden boxes jangled from the loose contents within. The weight was comforting. Every ounce was survival incarnate.

"We'll get more ropes from the northern wall!" called Zack. "It'll make it easier to get the goods inside."

"At least some good's coming from this," said Jodi, noting their efforts to help.

"They've got a lot of making up to do, but it's a start," Kurt muttered.

They were joined by the soldiers and the other fighters. Forming a human chain, the cabs were emptied in less than five minutes. An impressive stack of coloured steel and wooden boxes lined the stone. Kurt was filled with hope. Their days of cowering, waiting for the next disaster, were over.

"The guns are still inside the Hogs. We'll use them as seats for now and then winch them up when we get back."

Matt was the last to descend. Unable to use his legs, the powerful arms did all the work from knot to knot. Clarissa carefully dropped his crutches over the parapet. Peter and Jodi gave him as much help as possible around the aluminium supports. Joan leaned from the Warthog, grabbing his arms to help pull him aboard. Catching his foot on the low step, Matt clamped his eyes shut while the explosion of pain passed. Christina's cocktail was working, but a solid blow still sent slivers of white hot agony through each pellet wound.

"Sorry," said Joan.

"Don't worry, lass. I should've lifted my damned leg."

Slumping into the low, awkward seat, he could tell this journey was going to be hell.

"Kurt?" Holbeck called.

"Yeah?"

"What do you know of the route? Anything we should be aware of?"

"All I can tell you is it's clear all the way to the prison. You'll want to head south through the fields at the edge of town, though. The main road takes you straight to the entrance and it was crawling with the dead the last time we were there."

"Numbers?"

"Thousands," said Jodi. "Too many to count."

"Ok. Carpenter, Ewington, you're driving. Eldridge, Petermann, you're on the guns. The rest of you, buckle up. Kurt, if you could get the rest of your people stowed and join me at the front?"

"No problem."

Seeing everyone aboard and seated, he couldn't fathom the slatted steel siding. "Sergeant, what do we do with the rear gate?" Kurt shouted.

The soldiers laughed at his innocent mistake.

"It's RPG armour, Kurt. Shut the door and close it," replied Holbeck, climbing into the lead vehicle.

"I love you. Stay safe!" called Sarah.

Kurt mouthed the words back to her and slammed the door, before climbing in the front cab. Matt was shuffling, trying to find a position that didn't hurt so much.

"Sorry, mate. Did you want to swap places?" asked Kurt.

"I'll be fine, lad. If we could steer clear of any potholes, that would be swell."

"This is Britain, Matt. As well as death and taxes, the other certainty is shit roads and potholes."

"And women drivers. Fuck a duck!" Matt groaned.

"You can always walk if you want," teased Carpenter, flooring it.

Holbeck grunted and turned to Kurt. "What do we know about the prison?"

"It's got four walls and two main entrances. They've reinforced the front entrance with steel welded to the cage of the admissions area. It's like a holding bay for the prison vans while they load or unload the inmates. The rear gate is the same, but doesn't have the reinforcement. I think they

39

used it to move in and out as they herded the zombies around the front and sides."

Matt concurred with the assessment.

"What about the tunnels Jonesy was talking about?"

"There are three according to their engineer. We can check the tunnel at the farm shop to see if Jason left us a map. If it's not swarming with escaping cons that is."

"I think we should see the damage first and get an idea of what we're up against."

"Sounds good."

Kurt looked through the side window at the receding castle. The faces on the walls were too small to identify, but he was heartened to see a bustle of antlike activity around the new supplies. Sometimes the rumour of a brutal execution could work wonders on the attitude of the feckless. Not that he would ever carry out the slaying again. If justice was required, it would be done swiftly. The feelings surging through Kurt as Vincent was disembowelled scared him more than all the dead at the walls combined. He'd enjoyed it. What did that say about his suitability to lead?

Carpenter veered right, crushing through the same section of mangled bush the truck had passed through.

"You ok, mate?" asked Holbeck, seeing the look.

"Memories, that's all," Kurt replied as the huge fortress passed by. The last time they had been coming in the other direction, cruising up the River Arun towards the fateful battle in the upper bailey. Towards the death of John.

"Who'd have guessed how much could happen in such a short space of time? It's insane what we went through. And what we've got to do in the coming weeks."

"Just when we think things are on the up, another disaster hits us. I'd appreciate a break," Kurt muttered.

"Things always look darkest before the dawn," said Holbeck.

"Do you really believe that applies to the zombie apocalypse?"

Knowing what was coming their way, Holbeck fell silent. Their ordeal had only just begun.

CHAPTER 8

<u>6 Hours Ago</u>

Braiden came to a sudden halt, crouching between the bushes at the base of the castle living quarters. The glow of a passing candle flickered through the stained glass, growing dimmer as the holder moved deeper into the winding maze of corridors.

"That was close," whispered Sam.

"Too close," complained Winston.

"Stop talking. Someone will hear us," Braiden cautioned, barely audible in the ascendant darkness.

The light of the full moon didn't illuminate their position, merely adding another layer of gloom to anyone on watch. On the gravel drive of the greeting area, the outline of the eastern portion of the castle roof was sharply drawn by the cold, reflected rays. Braiden motioned for them to move forward along the flower bed, using the soil to mask their progress. The watchers were attuned to the crunch of the stones. Any noise and half a dozen torch beams would blaze to life, revealing them like prisoners caught under a spotlight. Instead of bullets, they would be dodging rapid fire questions and a hefty bollocking from Kurt. If truth be told, Winston would've preferred to outrun lead than face his stony faced accusations.

Keeping low, they quickly passed the last scraps of winter shed foliage and reached the archway leading to the upper bailey. The guards on the walls were pacing back and forth, their focus on the surrounding land. Braziers crackled as the logs inside burned, giving much needed heat to fight the December chill, and light to scout by. Kurt had helped Bob erect a series of platforms which raised the fire high enough to provide some light between the embrasures. Circular pools of yellow and orange glowed within the walls, throwing weak, half-moons of illumination on the frozen lawn. Lacking the discipline or knowledge, the sentries routinely turned back to warm themselves. Any night vision was instantly lost to the fire, which made their illicit manoeuvres that much easier.

"Now!" Braiden whispered, running across the open ground, and around the stagnant swimming pool. Filthy ice glittered from the frozen mire. Hands sprouted from the solid crust, the fingers of the undead trapped below frozen stiff. In time they would be dealt with, but for now they were harmless, imprisoned by both the deep sides and sub-zero temperature.

Braiden held up a fist as Jonesy had taught him, bringing the boys to a halt at the steps of the North Tower. The staircase was steeped in total darkness, no firelight or moonlight could reach them. Sam had picked this area for that exact reason.

"Psst." Sam held his breath, waiting for a challenge that didn't come.

"Psst," Braiden added, a little louder.

"You're clear, come on up," whispered Holly from the top of the stairs.

Clomping up the time worn stone, the soft soled shoes and secure packs masked their ascent. Blades were sheathed and muffled. Backpacks were strapped at shoulder and waist with nothing hanging loose. Holly had purposely allowed the fire to die down slightly, bringing in the sphere of potential exposure that much further from their means of egress.

"Are you sure about this? We're going to be in so much trouble," Holly whispered.

"We're sure," Sam confirmed with a nod. "Just keep quiet and we'll be back by tomorrow."

"What if your mum or dad finds you missing? The whole place will go nuts."

"If they do, just explain where we've gone and that we'll be back as soon as possible. We're going to steer clear of anywhere that could have loads of zombies, anyway."

"Yeah, with luck we won't even come across any," Winston added, trying to make the girl feel better. He knew she was afraid on their behalf simply because she hadn't been outside the walls regularly since the apocalypse began. The one time to retrieve the bows was a fairly sedate affair. It was impossible to explain that after a while the dead were just the dead, slow and dumb. In small numbers they were no threat at all, but you had to live it for yourself.

"Please be careful," she begged, hugging them each in turn.

"Careful is our middle name," Braiden whispered, approaching the battlement.

Three piles of knotted rope lay beneath separate merlons. Picking them up, they carefully spooled out the cord instead of tossing the coils. The thump of it hitting the ground could well draw the attention of nearby zombies, or even worse, humans. Winston was first over the edge, climbing down with a speed that belied his shrinking girth. Taking up position to guard the others, Braiden smiled in the shadows. He was really trying to win their friendship, not that it was necessary. Braiden was already fairly certain about him, not that he would show it. By far the biggest factor in the change of heart was discovering the portly youth eavesdropping as they plotted the mission. He'd feigned innocence, claiming that he was too scared to retreat in case the floorboards gave him away, and too worried of Braiden's retribution if discovered. They found him outside the door, awkwardly perched with one foot forward in a state of paralysis and flushed cheeks. Before Braiden could start shouting, Winston was offering his services and expertise to the cause. It had gone a long way.

"Right, from here on out we talk only in whispers," warned Sam.

"Wouldn't it be better to keep completely quiet?" asked Winston.

"Probably, but if we need to talk, it's in whispers, ok?"

Winston nodded, realised he couldn't be seen, and then whispered, "Sure."

No one needed to ask if they were prepared. All the gear had been checked in the bedroom twice before they snuck through the hallways. At a brisk pace, they would reach their destination before first light. If successful, they could then be home by lunchtime of the next day, ready to face whatever sanctions Kurt deemed necessary. If an issue arose, they were prepared for emergencies with extra food and water.

"Thank you," said Sam, cupping his mouth in an attempt to stop the sound travelling.

"Good luck!" Holly replied.

The sound of her scuffing feet as she walked back to her post signalled it was time to move. Spared scrutiny from the near dead brazier, the boys took their time in reaching the nearby treeline. A flash of sparks lit up the night sky behind them. Looking at the source, Holly had fed fresh logs into the embers which quickly set them ablaze. The retreating shadows were still a hundred feet away when the fire grew to its strongest.

"She's a great girl, Sam. You're lucky," said Braiden.

"I thought we weren't talking?" said Winston, surveying the gloom.

45

"We're whispering," Braiden replied.

"Semantics."

"What you and your wrist produce in the toilet is none of my business."

"That's... never mind," Winston huffed.

Braiden gave him a playful punch, showing he knew exactly what he meant. The blow filled his heart as surely as any words or kind gesture and Winston smiled to himself. Turning away from the meagre castle beacons, they waited for a minute while their eyes adjusted to the night. To their surprise, the crisp light of the moon was more than adequate to see by.

"I guess living by candlelight has helped our vision," Winston remarked.

"No hundred watt bulbs to mess our eyes up any more," Braiden agreed.

"Let's get going," said Sam, taking the lead through the undergrowth.

Now that they were alone, outside the safety of the ancient fortress, Winston's mind started to conjure all sorts of demons hiding just out of sight. Their razor sharp claws poised, ready to rend the flesh from their bones. Red, glowing eyes shuttered, waiting to snap open and terrify them. It was the one secret he would take to his grave. That every time he caved to the allure of sweet and savoury treats, he was shitting himself the whole time. What was it he'd heard once? There can be no bravery without fear? Tell that to his soiled underwear. Ok, that had only happened once when opening a larder door to find a rotting, bloated toddler on the other side. Being at the wrong height, she'd nearly bitten down on his unmentionables. A shrill yelp, followed by a hasty backstep and knee sent her flying back into her tomb. The sweets within stayed with her, and the house was never entered again.

"Can we talk?" Winston asked, quietly.

"I think we're far enough away from the castle now," whispered Sam.

"I'd like that," Braiden admitted. He too was getting the willies being outside without the adults for protection. Across the land, the mournful lamentation of the undead echoed through the trees. A chorus of dead-lunged doom, gurgling from the decomposing organs. No man alive could be held responsible for feeling a shiver run down their spine at the forlorn wails.

"It's funny how you kind of fade it out when you're inside," said Sam.

"You'd go fucking bonkers if you paid attention to it for too long," Braiden replied.

"You're right though. It becomes like white noise when you're safe, but out here you pick it up again. Survival mode, I guess," added Winston.

CHAPTER 9

<u>5 hours ago</u>

"What do you miss most from before?" asked Winston.

"Football training and youth club," replied Braiden.

"Sam?"

"I don't know. People, I guess. I mean, I know there's quite a few of us in the castle, but we're trapped together. Most of the new people we've come across are cool, but loads are just dicks."

"I hear that. I've had judgmental nuns. Then Mike and Debbie. Then as if that wasn't bad enough, an invite to be a plaything to Bubba in prison."

"You met a guy called Bubba?"

"Not in person, but I know he was in there waiting for me to come and be his wife. I'm way too pretty for prison," Winston replied, brushing a hand through lush, imaginary locks of hair.

Sam became serious at the memory of scouting the facility. The guards brutal execution at the wall. "I hope we can help the people in there. They don't deserve to be locked up like that."

"We'll find a way. And then we can kill those fuckers."

"That's another downside to the zombie apocalypse. The percentage of douchebags has risen sharply in the past few months."

"I know, we're stuck out here with one," Braiden teased.

"Hey! I know Sam can be a pain, but that's no reason to call him a douchebag."

Sam pushed him in the back. "I'm starting to wish there were even *fewer* people. Especially out here, right now."

"Sticks and stones may break my bones but words will only leave me sobbing in a toilet eating a whole tub of cookie dough ice-cream to numb the emotional trauma."

Braiden snorted. "Drama queen."

"Anyway, what do you miss most about before?" asked Sam.

"Internet porn," Winston answered candidly.

"Gay porn, more like," chuckled Braiden.

"I never cared much for it, but if that's your thing, fair play," Winston retorted, eliciting a snort laugh from Sam.

Braiden spluttered in faux outrage. "I only watched that four times. And it was only because the mouse stuck that I couldn't close the windows."

"I'll bet the mouse got stuck because you coated it in gentlemen's relish, you dirtbag."

"What the hell is *gentlemen's relish?*"

"White stuff. Slightly salty. Thick consistency."

"Ha! I knew you were gay. How else would you know what it tastes like?"

Winston lowered his voice further. "It's not like that. I just... it just sometimes..."

"It comes out a bit too fast," finished Sam.

Winston grimaced. "Yeah. I just got some blowback from the hose, that's all."

49

"Yeah, but you didn't have to swallow it," said Braiden.

"Protein's protein, mate. It's good for the complexion too, apparently. I bet with skin as smooth as yours you slather that shit on. Quick video on GuyTube. Pump, pump, squirt. Moisturise."

Sam stifled his laughter into the padded crook of his arm.

"It's more like, pump, pump, pump, squirt. I'm no virgin."

"I stand corrected. Pump, pump, pump, squirt. Then moisturise."

Braiden shrugged. "Pretty much. I couldn't afford creams."

"So you use your own. I like your frugal nature."

"What the fuck has wiping cum on my face got to do with ancient England? You're weird."

"Frugal, not feudal," Winston held his face in his hands.

Braiden grinned. "I know what it means. I might look like a dumb arse, but I have read a few books."

"You what?" Sam balked.

"Don't you dare tell anyone!"

"Openly admitting to smearing man juice on your face; no problem. Admitting to advancing your knowledge; threats of violence. It's weird how we operate..." Winston mused.

"I preferred porn with two ladies," Sam admitted, quietly.

"You mean lesbian porn," added Braiden.

"Yeah, but that sounded rude in my head."

"I preferred that too," said Winston.

Braiden raised a hand to make it a full three for three.

"They're so pretty," Sam gushed.

"And fit," Winston added.

"And naked," Braiden said, voicing what the others really meant.

"No more internet porn..." Winston lamented.

"It's going to be old magazines and cheesy, knock off DVDs from now on," said Braiden.

"We don't have electricity to power the DVD player," said Sam.

"Ok, just magazines then. Until Winston's hose lets loose and sticks all the pages together."

"I'll aim, I promise," replied the teen, holding up three fingers in a Scout salute.

"Into your mouth?"

"Like I said, protein is protein. We need to keep our strength up."

"I'll stay weak, thanks."

A rustle from up ahead stilled their movement. Silently slipping behind a thick oak, Braiden peered around the trunk. A small group of the undead were heading aimlessly through the same forest. Their trajectory was in a completely different direction, so he moved back out of sight and shook his head at the others. Waiting for the creatures to move away, they circled the tree to remain concealed. Winston held up his hands and blew into the thin gloves as quietly as he was able.

"Cold?" Sam whispered.

"A bit."

The crunch of shuffling feet across fallen twigs died away. Winston turned away and smiled to himself. His forays into the abandoned larders of decaying houses was always a lonely affair. Until that point, he didn't realise just how much fun he was having. Spending time with a couple of friends. Talking shit to each other. It was something he never would have believed possible. All because the dead decided to rise and eat the living. He was under no illusion that if the rampant cannibalism and fall of mankind hadn't happened, he would still be the same fat loser who hid packets of biscuits from his shame filled parents.

"Ok, we're clear," said Braiden.

"We can follow and kill them if you want?" suggested Winston.

"Nah, let them go. We've got enough to worry about."

51

"What food do you miss most from before?" asked Sam, eager to know more about his brothers. In much the same way as Winston, he was enjoying the opportunity to be a teenager again. Leaving aside the lurking corpses, of course.

"All of it," Winston replied.

"Yeah, but I'm talking about where your folks would take you for a birthday treat. You know, your pick of restaurant."

Winston and Braiden stared at him.

"I'm thinking we had massively different birthdays," Winston finally answered.

"I had to cook whatever was in the freezer. Chips and chicken nuggets mostly."

Sam looked aggrieved at his unintended insult. "I'm sorry, I forget sometimes."

Winston put an arm around his shoulder. "I was always partial to McDonalds."

"I'm a Burger King guy myself."

"I've always preferred KFC."

"At least we can all agree you're both totally wrong," Winston replied.

"What about movies?" Sam asked after careful thought.

"Action films," said Braiden without hesitation. "Things like *Jack Reacher* and *The Equalizer*. I love how they stand up for people who can't defend themselves." As the words flooded out, he suddenly realised that he had always been the bad guy during his formative years. Sam was the helpless victim. There were no heroes, not in real life. Only onlookers who were too scared to get involved, or often encouraged the behaviour.

Sam saw his face crumble and jumped in. "I liked them too. Now *we're* the heroes, trying to help the innocent. It doesn't matter who we were before, what we're doing now is what counts."

Winston clocked the exchange and caught the unshed tears in Braiden's eyes as he turned away. "I always liked horror. And comedy."

"We can tell," Sam replied.

"I can't help it if I'm hilarious."

"In your own mind," said Braiden.

"Even the finest comedians have critics."

"They also have fans," said Braiden.

"Ooh, tough crowd."

"I did like *Stepbrothers*," Braiden confessed.

"Will Ferrell is my all-time favourite actor! I love his characters."

"Who's the guy that seems to be in all his films?" asked Sam.

"John C. Reilly. He works so well as support."

Sam turned to Braiden. "You're John C. Reilly to my Will Ferrell."

"Fuck off. I'm the star of this show."

"You're both bit parts to the brilliance that is Winston. Never forget your place."

Braiden pulled out his screwdriver and showed him the pointy end.

"Ok, I can take the hint. I'll be the nameless henchmen that doesn't have any lines. I'm just here to get beaten up or killed."

"Nameless henchmen have a part to play in building up the main character. And by that, I mean me," Braiden replied.

"Or we could just all survive and be a trio of heroes."

"Like *Charlie's Angels*," Winston added.

"Weren't they all women?" scowled Braiden.

"Give me a break, it's the first trio I could think of," Winston replied.

"What about *The Three Musketeers*?" offered Sam.

"We don't have any muskets," replied Braiden.

"We've got the swords," added Winston. "If you class machetes as swords."

Sam withdrew the blade, a mischievous glint in his eye. Winston did the same, pointing at Braiden's as yet untouched weapon.

"What're you doing?"

"Just take out your chopper."

Braiden frowned and went to unzip his flies.

"Not that chopper, you dickhead," laughed Sam.

"I know." Braiden rolled his eyes and withdrew the blade. Holding it up, he looked around as if someone would witness his nerdiness. Sam and Winston joined him, the metal chiming gently.

As one, they all quietly cried, "All for one, and one for all."

CHAPTER 10

4 Hours Ago

"Shit," muttered Sam.

"Double shit," muttered Braiden.

"Triple shit," agreed Winston.

"Let's not go too far," cautioned Sam.

The sluggishly flowing River Arun passed before them. Hundreds of moons reflected on the rippling water as it made its way to the ocean to the south.

"We could swim?" suggested Braiden.

"I can barely feel my fingers as it is," Winston complained, wiggling the digits in his glove. "I'm buggered if I'm voluntarily getting in the water."

"How about *involuntarily*?"

Winston looked at Braiden. "If I go, I'm taking you with me."

"We can use you as a raft. We don't all need to get wet."

Winston's face dropped at the insult. "A fat joke. Good one," he replied, quietly.

"I wasn't on about your weight, dickhead!" Braiden replied, punching him on the arm. "I was talking about the amount of layers you're wearing!"

"You're like a blimp," Sam teased, poking at the deep insulation.

"I've only got two t-shirts, a sweatshirt, a jumper, and two coats on."

"And a thin set of women's gloves?" Sam added, pointing at the pink mittens.

"It's all I could find without arousing suspicion," Winston complained.

"Of course," Braiden conceded. "No one's going to ask questions when you're wearing those, are they?"

"I didn't wear them in the castle!"

"Not even when you were alone?" Braiden was unconvinced.

"Ok, maybe I tried them on for a bit alongside a nice dress and some high heels."

"And a wig?"

Winston shook his head. "Couldn't find one."

"We'll check the houses we come across, Winstina."

"Why, thank you," Winston replied in his best Southern Belle. "I must admit I'm not sold on the high heels, but the dress was certainly... freeing."

"I bet it was, weirdo," Braiden chuckled.

"Has the water stopped yet?" asked Sam, hopefully.

The gently flowing river was still passing languidly by at the bottom of the sloping bank.

"Fuck."

"I'm not going in there." Winston declared.

"I was only joking. We tried it on our way to the castle and it was a disaster."

"Peter nearly died."

Winston's eyes widened. "What?"

"He drowned. We brought him back."

"Technically, he brought himself back," Sam added, remember the coughing and spluttering as they prepared to do CPR.

Braiden shrugged. "Whatever. It was close."

"Too close," Sam agreed.

"At least he made it. Are we going to head left or right to find a bridge?"

"We could look at the map?" suggested Sam.

"I don't think the moon's bright enough to read it properly. Plus I don't really know what I'm looking for."

"Really? I had you pegged for a scout for sure."

"Too many people. Too much exercise. Too much nature."

"I thought you liked nature. You were always breaking out of the nunnery."

"I liked that I was able to find snacks. The walking through nature was a means to an end."

"What did you do in your spare time then?"

Sam looked at Braiden and they both said the words. *"World of Warcraft!"*

"The best game that ever was or will be," Winston replied, dropping to one knee and bowing his head to honour the memory.

"Rise, Sir Prancealot," chuckled Braiden, knighting him with the long bladed machete.

"Thank you, my queen," Winston replied.

"I'm not the one wearing dresses and high heels."

"So you say. How do we know?" Winston posed.

"You don't. I make sure the door is locked and blocked first."

Winston nodded, knowingly. "I thought so. You've got the legs to pull off a skirt."

"Why thank you, young man," Braiden cooed, fluttering a hand against his cheek.

"With all that online time, I bet you spanked your monkey plenty too," Sam teased.

"They didn't call me the hermit crab for nothing, you know," Winston replied proudly.

57

It took a second for the boys to conjure up the image of the crustacean; one small arm and one large arm. When it clicked they had to stifle their laughter in case it carried across the fields.

"You're one sick puppy," Sam giggled.

"I had one sock that was so hard I needed to crack it in half," Winston continued.

"Eww, gross!" Sam spluttered through his mirth.

"So did I," Braiden admitted, bringing more merriment. "Until my dad found it and beat the shit out of me."

The words were as shocking as a full dive into the icy water below. Smiles disappeared, laughter ceased like a closed tap. Sam knew of the abuse, but Winston had been in the dark up to that point. The honesty of his brother's admission proved to Sam that Braiden now fully trusted the other boy, otherwise he would have kept it a secret.

"I'm so sorry you went through that," Winston said.

"It made me strong," Braiden whispered, sniffing as a few stray tears trickled down his grimy cheeks.

"My mum and dad never laid a hand on me. They just hated me in a different way."

Sam pulled them both in and held them tight. "We're all the family we need now. I've got two awesome brothers, and you've both got a mum and dad that love you."

"Does that mean Kurt won't trim bits of me with his axe?" Winston asked, voice muffled by the clothing pressed tight.

"I give it a twenty percent chance he won't carve you up like a Christmas turkey," replied Sam.

"It's a chance. I'll take it."

"Has the water stopped yet?" asked Braiden, pulling away.

The mocking river continued to glide past towards the sea.

"Arsehole," Sam muttered.

Winston pulled his pack tight and stood tall. "Executive decision, we're going right. We follow it until we find a bridge."

"Lead on, Columbo," replied Braiden, waving an arm.

"I know you didn't just mean Columbus," Sam chortled.

"What's the difference?"

"One's a fifteenth century explorer, the other one's a hard bitten, glass eyed, cigar chewing American detective."

Braiden scowled. "Huh?"

"Just one more thing," replied Winston.

"What?" Braiden asked.

"It was his famous punchline! The murderer would think they'd got away with it, but Columbo would slap his forehead as if he was a moron, turn around, and then say those words."

"Then you knew they were busted," Sam added.

"You're both morons," Braiden complained, walking away.

CHAPTER 11

<u>3 hours Ago</u>

"That's the lane," Braiden whispered.

"You're sure?" Sam replied.

"Yeah, she said it was just outside the village. Twin brick pillars, with a forked track. One goes into the fields," Braiden indicated the muddy trail that led to a rusted iron gate. "And the other leads to three houses. The biggest one's theirs."

"Let's get moving then. What time is it?" asked Sam.

Winston checked his watch in the cold moonlight. "Just coming up to half past five. That gives us plenty of time to make it back by lunchtime. If we can get back on the wall we might be able to convince them we kept Holly company."

"It's worth a shot," agreed Sam.

"One problem," Braiden interjected. "We need to find out what happened to Christina's parents first."

"Ok, let's do it."

Leaving the concealment of the abandoned cars, they raced across the road and took cover by the wide stone column. The lane itself was empty, but the drone of undead in a heightened state of agitation came rasping from nearby.

"Ready?" Braiden asked.

Shucking off their packs, they tucked them away in deeper shadows. Winston weighed up the benefits of taking the battle-axe, then decided against it. Close quarters in a home setting wasn't ideal for such a large weapon. It would probably end up embedded in a block wall, with Winston trying to prise it free as the zombies bit his nuts off. Unsheathing the machete instead, they all proceeded down the tree lined drive. Shafts of moonlight lanced through the evergreen canopy, which they studiously avoided. Three sets of expensive wooden gates came into view. Two of which were closed, the electronic entry panels dark. The third, central pair, were broken away from the steel hinges. Shards of the shattered timber contained scraps of clothing and chunks of dried flesh.

"Whatever it was, there were a lot of them. See how fucked the bars are."

The thick, square steel struts which had held the gates in place were twisted completely out of shape.

"I think we're going to see how many in a second," Winston whispered.

The drive snaked out of view to the left, but each step forward increased the volume of the dead.

"That's got to be a good sign?" Sam whispered in reply.

"Something's kept them here," Braiden agreed, hopefully.

"Niiiiiiiiiice," Winston whispered almost inaudibly as the house came into view.

Dozens of zombies milled around among the shrubbery below the ground floor windows. Braiden scowled at the teen. "There's loads of them. What's nice about it?"

61

"The house. It's lush."

The house was indeed lush. Judging by the width, it would contain at least six bedrooms, notwithstanding how deeply it projected out onto the rear garden. Ivy trailed its way up trellising on the western wall. White glossed sash windows looked out over the ample driveway. Movement could be seen through every pane, both the partly broken of the lower floor and undamaged of the first. A quadruple garage lay to the left, both sets of doors fully open.

"It looks empty. Let's get inside and we can decide what to do next. I don't like being out in the open," whispered Sam.

"We'll follow you."

Using the darkness as an accomplice to their clandestine passage, they reached the garage without alerting the nearby horde. The dull drone of zombie communication and shuffling meandering were another useful tool in avoiding their ravenous attention. The crisp winter air took on the faint tinge of creosote, white spirit, and engines. Being out of the gentle, though frigid breeze, the temperature seemed to jump by several degrees. Winston took the opportunity to blow quietly through his hands, flexing the fingers to get the blood flowing. Sam was peering cautiously around the frame, thinking. Braiden was rapt on the silver beast before him.

"It's a brand new Mercedes AMG GT! Those things sell for like... Over a hundred grand," he marvelled.

"Looks like Dr Christina wasn't the only successful one in the family. It's a beaut," Winston agreed.

"The only way I could've afforded one of these is if I'd done a couple of bank jobs with my dad's mates."

"Don't sell yourself short!" Winston snapped. "You're smart enough to have done whatever you want."

"I'm dumb. Everyone knows it."

"Pack that shit in. You've managed to survive when most other people are dead... kind of dead, anyway. That's smart!"

Braiden ignored the compliment and circled the car, trying to peer through the windows. The gloom prevented any appreciation of the luxurious interior, so he finally gave up. Catching sight of a labelled drawer below the work benches, he pulled it out. Various types of glove were neatly laid out in two compartments. On the left were thick gardening, rubber, and other workwear. On the right were cycling mitts in men's and women's sizes.

"Winston, come here," he whispered.

"What's up?"

"Pop these on. They look a lot warmer than the one's you've got on," he replied, handing him a set of palm padded black cycling gloves. Slipping the thin, woollen ones off, Winston groaned in relief at the insulated softness of the new ones.

"Thank you, mate. They're great."

"Don't mention it," Braiden muttered, searching the racks for more treasures.

Approaching Sam, Winston carefully peered past him at the milling zombies.

"What do you think? Can we get in?"

"I've counted about three hundred in and around the house. There's bound to be more out of sight as well," he whispered.

"I think we can safely say that whoever's inside is in the attic," Winston added.

There was a marked increase in the agitation of the undead on the first floor when compared to the ground floor. Arms reached to the ceilings, the fingertips short by inches. No light spilled from the soffit vents or between the roof tiles. Other than the gurgles of the dead, no noises gave away any sign of an occupant.

"Is there any way we can get up there? Like how you did at your old house?"

"We can check around the back, but I doubt it. Our houses were all joined together and I snuck in an empty one on the end and jumped roof to roof. That whole place is crawling."

"What do you think our chances are of taking them on directly?"

"A few dozen, easy. A few hundred, we're supper."

"I'm not sure I like the sound of that," said Winston, falling silent. How could they clear the house without drawing any locals straight down on themselves? Fire always worked, but the houses sat atop a small knoll which would allow the glow to carry for miles. A distraction? Possibly, but what?

Unnoticed, Braiden had snuck away. He giggled in the darkness, causing them both to turn.

"What're you doing?" Sam gasped as a small light started blinking, quickly followed by two more. Then more. A familiar rattle of moving chain joined the low chuckling.

Emerging from behind the car, Braiden had attached several safety lights to a mountain bike. "Get back inside!"

"What the hell are you doing?" whispered Sam, furiously.

"Cardio!" He grinned. Pedalling slowly forward, he rang the bell. "Ding, ding, ding, mother fuckers!"

The undead loitering among the flowerbeds all turned in his direction. Several of those within earshot on the ground floor threw themselves over the windowsills and porch railing, landing heavily on the frost packed mud.

"He's crazy!" Winston whispered in Sam's ear.

"He's Braiden," Sam moaned, ducking back into the black shroud of the garage interior.

Doing a lazy circle, Braiden chimed the ringer for all he was worth. More cadavers flooded through the broken windows and open front door. Half of those on the upper floor started to peel away from whatever was in the loft, heading towards what he assumed must be the stairs. A few managed to smash the glass, before swan diving onto their unfortunate brethren below. Two more circuits and it became too dangerous to continue. Those that were engaged were now intent on eating him, the others would need to be dealt with another way. Lowering the gears, he pulled a wheelie and pedalled furiously for the shattered entrance.

"Feeding time! Come and get it," he called, skidding to a halt when he put too much distance between them.

The lights strobed from the frame and his coat, reminding him of a long forgotten Christmas. His father, drunk and high, had got it in his head to get a tree and decorate it. Disappearing with a wood saw, he returned twenty minutes later with the top section of a nearby pine from the local park. Unable, or more likely unwilling, to buy lights, a neighbours garden hedge was duly stripped of their own pretty LEDs. After planting the hacked tree into a bucket of builder's sand, Lennie attempted to add a plug to the torn wires.

Braiden peeked nervously from the filthy lounge curtains, only to find the victims of his father's endeavours pointing at their house. Anger and impotency were plain to see. The husband threw his arms in the air in a 'what do you want me to do?' gesture and the wife stormed off in disgust. Braiden thanked whoever was watching that the man was sensible enough to leave it alone. Getting smashed to pieces over a fifteen pound set of novelty lights was not a good way to start the holidays. Finally succeeding in outsmarting his uncooperative fingers, the plug was on. Wrapping the bulbs haphazardly around the branches, Lennie switched them on. Congratulating himself on a job well done, he headed to the fridge for a fresh can of high-strength lager. Stumbling from the lounge, he completely missed the cables melting from the increased voltage. The plastic coating burst into flames, causing the electrics throughout the whole house to trip out. Upon seeing the smoke and Braiden desperately stamping out the blaze, Lennie was lost to reason. The ungrateful little shit had caused it, and he needed punishment. A split lip, severe bruising, and two fractured ribs were Braiden's Christmas present for preventing an inferno.

"Wanker," he spat, wiping away the confused tears. Why was he still so broken about the loveless paternal relationship? He had a new family now. A better family. Perhaps it was the inescapable knowledge that those responsible for his existence on this earth valued him less than an animal. His mum vanished without so much as a goodbye or I love you. He was worthless. Totally worthless.

"Bitch."

Reaching the road, he came to a stop to allow the merry band of rotting fuckwits a chance to catch up. The growing winter wind chilled the flowing emotions on his cheeks. Biting down on his hand, the physical pain quickly surpassed that of his damaged soul. Tasting blood, he looked down to see the broken skin.

"I'm glad you're dead," he sneered to the ghosts of years past. Through the raw grief, he remained unconvinced by the words coming out of his mouth.

Satisfied the zombies were close enough, he set to pedalling again. Their destination was only about fifty yards away now, around the next bend in the road. Chiming the ringer, he cycled leisurely, zigzagging along the darkened road as if trying to dodge the unwanted memories. The crash barrier came into view. Hit by a speeding lorry, the impact dissipating steel was torn apart, each side splayed out over the steep sided embankment. In the harsh light of the full moon, Braiden could make out the darkened shell of the burned cab. The flames had made it partway through the trailer before guttering out from lack of fuel. *Eddie Sto* was all that remained of the well-known company name.

Hopping from the saddle, Braiden lined the front wheel of the bicycle up at the edge of the drop. Cranking the ringer for all it was worth, he waited for a decent number of the undead to round the corner before propelling it forward. Ducking behind the barrier, he scurried low, allowing the intact metal to hide his escape. Reaching the sizeable block of a concrete support, he stopped and dropped to the ground, peering through the gap.

"Fingers crossed," he whispered as the bike finished bouncing and skidding, shedding the flashing bulbs.

Lured by the sound to the precipice, the lead zombies caught sight of the strobes and followed. The stony embankment was no kinder to the decomposing corpses than the lorry or twisted bike. Made instead from rot weakened flesh, the bodies crunched and squelched as they descended. The oldest among the horde, whether fresh risen from the grave or turned at the outset of the apocalypse, broke apart completely, the decay too advanced to hold against the jarring impacts. One by one they followed, until the threat was nothing more than a wet mess of shattered, sundered, and broken things.

"Holy shit," Braiden muttered. It worked far better than he had dared to hope. In fact, he was fully prepared to lead them away at a light jog for a mile or two, before doubling back and sprinting to the house.

Standing up from the concrete block, his outline stood in stark relief against the lighter sky around him. Milky eyes saw their quarry and could only groan and salivate at the meal they would forever be denied.

Braiden answered their gurgled excitement with a wanker sign.

CHAPTER 12

2 Hours Ago

"How did it go?" whispered Sam as Braiden ducked into the garage.

Taking a few deep breaths, Braiden opened his mouth wide to minimise any gasping. "All good. They're fucked up at the bottom of a ditch."

"Good work!" Winston gushed.

"Don't be a kiss arse," warned the sweating teenager.

"Sorry, I'm still trying to find the right balance of kiss-assery and teenage indifference."

"You'll get there," Braiden grinned, wiping at his brow.

"What now?" asked Sam.

"We have to go in and clear them out. Or we can try and goad them out onto the front porch and kill them there?" Winston replied.

"There's a set of ladders at the back of the garage, I saw them on my way back. We could try and set them up so you can reach the attic."

Sam discounted the suggestion immediately. "Nah, if they're anything like my dad's set they'll rattle and clank like a bastard. I'd get halfway up and the zombies would knock them over."

"Which would buy time for me and Braiden to get inside safely," exclaimed Winston.

"Fuck you. I'm not a diversionary snack." Sam flipped him the bird.

"Hand to hand it is then," Winston replied, swooshing his machete.

"We're going to be in trouble if we get covered in brains and blood. We might not be able to slash and keep back like we can in the open."

"Masks as well as armour?" Sam replied.

Winston grimaced. "I hate wearing them but I think it'll be safer. I'll eat almost anything, but zombie is taking it a bit too far."

"What if we slapped a shit load of barbecue sauce on them?"

"Then get the grill fired up, baby! We're having zombie steaks!"

Fastening the protective visors, the three teenagers slowly broke cover. The remaining zombies within the property were either too caught up in reaching their prey, or zoned out thinking undead thoughts. It allowed the trio to make their way to the front porch without being discovered. Winston looked around, deep in thought. Before Braiden and Sam could climb the six steps to the small veranda and smashed front door, he held them back and raised a clenched fist. They dropped out of sight into shadows by either side of the small stairs and waited.

Retracing his path back to the garage, Winston retrieved a coil of spooled washing line cord still fresh in its packaging. Peeling the brittle plastic away, the sound seemed eerily loud in the hush of night. Re-joining Sam and Braiden, he indicated his plan wordlessly. Both gave the thumbs up, so Winston knelt on the lowest step and carefully moved up towards the thick newel posts. Tying off one loose end, he proceeded to loop the thin twine back and forth around the opposing supports until they became strong enough to withstand their purpose. Tugging on them forcefully, they held fast.

"Here goes. Be ready," whispered Winston.

Sam and Braiden rose, taking position nearby. Rapping gently against the bannister rail, Winston waited.

"Harder," urged Sam, watching the empty doorway.

Winston hit the flat blade against the wood again with more force. The sharp reports sounded deafening compared to the earlier unwrapping. From within, they could hear the subtle change. Vacant gurgling died away as the noise caught their attention. Some of the more macabre castle survivors attributed the groaning to wails of torment. What if the zombies were aware of themselves slowly rotting? What if they could feel the pain of decomposition as it ate at their bodies, but were forever trapped in mute silence within their own minds? Sam had suffered nightmares on at least three occasions since that discussion.

"We're in business," said Braiden as the first zombies staggered over the threshold.

Foot catching on the taut hazard, the first woman toppled headfirst down the steps. Her mouth made contact with the lowest tread, shattering teeth and tearing her jaw away.

Sam winced. "Ouch."

Before she could stand and show the gory wound, Winston opened a rent in the back of her head. One became ten, all collapsing over the tripwire. Slashing savagely, the boys were surgical in destroying the creatures. Open skulls spilled brains that trickled down the brick faced steps. Ten became thirty, and with the way becoming blocked, the undead separated and pressed against the wooden porch railing at either side. The timber strained, beginning to split.

"Get back. It's going to give!" ordered Braiden.

Losing the battle against the weight, the wood cracked, pitching the corpses from the porch.

"Let's get inside. They won't be able to get back up the steps," said Sam, cautiously treading between the slain zombies.

Following behind, Braiden marvelled at the reception room of the huge house. It was larger than the entire lounge of his modest, two bedroom council house. Six open doorways and a double wide central staircase gave the dead too many routes of attack, so Sam indicated the room to the right.

"We can funnel them through the door," he explained, pushing aside a grasping monster. It went down hard, toppling a table with an antique lamp atop the varnished top. It hit the carpet with a dull thud, causing several pocked, grey faces to peer down from above.

Braiden gawped at the size of the destroyed lounge which would be larger than an entire floor of his old home. *This is what hard work gets you,* he thought. *Why couldn't you have stayed, mum? Why didn't you push me to work harder in school?* Probably because she was a heartless bitch who was too caught up in trying to get away from him.

"This is good," Sam said, breaking into his sad thoughts to point out further doors leading from the lounge. "We can go room to room, leading and killing them. Winston, you check the path ahead. Me and Braiden will do the dirty work until we get tired."

"Sounds like a plan," he replied, rushing across the room.

"Bray, help me move the sofa. We can use it to give us a barrier."

Hefting the deceptively heavy leather couch, they quickly shuffled it across towards the door. Zombies were already filtering through, slowed by their selfish need to feed as they wedged shoulder to shoulder between the jambs. Hands began to clap against the lower panes of the lounge windows from the porch fallen. Thankfully, the raised construction of the property ensured they could only add an irksome distraction rather than any further danger.

"Ok, good," said Sam, dropping it short of the nearest creature.

"Hello, officer," said Braiden.

The unmistakeable police uniform was tattered and filthy. Protected by the stab vest, most damage had been done to the arms and legs. As he moved, the deep, festering bites pouted like small mouths. A single swipe from Braiden severed the head which went thudding across the hardwood floor. Resting on its side, the jaw still snapped.

"Hold them back," he barked, dragging the decapitated body around the blockade.

"What're you doing?"

"I've always wanted to try this," he replied, removing the taser from the duty belt.

"Do we really have time for this?" Sam complained.

"We've always got time for a little fun. How's our rear?"

"All clear," Winston replied, peeking through a crack in the second door. "It goes into the kitchen. I think they've all headed through to the main hall."

"Sweet." Raising the taser with X26 imprinted on the side, he inserted the cartridge and aimed at the nearest cadaver. A single bite wound on her neck had killed her, the ragged tubes of severed arteries clearly visible. Other than the grey, weeping flesh, she was among the least damaged corpses Braiden had seen for a long while.

"Do you even know what you're doing?"

"Yeah. PC Macey showed me how they worked when I was last locked up. He was cool," Braiden replied, deep in concentration.

Sighting the red dot at the woman's chest, he pulled the trigger. The prongs exploded from the weapon, embedding deeply as the crackle of voltage surged down the curled wires. Paralysed from the electricity, she fell face forward onto the sofa. Five seconds passed until finally the chittering stopped. Instead of shaking it off and getting up, she simply laid there in the same position.

"Is she dead?" asked Sam, cleaving his own zombie.

"I don't think so," Braiden replied. Staring at her open eyes, the irises were still visible beneath the milky coating of decomposition. They moved, fixing him in their gaze. Still, she remained motionless.

"I think the shock fried something in her brain."

"Who gives a shit? Kill her and help me."

Pocketing the weapon and the two spare cartridges, Braiden drove the screwdriver into the top of her head. Sam was darting in, slashing, then dodging back. Joining his brother, Braiden pulled his own blade.

"Don't kill enough that they block the way," Sam warned.

"Gotcha," replied Braiden.

Forced to march over the dead zombies, at least half of the reanimated toppled and fell from their lack of coordination, making for easier kills. Casting a look back, Winston was still watching the kitchen for any threat. By the time they reached the door, a trail of corpses lay in their wake.

"There's still too many," Braiden grumbled as the lounge slowly filled.

"Get back into the kitchen," said Winston, ushering them through.

Closing the door, he was heartened at how sturdy it felt.

"My arm's aching. I need a break," said Sam, breathing heavily.

"We can always retreat into the back garden?" offered Winston, pointing to the rear entrance. "We've put a big dent in their numbers already."

"What about those that fell?" asked Sam.

The dull rapping was still constant from the other room. "They're still at the windows. I can lead them away if I need to."

"Ok, garden it is."

Retreating into the darkness of the rear yard, they hunkered down by a pair of garden sheds.

"What's the plan, now?" asked Braiden.

"We rest for a while and then head back in," said Sam.

Winston watched the shadows on the upper floor slowly empty as the undead hobbled down the stairs. "I don't mean to be a killjoy, but what if they aren't up there?"

"What do you mean?"

"I mean, they must've heard us by now. Why not try and help? Or cry out?"

Braiden stared up at the roof. "They're just asleep. Or too weak to call out."

"Yeah, it's probably that, Bray," Winston replied, hating himself for the doubt on his brother's face. "Can you imagine how happy Christina will be when we get Mr and Mrs Hargis back to her?"

"We'll be heroes," said Sam, patting Braiden on the back.

"How many do you figure are left?" asked Winston.

Sam carried out a quick tally. "A hundred or so."

"Did you want to fight them?"

The two teenagers turned to Braiden who was facing towards the open fields beyond the home.

"What did you have in mind?" asked Winston.

Braiden pointed out a pile of darkness in the gloom. The cloud passed and the cold rays of the ghostly moon illuminated the unburned branches and assorted rubbish. A subtle change had occurred in the sky, hinting at the onset of sunrise.

"A fire?"

Braiden nodded to Winston. "A fire."

Sam was game. "Why not? Anything to make our lives easier. Daylight will stop it being too obvious from a distance too."

"Winston?"

He agreed. With morning rapidly approaching, it was the safest option.

Braiden left them crouched in the shadows while he sprinted around the house using any available cover. In less than five minutes he was back with an open bottle of clear liquid. Sam had been around Kurt and their home decorating projects enough to recognise the smell of white spirit.

"When I say go, use those bushes to head back around the front. Most of the dead are trying to fight their way back inside the house up the steps, so you should be ok. They didn't see me, after all."

"Gotcha," replied Winston.

"Back in a jiffy, mo-fos."

Sam and Winston waited patiently while their brother doused the pile in the liquid.

"Go, go, go!"

Braiden waited for them to get out of sight before striking his lighter. The blue flame crept greedily over the wood, curling and igniting deeper into the huge pile of rubbish with a dull whoomp. The outer layer was still a bit damp from the night frost but with the accelerant, the moisture hissed away and the pyre started to crackle.

Keeping low, he coaxed the fire with slow, steady breaths. Every time he thought it was going up, the flame sputtered. The firelight, though weak, was still too bright, so Braiden escaped the growing swathe of flickering yellow and moved behind the bushes to watch. If the fire petered out completely, they would have no alternative but to fight. He wasn't particularly bothered either way. A few minutes passed as the two elements went to war, neither giving an inch. Braiden was all but convinced it was a lost cause until something flared. The core of the fire grew in strength and in no time the flames were climbing into the night sky, the water defeated. Shielding himself from the light in the way Jonesy showed him, Braiden watched the cadavers stagger from the house. Reluctant to leave the marginal heat supplied by the growing inferno, he sighed and backed deeper into the shadows before making for the front of the property.

"We're in business!" he whispered, joining the others back in the garage.

"Do you think it'll keep them occupied long enough?" asked Sam.

"It's a big pile, so probably."

"Let's get it done, then. I can't wait to meet them," said Winston, trying to convince himself.

Breaking cover, the trio moved back to the steps and butchered the zombies who were unable to make it past the bodies. Pulling them aside, they carefully entered the house again.

"Deja-vu," said Sam.

"You got that right," replied Braiden, moving back through the lounge. The blonde lady was still rigid, even in death. Peeking into the kitchen, the tail end of the undead was patiently pushing through into the fading night.

A starburst of sparks soared up from the fire as one of the zombies got a bit too close and toppled on to the pyre.

"We'll need to be quick. I didn't figure the dickheads putting the fire out by committing suicide on it," muttered Braiden as another shower of embers fluttered up on the waves of heat.

"How many left?" Winston asked over his shoulder.

Three. Two. One. None. "That's the last of them," whispered Braiden, pushing through and crawling to the open door. Closing it slowly, he dropped the handle and let it go only when the door was closed. Twisting the key, the route was secured.

"Ok, back the way we came. There may still be zombies, so be on guard."

"Yes, boss," grinned Winston. His amusement at the take charge teenager disappeared at the foot of the staircase. In less than a minute, they would know for certain if their mission was a success... or not. Too much hope rode on the outcome. Too much goodwill needed to be repaid. They *were* up there! The reunion of parent and daughter would be spoken about in the histories of the zombie apocalypse.

Why then wouldn't Winston's feet move?

Sam displayed the same hesitation, staring at the first step.

"It's only zombie juice," snorted Braiden, missing, or more likely ignoring, their doubt.

His trainers squeezed the liquid rot from between the thick pile with each step.

"Gross," said Winston.

"Gross," agreed Sam.

"Come on!" Braiden reached the landing and disappeared from sight.

"I hope they're up there," sighed Winston.

"I hope so too," agreed Sam.

Jogging up the stairs in pursuit, they tried to keep to Braiden's steps.

"Fucking son of a fuck!" Braiden snarled.

"Oh dear," said Winston.

The curses pouring from the third doorway were low, but filled with disappointment.

"What is it?" asked Sam, entering the bedroom.

"Rats. It's fucking rats," he said, rage turning to weary acceptance. He dropped the torch into Winston's open palm, before slumping on the bed.

"How can you be so sure?" said Winston, climbing up the freshly dropped access ladder.

"The size of the droppings," said Braiden. "Plus I saw one scurry back into the nest. You can see it by the chimney."

Winston climbed the first few rungs, and scanned the loft. Finding the chimney, he aimed the beam and found the pile of shredded paper and linen. The fearful creatures shuffled around inside, causing it to jiggle as if a living thing.

"Shit!" Winston hated that his hunch had proved correct.

"Nothing?" asked Sam.

"Nothing I can see. I'm going to take a look around. Keep an eye on the party," Winston said, pointing at the windows and the burgeoning dawn.

Climbing out onto the boarded loft, he kept his head bowed to prevent a painful connection with the rafters. A rat peeked out from the gnawed strands of its nest, then quickly retreated when Winston looked in its direction.

"I'm not here for you, buddy. You're safe."

Moving amongst the relics of years past, Winston felt at ease. The loft of his own home was often a refuge from the toxic environment on the floors below. Scanning through the dusty albums, he could almost convince himself that the smiles in the family snaps weren't forced. That the love on display was real, not some sham for the photographer that flicked off as readily as a switch when their backs were turned. The black and white pictures of his grandparents were by far his favourite. Lacking colour, they still conveyed more warmth than the newer photos with his own parents. Love positively radiated from the dull images. It was in the eyes. The smiles. Even the postures. Maybe they had too much love inside, and by bringing their light to the world, his own blood kin were starved of the nutrients to nurture the same emotions. God, how he missed them.

"Anything?" called Sam, quietly.

Swallowing the lump of concrete in his throat, Winston continued the search.

"Nothing yet," he replied.

Moving past the huge chimney stack that served several of the rooms, he found the source of part of the rat's nest. Duvets, blankets, and pillows were laid out neatly on two camping beds. At least they had been. Evidence of the rodents messing with the neatly made sleeping areas were obvious in the missing corners, torn seams, and spilled feathers. Empty bottles sat alongside bottles filled to the brim with yellow liquid. Winston didn't need to be a survival expert to understand it wasn't apple juice fermenting in the containers. A sealed picnic box sat against the aged brickwork of the chimney. At the bottom, a neat hole had been chewed through the blue plastic to get at the contents within.

"You've got it made up here, don't you?" he said to the twitching ball of textile and paper.

"What's that?" said Sam.

"They were up here," Winston confirmed. "There's two beds."

"But no sign of Christina's folks?"

"Nope, nada."

A shredded envelope was strewn across the second bed. Winston picked up the fragments and found the letters CHR and IN written in black ink. The seal had been licked and pressed, but the accompanying letter was nowhere to be seen. Checking beneath the thick canvas of the bed liner, nothing was concealed in the dark recess.

"You little buggers!" Winston scolded as he looked closer at the nest.

Thin strips of the secret contents were woven into the fabric of the rat's home. The ink was the same colour, with the same handwriting style. Reaching for the paper, a thought suddenly popped into Winston's head. A dozen rats, all hungry after the picnic food ran dry, pouring from the nest. Scurrying up sleeves, trouser legs, down collars, nipping, tasting, then feeding. And Winston, beating against the padding of his many layers, doing no damage at all to the creatures feasting on his tender flesh.

"Fuck that," he said, stamping down on the boards.

Three black creatures flashed out of the nest, disappearing instantly in the loft insulation and shadowed nooks.

"Sorry!" he said.

With three chewing away on him, it would've been the slowest death imaginable. He shuddered at the thought.

Kneeling by the empty den, he picked carefully at the bits of letter so he didn't cause too much damage. Seven pieces were retrievable without tearing the sphere of cloth and paper to pieces. He hoped it would be enough.

Taking the scraps with him, Winston scurried down the creaking ladder and showed the teenagers his prize.

"Who's good at puzzles?"

They stared at him blankly.

"Oh, so because I'm a nerd, you think I'm automatically good at puzzles."

They slowly turned their faces towards each other, then back to Winston.

"Yeah."

"Ok, I am," he admitted, passing the torch to Braiden.

Lining up the slivers, he studied the teeth marks. One was a corner piece with a greeting, so he discarded that immediately. Some edges lined up, while others were obviously separate pieces without the adjoining length.

Nothing. No clues.

Winston resigned himself to entering the loft again, and spent close to an hour gently filtering through the nest with as much care as he could muster. When he was sure he had all the available pieces, and that any others were lost to them, he descended the ladder. Braiden was asleep on the bed, and Sam was watching the funeral pyre outside with grainy eyes.

"I've shut all the doors," Sam explained. "I think we should try and get an hour or two of sleep before we head out. I'm kinda zonked."

Winston's adrenaline was ebbing away following the fighting and discovery of the treasure locked in strips of sacred parchment. Well, technically it was A4 paper, but the excitement was real. He yawned.

"I'll just get this all lined up first, then I'll spot you for an hour. Deal?"

"Deal."

Another fifteen minutes passed while they rearranged the strands. Braiden woke up, checked his watch, yawned, and then headed for the window.

"Nice to see they've mostly cooked themselves," he said.

Below, the wide circumference of black and red embers contained dozens of bodies. Some were still struggling within the dying flames.

"Idiots," he muttered. "What does it say?" he asked, returning to the dresser table.

Sweet words of love and hope could be read. Pride at Christina's achievements. Apologies about not always being there for her. Heartfelt and warming. But it was a part of a name that caught their attention.

"There!" said Sam.

"What does it say?" asked Braiden, leaning closer.

"Pulbor," replied Winston.

"And that?" Sam pointed.

"Safe. Try to make."

"And I bet the missing words are "it to"," Braiden added.

"It's got to be Pulborough. It's the only town I can think of near here."

From above came the faint squeaks of angered rodents as they investigated their ransacked home. Winston grimaced, "Oops. I think they're pissed at me."

"Who cares? We know where they are. A quick nap, and we hit the road."

Hope was not lost, after all.

CHAPTER 13

<u>**Now**</u>

"Do you have the map?" asked Braiden.

Winston ruffled in a side pocket and pulled out the plastic wallet. Unfolding the paper, he creased the surplus pages to show only the local area and placed it on the bedside table.

"We're... there," he said, pointing. "There's Houghton village. Christina's folks are..."

They all scanned the names and contours of the land, finally finding the location.

"There!" Braiden finished.

"Fuck my life!" Winston moaned.

"Fuck *our* life," countered Sam.

Braiden's dirty fingertip had picked out a point due north. Using the scale marker, he did a quick calculation. "Another four and a half miles by the looks of it. And that's as the crow flies. I doubt we'll be able to go in a straight line."

"There goes our chance to sneak back in before dad finds out we're gone," Sam sighed.

"As if he wouldn't know. Your dad *knows* everything. He *sees* everything," Winston groaned. "He's going to introduce me to the sharp end of his hatchet."

"Or war pick." Braiden piped up.

"Yeah, or that."

"Or his hammer," Sam finished, helpfully.

"Now that we've cleared it out, I think I'm going to move in here," Winston declared, looking around his new home.

"Dad will find you."

"Do you really think so? I'll have to keep heading north to try and outrun him. I can try and survive on a couple of hours sleep a day."

Sam shook his head, sadly. "It won't be enough."

"You're fucked," said Braiden.

"I can always plead for mercy. Do you think he'd believe you both forced me into it?"

Braiden looked at Sam. "Probably, but you're still getting the axe."

Winston pondered the situation, rubbing his chin. "Ok, disguise it is then. I'll shave my head and pretend to be a Buddhist monk. There's bound to be some orange sheets or material lying around I can turn into a smock."

"That might work," said Sam.

"Really?"

"No, you'll just die bald and dressed in Aunt Vera's lounge curtains."

"Fuck my life!" Winston wailed.

Sam and Braiden burst out laughing while trying to shush the overdramatic teen.

"If I was a horde, you'd all be food right about now," growled a deep voice from the hallway door.

Braiden spat out a few choice expletives. Sam swung around defensively with machete raised. And Winston let out a shrill yelp of surprise.

DB stepped through the doorway. Even in the gloom of the winter morning they could see he wasn't happy.

"What the hell are you playing at? Do you want to get yourselves killed?"

"How... how did you find us," blurted Sam.

"And how did you know we were gone?" asked Braiden. His heartrate was slowing from two hundred beats a minute to its normal eighty now the shock had worn off.

"Is Kurt going to cut me?" Winston gulped.

"One at a time!" DB grumbled. "We found you because you're so bloody predictable. Did you think we wouldn't find out about your questions to Christina earlier?"

Winston looked at the others. "I told you we came on too strong."

"Strong? She had you clocked after the first sentence. You were as transparent as glass. What village? What house? Any obvious features?"

Braiden shrugged. "Ok, fair point."

Sam frowned at his earlier statement. "We?"

"Jonesy's at the front door keeping watch."

"Is he pissed off?" Braiden asked.

"No, which is why I'm up here to give you a well-deserved bollocking. He's more likely to shake your hand or give you a high five."

"I've always preferred Jonesy," Winston remarked sarcastically. DB growled and the teenager shrunk away.

"Two. Christina came to me when she grew too worried. The only safe place to get out of the castle unseen is from the northern end, and who did we find on guard? Your friend, Holly."

"She gave us up?" said Sam.

"Instantly," DB replied.

"Snitches get stitches," muttered Braiden.

"You can't trust anyone." Sam felt betrayed. She'd promised!

DB could sense the boys' disappointment. Marching forward, he grabbed them by the arm. "She was scared shitless for you, even though she wouldn't admit it when you left. When we asked her where you were she was so relieved to get it off her chest. I swore we'd bring you home safe."

"We're fine. We don't need your help," Braiden seethed, pulling his arm free.

Sam knew the attitude all too well from the times when teachers would challenge his behaviour at school. The downcast eyes, the gritted teeth, the clenched fists. DB represented another form of authority, and the teenager was responding in kind.

"Hey," DB snapped, rounding on the boy. "I know you can handle yourselves! I've *seen* you handle yourselves! The bodies everywhere in here, plus I don't know what that mess is in the back garden, and the trick you pulled out on the road show you can handle yourself! I'll admit, we weren't as worried as Holly." DB paused to let the words sink in. "But! That doesn't mean we can just let you go wandering off without making sure you're ok! You know the type of people that might be out here now. What if you'd run into more than just zombies?"

"We'd have hidden like you and Jonesy taught us," Braiden replied, meeting the soldier's gaze. Some of the fire had left his eyes, a sign that DB was talking on his wavelength.

DB smiled despite his anger. "I'll bet you would've too."

"And three?" Winston inquired, uncertainly. He could already feel the sharp kiss of steel.

"No one knows but us, Christina, and Holly," he lied. "I'll do my best to keep it that way."

"Thank God!"

"At least you won't need to shave your head and wear an orange dress," DB chuckled.

"How long were you listening?" Winston spluttered.

"Long enough."

"I might still wear the dress," Winston added.

85

"What you get up to in private is none of my business. Now let's get you home," DB replied, turning towards the door.

The boys remained motionless. "We didn't find her parents," said Sam.

"They're here," added Braiden, pointing at the map.

"Christina wants you home. She doesn't want you in danger, not that she doesn't love you all for trying." He came close to explaining their terrible timing and coincidence of the Gypsy attack, but he decided against it for now.

"We're not going back without finding them," Braiden said, resolutely.

Sam and Winston stood side by side with the hellraiser, defiance written plainly on their faces.

"You saved *us*, she saved *you*, *we're* saving her mum and dad," said Sam.

"Trying to," Winston added.

DB appraised the fearsome youngsters and smiled again. Their foolhardy logic was undisputable. "You little fuckers are gonna be the death of me."

"So you'll come with us?" asked Sam, eagerly.

"Yes, we'll come. On one condition."

"What's that?"

"If we don't find them at the next location we call it off for now. If they aren't there it'd be like looking for a needle in a haystack. Not to mention the reality..."

"What do you mean?" Braiden asked.

"Bray, if they aren't here, and they aren't there, how many safe places are there?"

"You mean they're probably..."

"Yeah."

"I understand," he replied, morosely. In their youthful minds, failure had never entered the equation. They *knew* Gail and Don were ok. They *knew* they would find them. And they *knew* that Christina's kindness would be, in some small way, repaid. The rodent infested house was the first blow to their theory. Braiden hoped that upon

86

finding the settlement, they wouldn't be hit with the knockout.

"Did you want to raid the kitchen for some bottles of water?" DB asked as they stepped carefully around the gore.

Winston pulled a face, remembering the cloudy yellow bottle above, and DB scowled at him.

"Nah," Sam replied, "Our canteens are in our backpacks by the front gate. We couldn't fight with them."

"I had a feeling you were going to say that," DB said with relief. "I was going to tear you a new one if you came out here unprepared."

"We've got everything. First aid kit," began Braiden.

"Not that it would do much good if we got bitten," Winston chimed in.

"I've got this just in case," Braiden replied, pointing his screwdriver. "We've also got food for a couple of days. Wet weather gear. Stuff to start a fire. A tarp to make a shelter. Torches just in case. Plus the water."

"We could still check the kitchen..." Winston suggested.

"For snacks?" DB chuckled.

"Knowing how fit Christina's parents were I was expecting more chia seeds and kale. But they might have a forgotten pack of chocolate digestives in the back of a cupboard somewhere."

DB pondered for a moment. "You've already done the leg work in clearing out the dead. We may as well bag up any food to take back with us. It could buy us a day or two."

"Even if it does taste like shit," Winston muttered.

"You mean healthy?" DB replied.

"Sounds the same to me," remarked the unimpressed teenager.

CHAPTER 14

"What took you so long?" asked Jonesy as they left the house.

Glancing down, he saw the fully laden double layered shopping bags.

"We struck gold, brother," DB replied. "Enough rice, pasta, and canned goods to last us all a week. At least."

"Canned cabbage. Canned pickles. Canned kale. Canned crap," Winston complained.

Jonesy raised an eyebrow.

"He's just salty because we didn't find any food high in saturated fats," DB explained.

"Not even a solitary bag of crisps," Winston sighed.

"Bollocking delivered?" Jonesy asked.

"Signed and sealed," DB confirmed.

"Can I say my bit now?"

"No! They know you think they're bloody heroes. Heroes who need a good arse kicking!" scolded DB.

Jonesy was cradling his rifle, chest puffed like a proud father. The cheesy grin on his face was infectious and

DB found himself smiling along. "I told them they're going to be the death of us. Don't encourage them for fuck's sake."

"Risking their lives. Unwilling to leave a good man and woman behind. Braving the cold and zombies to do what's right. Sounds like a certain two hundred and twenty pound, six foot six soldier I used to know," mused Jonesy, rubbing his chin in mock contemplation with his free hand.

"It's more like two hundred and ten now," DB laughed. "And that's not helping!"

"Ah, cut the kids some slack. How's this any different to us fucking off from Thorney to help our boys at the hospital in Chichester?"

"And they haven't got a target on their back from a lunatic with access to long range snipers," DB agreed.

"Long range snipers?" asked Braiden.

"Drop shorts," added Jonesy.

"Huh?" Sam was lost.

"Artillery, boys. Gunnery teams."

"Like your friend who helped us in Chichester?" asked Sam.

The memory of Bennett's actions to save their lives still burned brightly. They would find some way to repay his sacrifice, that was a promise.

Sam saw the sadness and kicked himself. "I'm sorry. I didn't mean to bring it up like that."

"It's ok, mate," Jonesy replied. "He was a damned good man. I'll tell you about our tours in Afghanistan one day. His close cover saved our arses more than once."

"I'd like that," Sam replied and the two other teenagers nodded eagerly.

"In the meantime," Jonesy said, standing straighter and banishing the haunting guilt, "let's stow the food and get a move on. I've gotten soft in my old age and want to get back by the fire."

"We can look for a pipe and slippers while we're out here if you want?" suggested Winston.

"I'm not *that* old," Jonesy started to protest, then reconsidered. "Though a nice pair of slippers to potter around the castle in do sound tempting."

"We've got a bit of a problem, brother," said DB.

"What sort of problem?" Jonesy stared around, searching for a threat. "Do you mean?"

DB shook his head. He wasn't talking about the prison assault. "The problem of three obstinate little fuckers and knowing that Don and Gail left here to take shelter in a village a few miles due north."

"What're we waiting for then?" Jonesy replied without any hesitation.

DB groaned. "I was hoping you might help me talk some sense into them."

"We're already out here freezing our nuts off. What difference does a few miles make?"

"Exactly," said the boys in unison.

"Death of me," DB muttered, walking towards the broken entrance. "Little fuckers."

"Hold on a second," called Braiden.

"What's up, mate?"

"I found these inside while we were fighting," he replied, holding up a fob with the Mercedes logo. "We could travel a couple of the miles in style?" Braiden pointed at the rear of the AMG.

Winston agreed eagerly. "Yeah, the roads are pretty empty out here in the countryside."

DB scowled, but his eyes traced the slick contours of the shadow shrouded luxury vehicle. "What about the noise?"

"We'll be fucked if we bring a horde down on our heads," added Jonesy.

"We just keep the revs low. They're fairly quiet as long as you don't gun it."

"And how would you know?" DB asked.

"You mean did I ever steal one?" Braiden bridled.

DB threw his hands up in frustration. "Fuck me! No, I just asked a question. You need to let this woe is me shit go, mate. I didn't have the easiest time as a kid being raised in London, either."

"You didn't?"

"Hell no! My old man left when I was ten. He didn't even say goodbye."

Braiden held DBs gaze as his own memories returned again.

"I was one of the only black kids on my street. And I was a fat little fucker to boot. I used to get beaten on my way to school, get beaten by the teachers at school, and then get beaten on my way home."

"Really?" gasped Sam.

"Nah, the teachers were actually pretty cool. They tried their best to give us a shot in life which was more than most people. But the other kids? Every... single... day. It got so bad I tried to kill myself. Luckily, mum found me and the hospital pumped the pills out of me."

"Whoa," Winston exclaimed. The thought of the fearsome soldier being the victim of any kind of physical assault didn't compute, let alone the situation becoming so grim he felt the only way out was suicide. Even during the darkest days of his own adolescence at the hands of the school bullies, ending things had never entered his mind.

DB continued with a sad shake of his head. "I had two choices; let them win, or fight."

"So you fought?" asked Braiden.

"No, I made my second mistake as a kid. I joined a local gang."

"I'll get her started," interrupted Jonesy, taking the key fob.

"What happened?" asked Braiden.

"The usual shit. I did a bit of running for the top boys on the manor, hash and sometimes harder stuff. The police weren't aware of who we were and how many of us were doing it. Nowadays they're a little more savvy, with all the county lines drug running. Sorry, *were*. I made a bit of money which helped my mum out. She knew where it was coming from, I know she did, but she kept out of it because

I was finally making friends. She didn't know how dangerous they were at the time."

Jonesy had started the Merc and backed the vehicle out of the garage. Apart from the crunch of tyres on gravel, the engine was purring like a kitten, making very little noise.

"Load up the gear and we'll be on our way," Jonesy said, climbing from the driver's seat.

"We'll get our bags," offered Winston.

"And I'll get the food," said DB.

Jonesy popped the boot open as the teenagers ran towards their stashed belongings.

"They done well, didn't they?" he asked as DB stowed the bags.

Looking around at the piles of corpses, he allowed himself a smile. "They're a three man wrecking crew. I can't believe they didn't get themselves in the shit."

"What did I tell you?"

"Yeah, yeah, you were right. I can't help it if I worry about them."

"I know, mate, I do too. It's the apocalypse, though. We're all in danger every minute of every day. It'll fuck with our heads to dwell on it too much."

"I know."

"In the boot?" asked Braiden as he approached.

"Please, Bray. We can just grab them back out when we run out of road."

"Ok."

After loading up, the five climbed back inside the car.

"Oh. My. God," groaned Winston as his bottom made contact with the heated seats.

"Thought you'd like it," chuckled Jonesy, shifting into drive. "Do you want the heaters on?"

"Yes!" Winston exclaimed.

"No," replied Sam.

"And can you turn the seat heaters off, please?" asked Braiden.

"What for? What's the point of having a ride if we can't enjoy it?"

"Grandad was the one who taught us about acclimatisation. We're going to be out in the freezing cold again shortly, so I'd rather just stay cold."

DB looked across at his partner. "They make a good point."

"No they don't!" Winston moaned. "Their point's rubbish. I want a toasty warm bum. And warm air blowing in my face. And a McDonald's breakfast."

"Best I can do is some steamed kale," offered Jonesy.

"I hate you," Winston huffed.

"You love me," Jonesy countered.

"Ok, I do," he agreed. "But my stomach and arse hate you. I can't control their opinions."

They turned left out on to the main road, staying below twenty miles an hour which seemed to be an ideal speed in terms of engine and road noise.

"What happened next?" asked Braiden, still fixated on the soldier's youth.

"You want me to go on?"

"Please."

"Ok. Our crew was growing and I was invited to step up, to become more involved. They saw how well I moved their gear. Being fat and nerdy looking meant I was completely invisible to the old bill. They liked that. Part of my initiation was getting beat to shit, which was no different to any other day. That was the easy bit."

DB paused, remembering what came next. A feeling of revulsion twisted his stomach into knots.

"The final part was going into Peckham and finding someone from the Peckham Boys."

"Who were they?"

"One of our rivals. They were run by a heavy mob from Albania, real gangsters."

"What did you do?" asked Braiden. He could tell it was bad by the conflict visible through the rear view mirror. DB was wrestling with a long buried guilt.

"We went there alone. The risk was a part of the initiation," he replied, skirting the question as he thought how best to admit his crime. "If we were caught, we'd be lucky to make it out in one piece."

Nearly a full minute passed in silence as everyone waited for him to continue. Hedgerows gave way to a small village. Figures could be seen moving around in the gardens and car park of the local inn. Jonesy expertly steered around any blockage, including mobile varieties. One gave them a fright as it beat on the glass as they passed.

"It wasn't like it is today in London. Life still had meaning, back then. There was still respect."

He fell silent once more. The village receded to their rear as fields opened up before them. A solitary scarecrow was mounted on a cross of rotting timber. Deeper in the farmland, undead scarecrows wandered, instilling more fear than the straw stuffed dummy.

"I killed a kid. He was my age, about thirteen," DB finally said, the words choking out. "I didn't mean to. We had to cut them, that was all. Leave them scarred so they would be a warning to all their friends. He... he saw me. Just as I was about to lunge out of the shadows, I hesitated. He pulled his own blade. We fought... I can't remember what happened next, only being laid on the ground. I thought I'd been stabbed, there was so much blood. He was facing me. His mouth was moving, but he couldn't speak. Then he was still. I saw my knife sticking out of his chest."

"Fuck, I'm sorry, mate," said Jonesy. This was as new to him as it was to the three dumbstruck teenagers in the back.

"I was treated like a hero. They idolised me. The fearless fat kid who murders their enemy," he laughed sickly, shaking his head. Flowing tears glinted on his cheeks in the morning light.

"Sorry, DB. That's tough," said Braiden, reaching forward to pat his shoulder.

"You know the worst thing? I never got caught. I never paid for my crime. He was buried, and I went on living. I can still see his eyes when I go to sleep. The way they just glazed over. They were brown."

"I hate to ask," began Winston, cautiously, "but why become a soldier? You'd be forced into doing the same thing, wouldn't you?"

"You know what, mate, I never really thought about it until you asked me. When mum found out, she moved us away to the Pennines. A ratty little town with no jobs and no prospects. If I'm honest, I think I joined the army to die."

"You wanted to commit suicide again?" asked Braiden.

Things clicked in Jonesy's mind. "No, not suicide. He wanted to die saving people."

DB laughed again. Wiping at his face, he laid his head back against the headrest, as if the weight of memory was suddenly too heavy to bear.

Jonesy continued to explain. "Whenever we were out on patrol from Camp Bastion, this crazy fucker would always volunteer to take point. Whenever we got into a firefight and one of us took a bullet, he would charge in to drag them out. It's all starting to make sense."

"Didn't work though, did it? I'm still here."

"Seems to me, someone had other plans for you. How else could someone as big as you avoid getting shot in the arse?"

"Or anywhere else," DB added with a saddened chuckle.

"You didn't mean to do it, that's what counts. You were scared. It was an accident. You've made up for it a hundred times over," said Jonesy.

"Doesn't bring him back, though, does it?" DB replied. Turning away, he looked out of the window, seeing nothing but the vacant brown eyes, and blood. So much blood.

CHAPTER 15

"I guess this is the end of the road," said Jonesy, coasting to a stop in the middle of the street.

The junction was full to brimming with burned out cars. Parked up neatly by the wreckage were further vehicles who had arrived after the crash. Whatever was pursuing the missing people had been terrifying enough for them to just bolt, leaving the doors open to the elements. Jonesy remembered the sight of the growing Emsworth horse as it ate its way through the stream of traffic trying to reach their barracks. He prayed at least some of them had made it to safety.

"I can see the station through the trees," said Winston, pointing.

"That means the trainline should take us all the way to Pulborough. Another..." Jonesy studied the unfurled map pressed against the steering wheel, "half mile or so."

"Leave the food or take it?" asked DB.

"We may as well leave it. We'll have to come back this way regardless, so it saves us humping it," said Jonesy.

They climbed from the car and slipped the backpacks on. Jonesy locked the Mercedes and slipped the fob out of sight in the front wheel well.

"Who's going to steal it out here?" DB chuckled.

Sam and Winston slowly looked at Braiden with smirks on their faces.

"Fuck you both. I want to be an only child again!" he muttered before storming off.

"Let's get our asses moving. I think sitting comfortably has messed up my back," DB groaned.

They ignored the easy to access crossing by the station, opting to head across one of the fields and fence hop instead. The stations seemed to have taken on a significance to the dead who sought them out to wait on the platform for a train that would never come. It reminded Sam of a Romero film he had seen. The characters discussed the behaviours of the dead and why they congregated in places that were once part of their living lives. This trail of thought naturally brought him to the musings of the castle survivors in that the people were still aware inside their new, rotting frames. Sam quickly changed his thoughts to that of Holly to banish the horror.

"Oh shit, this can't be good," muttered Jonesy at the sight of the rising plumes of black smoke in the distance.

The sounds of battle, though faint, were well known to the soldiers, a constant companion on the killing fields. The arena and enemy were different, as were the means of waging war. Gone was the chatter of automatic weapons, the crack of detonating grenades. The one remaining constant was the fear in the cries, the shrill screams of the injured and dying.

"Let's move!" DB ordered.

Securing their belongings, they moved to the side of the rusted train track and pursued the sprinting giant towards Pulborough town. The steel lines stretched on, bending around a corner towards a bridge.

"Mind your step!" called DB without breaking stride. He danced expertly from support to support, missing the gaps completely. One false step, combined with the impetus, would likely snap his leg like a twig. Jonesy and the boys were more cautious, hopping carefully between the thick ties.

As they all reached the other side, DB came to a sudden halt and held up a hand. They dropped to their knees while he checked ahead through the rifle scope. The station was totally deserted. Considering the raging chaos in the near vicinity it was to be expected. Undead from miles around would be drawn to the noise so they had to move fast. Bypassing the empty platforms ahead, they dodged over the flattened railway chain-link directly into the station car park. Jonesy traced the well-trodden path of the horde back along its route to the west. The crushed foliage and footprints stretching across the field to the woods beyond indicated a sizeable force.

"They've only come through recently," noted Braiden. Insects writhed sluggishly on the ground, perishing after falling from their rancid, fleshy home.

"How can they survive in the zombies?" asked Sam, grimacing.

"Ask the scientists if we ever find any," replied DB, dismissing the question. "I don't like the look of this one bit."

"When's there ever been anything to like about this shit?" asked Jonesy.

"I'm talking about the numbers. This is only from one direction," DB explained, indicating the fresh, grave rot smears marring every vehicle panel and window in the area like some crazed abstract art.

Jonesy sighed in frustration. "You think we might be out of our depth?"

"We've got a couple of hundred rounds and the Three Musketeers. What do you think?"

Jonesy looked at his friend, to the gore coated boys, then back to DB. "I think the zombies are the ones in the shit."

"You better believe it," said Winston, hefting his axe.

Sam and Braiden let the glint of the morning sun on their blades do the talking.

"This isn't the time for bullshit heroics! People are dying nearby. They're dying bad. If I get a sniff that we're outgunned, I'm pulling the plug. Understood?"

Braiden mumbled something under his breath.

"Bray, I'm serious! I know how bad you want this, but you're not just taking on a rag tag group of leftovers inside a house. This is a fucking horde!"

Jonesy agreed. "You can hear by the moans, mate. They're louder than the... the other sounds."

"You mean screams," finished Sam. It was true. The combined audible strength of the undead was drowning out the living. As each life was snuffed out nearby, the balance shifted ever further in favour of the dead.

Braiden wasn't dissuaded. The old look was back; face lowered, cheeks flushed, teeth clenched. "We have to try."

"We're wasting time," finished Sam, standing shoulder to shoulder with his brother.

"We've got our first customers," DB growled. Slipping the mask down over his face, he withdrew the spiked mace from his belt. "I've got these. Recce round the corner while I'm busy."

Jonesy stared hard at the boys. "You stay on my arse, just like when we scouted the prison, got it?"

The three teenagers nodded. Despite the bravado, they were well aware that this was a deadly situation. One mistake could see them walking back to the castle as a drooling ghoul.

Staying low, they slipped between the cars and ducked behind a garden wall. Jonesy scanned ahead, while Winston risked a glance back. Just in time to see the spiked weapon bury itself in a female zombie's cranium. Both eyes popped from the sockets, forced out by the expulsion of the mashed brain. Wrenching it free with a helping boot to her chest, DB caught sight of them and followed.

"Whatever's happening, it's around that corner," Jonesy whispered.

A small group of undead were shuffling towards the fighting, showing the way. Some were naked. Some were fully clothed. More were missing garments that had been torn loose during their deaths. All bore the same grey and yellow tinge to whatever skin remained. The same jellied slime of decomposition glistened in the rising sun, reminding the group of common garden slugs. The similarity to the unshelled molluscs ended there. Slugs weren't hollowed out husks, bereft of juicy organs. They weren't missing faces, limbs, and skin. Or hefty chunks. Or, in some cases, most of the body's meat and muscle, leaving a wetly rattling skeleton.

Joining them at the brick wall, DB crouched down, awaiting further instruction. Jonesy raised a flat palm and chopped it forward. Breaking cover, the five moved in a line to the opposite building and hugged the concrete render. The ravaged stragglers either missed their surreptitious movement, or ignored them in favour of the shrieking meal on offer nearby. Motioning towards the broken door of the home which covered their movements, they filed inside. They quickly cleared the ground floor, finding nothing except for a toddler chair covered with brown crust. Ignoring the heart-breaking discovery lest it rob them of resolve, they moved upstairs, finding nothing. Gathering in one of the rear bedrooms, they kept out of sight.

Jonesy stood with his back to one of the walls, an empty white cot to his left. The pink paint and general décor indicated a girl. Pictures of a beaming baby with a mess of red curls confirmed it beyond all doubt. Cursing whichever fucked up deity that would allow the innocents to become such easy prey for the dead, he had to put it out of his mind. Like any war, civilian casualties were guaranteed. Squeezing his eyes shut, the fate of the poor child was locked away inside a secret compartment in his mind. It was the only way he could cope with the horrors of the pre and post-apocalyptic world. Opening them, the four looked on without judgement, only anticipation. Snatching a glimpse around the curtain for a split second, Jonesy saw everything. The road opened up to a large traffic light junction. One of the branches led to a housing estate similar to the one he grew up in. Set in a square, the four rows would face inwards to a green with small play area. What had been designed to foster community spirit among the inhabitants, had also provided a neat little enclave. Up until now. Every outer window and doorway was boarded with heavy ply. The sturdy material bore the hallmarks of a protracted siege; claw marks gouging the wood, congealed green blood, almost black from the length of time, coating the surfaces.

"Shit," Jonesy muttered, waving them over.

They kept well back in the shadows, but could see what was unfolding.

"They sealed the houses with a bus?"

"Two buses," Winston added.

The road across the way was blocked by a pair of coaches tipped on their sides. The undercarriage was a solid mix of axles and plating that kept the undead at bay. From their angle they could make out the interior of the closest vehicle was packed with heavy appliances, rubble, and mud. A line of cars stretched into the estate, bumper to bumper, providing an extra brace to the fortification.

"It's kind of like the HESCO walls we had in Afghanistan."

"HESCO?" asked Sam.

"They're rapid deploy wire mesh and fabric wall sections. A truck drops them in a row and we filled them with soil and sand," replied Jonesy. "The only difference here is they've done it with fifty seater coaches."

Hundreds of cadavers pushed and beat against the blockade, to no avail. The weight was enough to keep them out.

DB was looking around, puzzled. "How are the zombies inside, though? There's no breach here."

A haphazard wooden structure had been built atop the defences to provide a higher barrier and a vantage point for observation. One side of the frame was burning fiercely, but the source of the blaze was a mystery. Between the gathered corpses they could see the flat bottomed fuel tanks of the buses were intact and unburnt.

"Fucked if I know. There're bigger fires over the other side, we need to move position and see where they're getting in."

Sam, Braiden, and Winston moved towards the stairs until Jonesy stopped them.

"Boys!"

"Yeah?"

"There's going to be thousands of them."

"So?" Braiden muttered. He knew what was coming.

"I'm just saying; be prepared. We may need to fall back like our arses are on fire."

"With, or without *them*," DB added for clarity.

It was a bitter pill to swallow, but Braiden slowly nodded. He would've given anything to reunite a daughter with her loving parents, a situation that would never occur in his own life. Perhaps it wasn't to be.

"You're a good lad, Bray," said Jonesy, patting him on the back. "Let's get moving."

CHAPTER 16

"There it is," said DB. "We've found our breach."

"We're not getting through that lot," Jonesy replied.

A convenience store with the name Patel's was a smoking shell. The inside of the shop was still burning in places, but the conflagration that had gutted it was over. The flat above was another matter. Flames roared from the shattered windows, while plumes of black smoke poured through collapsed sections of the roof structure.

"It'll all come down soon. You can see the brickwork's already sagging from the heat," said DB, noting the widening cracks.

"What the fuck's happened here?" Jonesy spat, his own frustration boiling over.

A dozen sheets of reinforced ply were neatly stacked against the wall to the side of the storefront.

"If I were to guess, someone's taken them down in the night and then lit the fire to stop the people from trying to seal it again."

"But who? And how? And why, for fuck's sake?"

"The prison?"

"Surely this is too far for them?"

"Another group then?" Jonesy's words were laced with dread. It was hard enough to contend with two factions of lunatics. If other bands existed who would use such calculated premeditation to murder a fellow group of survivors, humanity was truly fucked.

"It doesn't matter right now. What we need is a plan."

"First things first, we need to see if there's another way in. There's God knows how many down there," Jonesy said, pointing at the crowd.

Winston tried a quick headcount. "Close to a thousand I'd say."

"With more coming," said Sam, pointing down the street at the newcomers.

"And we're not getting over the coaches, either. The whole platform is probably on fire by now."

"I might have an idea," said Braiden.

"Let's have it, mate."

"This is just like our estate in Emsworth, there'll be alleys and other roads. We just need to keep looking for an easier way in."

"Ok, let's do it. Time's running out and we're going to be fighting as we go."

"Everyone check your masks and armour. I don't want any fuckups," said DB.

A quick check was carried out to the soldier's satisfaction. Bounding down the stairs, the five exited the house and headed away from the failing fortification. DB and Jonesy switched to the flanks, while the teenagers held the centre. Moving down the road between abandoned cars and empty pavements, they all felt the loneliness closing in. None of them had been here, but it resembled a normal town found up and down the country. Bustling shoppers jostling for position. Irate drivers trying to do the same on the packed roads. The only travellers on the ghost roads now were the dead. Their only goal, to feed.

"Heads up," Jonesy warned as a sizeable group appeared. The newly summoned undead were massing.

The warriors all moved apart to give each other space. Winston lunged forward, slashing down with the axe. Using a restraining hand to pull the blow on the long handle, the heavy blade only cut through to the sternum, separating the man's head. As the creature slopped to the ground, Winston noticed the familiar McDonald's uniform.

"Mmmmm, Big Mac," he drooled.

"What?" DB spat, sideswiping a woman with the mace. Skull caving in, the power of the blow nearly took her head clean off. The deep bite marks on the side of her neck tore, causing the crushed skull to flop onto her shoulder.

"Just reminiscing," replied the teenager, his tummy grumbling at the memory of the sauce.

"Don't reminisce. Kill!" snapped Braiden. Expertly darting around his prey, he lanced through the temple. All unlife fled the zombie as it dropped, the neat puncture oozing black matter.

Sam was keeping his distance, hacking with the long bladed machete without putting himself in reach of the dead. Foreheads split open like cracked eggs, expelling the riven grey contents onto the ground.

"Mind your step!" warned DB, mostly to himself as he came close to slipping over on a patch of gore.

Winston started merrily humming a tune. Fully warmed up, he struck the next zombie with a devastating upswing. The axe separated the rib cage, cleaved the chin, before leaving through the top of its head and lifting the monster a foot off the ground. Something in his shoulder flared in pain from the awkward angle of the stroke. Promising the pained muscle to keep it simple in the future, he moved on to the next corpse.

"More to the left!" Jonesy called.

A quartet of school children in matching green blazers headed the pack. The plastic bags used to suffocate themselves were still wrapped tightly around their heads, shrouding the faces in polyurethane camouflage. Four blackened tongues probed against the plastic, the weight of spilling drool pooling in the bag at the neck, pulling the covering tight.

"Fuck, that's disgusting," muttered Sam.

"At least they haven't been eaten," responded Braiden, shrugging. "That could've been us if Miss Blume hadn't saved us."

"But suffocation?" Sam groaned. It hit too close to home after the outbreak involving Jasmine.

"They must've been trapped and used what they could. I'd rather that than be a dead fuck's next meal."

"I guess."

Winston was equally appalled by the inhumanity that forced the youngsters into such a drastic action. Swinging wide, he knocked all four down with one strike. The soldiers finished off the hooded monstrosities, putting them out of their misery.

Sam smiled gratefully, though it looked more like a grimace. Braiden joined him and stabbed and slashed until another six were killed. Taking a step back, Jonesy, Winston, and DB stepped in to let them catch a breath. Most of those remaining were crawlers; zombies so damaged they could only drag themselves across the unforgiving ground. Winston buried the battle axe in the nearest creature's head, nearly crippling himself in the process from the jarring impact. Letting out a cry of pain, the weapon clattered to the road. Shaking his hands, he tried to flex the numb, tingling fingers. Braiden retrieved the axe for him and moved back behind the soldiers who were trying not to laugh.

"Dumbass," he said, shaking his head.

"I think I might've been a bit overzealous," Winston replied, wincing.

"No shit, Sherlock."

"Ok, leave the others," Jonesy ordered. None were capable of doing much pursuing, only leaving bits of themselves behind.

"We've seen the south and west of the estate, that leaves two more roads to check," Braiden explained.

DB took the lead as they neared the junction. Peeking around the back of a milk truck, Braiden's information was on the money. Twenty four homes stretched away, broken into terraces of six. The back yards were, conversely, on the main road, while the frontages opened up onto the unreachable green beyond. Low brick walls encircled each home's postage stamp sized patch of garden. Once filled with flowers, grass, or in some cases discarded appliances and furniture, they now held the dead.

"There's hardly any of them," DB said over his shoulder. "I say we run past and ignore them. Is everyone ready?"

Four confirmations came and he left cover. Jogging down the street between the vehicles, the zombies saw the movement and gave chase.

"There's the first alley!" called Braiden.

"It's blocked solid all the way to the roof. No way through!"

Rising six feet in the small opening was a concrete block wall. The cement joints were uneven and sloppy, evidence of the hasty erection. More debris was piled and stacked behind to give an impassable barrier.

"They've got a builder in there by the look of it!" remarked Jonesy.

"I wonder if they can build more castles?" asked Winston.

They continued on, ignoring the question. A small group of undead were converging in their wake, still in numbers too low to be a threat. Each of the other two alleys were blocked in the same fashion. At the third, several cadavers were knelt down in a circle. The tearing sounds meant one thing; food. Whoever it was had climbed the blockade and chanced the fall. Fifteen feet and panic assured failure. One of the dead held a coil of intestines aloft like a prize, before tearing at the flimsy tube with eager teeth. Staring at the group, he slowly chewed, weighing up whether to give chase. The warm banquet proved to be the easier meal and he tore another length from the digestive tract.

"It's not one of them," declared Braiden.

"No way!" agreed Sam, eternally optimistic.

Braiden knew he was only being supportive and loved him for it. He didn't explain that he'd caught a glimpse of the victim's face. The silent, screaming mouth seared onto his memory. The missing eye. They were too young to be either Gail or Don.

"That's where they got all the gear!" said DB, pointing ahead.

A Travis Perkins builder's centre lay a hundred yards away down the next road. Like Hansel and Gretel, a trail of materials marked the route the scavengers took in claiming the goods. Split bags of sand. A stray block here and there. Boxes of spilled screws. Spars of milled lumber. Littered amongst the inert were truly dead corpses, their heads split open.

"Bastards!" Jonesy spat suddenly.

"What's up?" DB called back.

"These people were surviving! I'm going to fucking kill whoever did this!"

"Cool it, bro. We don't even know if the people inside are good or bad. They may've had it coming."

"Fuck that! Somehow these people got word out that there was safety here. They took people in!"

"They could be cannibals stocking up the larder! No assumptions!"

Jonesy huffed. DB was right.

"How could they do it?" asked Winston as they reached the final corner.

"Get word out? It can only be HAM radio," replied DB.

"Things went to shit so quickly. I'm amazed they had time to secure the estate, let alone send out a call for survivors."

"Probably the same thing that's happening now," said Sam as they reached the final corner.

Eyes turned to him questioningly.

"The zombies are drawn to fire and noise. If something big was going on nearby, the people would've had a good window to get their defences up. Now we're using the same thing to get to them. Hopefully."

DB nodded. "A few people with their lives on the line can get a hell of a lot done."

"We can ask when we've got them out safely," finished Jonesy.

Another shriek reached a pitch of unendurable agony before cutting off with a dying gurgle.

"This is it. Finger's crossed," said DB, looking back at Braiden.

"I'm ready," he replied.

The street was similarly quiet. In total, only a dozen undead wandered around aimlessly. A larger group of perhaps thirty were crammed against one of the alleys.

"They can see something," said Jonesy.

"Let's cross the road to get a better angle."

Following DB, they saw what had the zombies so riled. A woman and child were perched atop the blockade, clutching at the roof of the house for support. DB couldn't make out if they were more afraid of the undead or the height and precarious nature of their platform.

"That's going to be our way in!" declared Jonesy. "We clear the road and use those ladders to get up."

Two sets of double extension ladders were secured to a van halfway down the road. Upon seeing the group, the woman tensed and prepared to scream for help. Jonesy waved her off frantically, before holding a finger to his lips. Beyond terrified, still she understood the command.

"Sam, your dad's a plumber. Do you know how to get those clamps off?"

"Yeah, piece of cake."

"Ok, Braiden, cover him while he's getting them down. Winston, you're with DB on the main group by the alley. I'll pick off the lone zombies following in the last street. Once we're clear we get one ladder up this side, and one down the other."

Knowing what they had to do, they separated silently to their individual tasks. Sam chose to climb straight onto the roof of the vehicle instead of straining from the sides. The steel panel clunked from the shifting weight, but Braiden was there to protect his brother. Jonesy raced between targets, slashing once for each head and then moving on before the bodies had time to fall. So rapt were the reaching zombies on the sweet meat above, DB and Winston cut them down effortlessly without drawing their attention.

"Oh, thank you! Thank you, so much!" praised the woman. Turning to the little girl, she pulled her tight. "See, honey, I told you we'd be rescued. The army's here now."

"Sorry to disappoint you, lady, but the army's gone. We're just two more deserters trying to stay alive."

"I don't care! Please hurry, there are people still inside!"

Tossing the rotten bodies over the low walls of the neighbouring homes, they cleared a path for Sam and Braiden who came clattering over with enough noise to reawaken the newly dead.

"How sturdy is that thing?" DB asked.

"Solid. Once Irish finished the walls, we packed it tight with everything we could find," she replied.

Throwing up the first ladder, the woman quickly stepped onto the rungs. Beckoning towards the little girl, she held on tightly to an upturned chair leg and refused to budge.

"Come on, honey. It's perfectly safe."

Unconvinced, the child increased her limpetlike grip on the thick wooden leg.

DB could picture a huge clock, each tick of the second hand gonging deafeningly like an omen of doom. "We don't have time for this. I'll get her! Come on down."

Moving as fast as her trembling form would allow, she fell into the arms of Jonesy who steadied her.

"Thank you."

"What's her name?" asked DB.

"Tara."

DB took the steps two at a time, the aluminium frame bouncing from his weight. Reaching the top, he smiled warmly. "Hey, Tara. I'm DB. I need to get you down, sweetheart."

She shook her head firmly.

"Do you know why they call me DB? It used to mean Dough Ball. I was *so* fat I couldn't even fit through a door," he said, puffing his cheeks out.

She smiled slightly, but held on for dear life.

"I was so fat, I broke every chair I sat on." He made a groaning sound and finished it with an explosion. Bracing his legs on the rungs, he used his hands to demonstrate it blowing apart.

She giggled. "You're not fat. You're tall, like a giant."

"Other kids used to tease me. I bet you wouldn't, though. You're way too nice."

"Callum used to pull my hair at school. I didn't like him. I bet he would've been mean to you too."

"Callum sounds like a poopy bum head," DB stated, triggering more giggling. "How about you come with me and your mum?"

"She's not my mummy," Tara said quietly.

Cursing himself for breaking his own rule on making assumptions, DB expected the girl to completely clam up. Instead, she surprised him by letting go of the upturned table.

"My mummy's in Heaven with my daddy," she said, holding her arms out.

"So are mine, sweetheart," DB husked, picking her up. She weighed next to nothing and DB had her down in moments, passing her back to the woman.

"Is there a ladder on the other side, ma'am?" Jonesy asked the woman.

"My name's Emma," she replied. "And no, there's no ladder. We had to climb the rubbish."

"Boys, stay here and keep them safe. Sam, pass the second ladder up once we've got to the top," said DB.

"Remember, you might still have company any second now from the last street. I saw a few rounding the corner. If it gets too much, whistle, then get the hell out of here."

Braiden was hovering, staring at the young lady. "Are Gail and Don in there?" he asked tentatively.

She looked confused. "Who's that?"

Her words hit him like a physical blow. Lowering his face, he moved away to be alone. DB pulled a face at the other boys that said *keep an eye on him.*

Braiden stopped suddenly and turned, his eyes blazing in anger. "I want to go."

"We've got this, Bray. Keep the girls safe for me," said Jonesy, scurrying up the rungs in pursuit of DB.

Sam was ready, the second ladder in hand. Offering it up, the soldiers pulled it up and dropped it over the other side with a crash. The noise didn't travel, the high alley containing the impact.

Sam was heartbroken for his brother and moved to console him. "It's ok, mate. Dr Hargis is a strong lady. At least she'll know now."

Emma frowned. "Wait, did you say, Hargis?"

Winston nodded. "We came looking for the parents of our friend."

"I didn't know their first names," blurted Emma. "I always called them Mr and Mrs Hargis."

Braiden tensed and rushed towards the ladder.

"Wait! They're not in there at the moment. They went on a supply run two days ago."

The teenager turned back to her, eyes frantic. "But they *were* here?"

"Yeah," she nodded enthusiastically.

"Alive?"

"Erm, yeah," she replied with a little less vigour at the strange question.

"Where did they go?" he demanded.

"I'm not sure... I don't get told these things."

Sam moved fast to interject. "Remember the deal. They're probably safe out there."

"Oh, they'll be fine. They're two of the best runners we had. Sometimes they would be gone for days, but they always brought back a stack of goodies."

"We need to find them!" Braiden snapped.

"No!" declared Sam. "We've done enough for now. We can give Christina hope. Right now, *they're* the most important thing." He pointed to the out of sight battleground raging on the estate.

"But..."

"No buts! Dr Hargis said they were survivors."

"If I could make it out here burgling snacks, they are," said Winston. "And by the sounds of it, it isn't the first time they've done it either."

"Not even the tenth," Emma confirmed.

"We'll leave information somehow before we go. We'll tell them where we are," said Sam. Dragging Braiden into the next garden, they started to score a message onto the ply.

"In the meantime, we've got a few party crashers," Winston added.

Turning to see the approaching zombies, Braiden withdrew his screwdriver and left the half carved instructions. "I've got these!"

Winston raised an eyebrow and Sam shook his head. As the youth marched off, he whispered, "Sometimes he needs to let off some steam. He'll be fine."

"Tara, I need you to look at me, honey," Emma cooed, shielding her from the horror as Braiden begun slaying the creatures.

CHAPTER 17

"Hold here while Kurt and I check the farm shop," ordered Holbeck.

The soldiers jumped from the Warthogs and set up a perimeter, watching the sprawling fields. Small groups of the undead were traversing the farmland, but not in numbers that posed any threat. The explosion was sudden, the sound gone as soon as the shockwave dissipated. It wasn't like their firefights, the protracted bedlam of combat. Most of the undead who weren't already in the area lacked a focal point to head towards and had probably returned to their vacant wandering. Peter assured his colleagues they could handle them hand to hand to save ammunition.

"After you, Kurt."

The two men moved between the houses. It was all new to the sergeant, but old hat to the plumber. Sights from weeks ago guided him the correct route without having to pause.

"We're nearly there," whispered Kurt. "We just pass that promenade of shops and it's down a side street."

"I don't hear anyone," replied Holbeck, pistol in hand.

"Me either. Keep to the shadows anyway."

Holbeck nodded and Kurt hugged the glass frontages of the retailers. Ducking into the entrance alcoves, he waited after passing each one. The buildings were fully deserted now. Glittering on the floor across the road was the shattered glass from when Jonesy had taken the boys on their reconnaissance mission. Two other panes were smashed in a similar fashion, the festering occupant drawn out of their home in the recent past. It may have even been the explosion itself that caught their attention and pried them from undead self-isolation.

"There," whispered Kurt.

"Hold here while I take a look," replied Holbeck.

Moving to the corner, he kept his pistol lowered. Snatching a quick glance around the edge of the brickwork, he visibly relaxed and waved Kurt over. "It's all clear. Nobody there."

Remaining cautious, the pair ran down the short alley. Kurt could see the thick sheet of plywood was undisturbed. Pointing to his eyes, he then indicated the cover to the soldier.

Kneeling at the edge, Holbeck carefully lowered his head. Placing an ear to the timber, he concentrated before shaking his head. Indicating Kurt should lift it, Holbeck aimed at the rim. Kurt took hold of the wood and mouthed; three, two, one, before yanking the covering. The tunnel was empty except for the aluminium stepladder. A faint groaning carried down the dank passage.

"Undead," Kurt whispered, dropping the ply.

"Agreed. Let's see if your friend left a message," said Holbeck.

Kurt moved towards the car Jodi had identified. The front door was open, just as they had left it. Opening the glove box, a small map was hidden beneath the car's information pack and several discarded parking permits. Unfolding it, three tunnels were highlighted. On two the ink had faded slightly, while the third was a fresh red dot.

"We're there," Kurt explained. "The next tunnel comes out to the east of the prison."

"Then let's move."

Backtracking to the Warthogs, they found a scattering of fresh corpses around the vehicles. Louise was washing gore from her machete from a spare water bottle she had brought along.

"No good?"

"The dead are in the tunnel. We didn't go down and see how many," explained Kurt.

"Ok, everyone mount up. We're heading east."

The armoured monsters grumbled away, leaving the heartbroken dead to wail and gnash their teeth.

"Which way should we approach?"

Peter pointed towards a group of huge warehouses. "If we head through the industrial park, we come out facing the eastern edge of the prison."

"That steel fence looks pretty sturdy," said Holbeck, doubtfully. If it was a Hollywood movie, Carpenter could charge straight at them and crash through. This was real life, and the likelihood was that one of the thick struts could damage the rubber caterpillar tracks or vital hydraulics beneath the cab itself.

"There's going to be a gate at the rear for emergency access. It'll be right around the corner," said Kurt.

Winston had explained the area in great detail following his discovery of the damaged NHS supply building. Anything to curry favour with his new guardian. Kurt smiled at the thought of the awkward teenager and how well he had fit in to their disparate band of survivors. He would still give him a hard time to keep him on his toes, though. And the mother of all bollockings when they got back to the castle.

"There it is, Sarge. Want me to ram it?" asked Carpenter.

"Don't do that," warned Kurt. "It's one of the solid gates with those latches that you pull across. You know, the really thick ones. Get close and I'll shatter the padlock."

"I can pop off a couple of rounds," offered Petermann from the turret.

"And bring the whole horde down on our head? Think, Soldier."

"Sorry, Sarge. Just eager to get in the fight."

"Give it ten minutes and we'll be up to our necks in the dead. There's no rush, Corporal."

"Understood, Sarge."

Carpenter ground to a halt and Kurt hopped from the cab. Taking out the war pick, he aimed and struck at the heavy duty lock. Three blows and the internal mechanisms shattered, releasing the shackle. Tossing it away, he slid the central latch free. Reaching through the thick bars, he pulled the bolts from the ground and swung the huge gates wide open.

"Follow it straight," said Kurt as he climbed back aboard.

"Want me to stop so we can close them?" asked Carpenter as she trundled through.

Kurt shook his head. "No. They'll give us some cover if we have to retreat in a hurry. We can shut them during the escape. It'd take a thousand zombies to force their way through those things."

"Good thinking," complimented Holbeck.

"Sometimes us civvies can be useful, Sergeant," Kurt replied.

"Sometimes," he agreed. "Rarely."

"Hater," Kurt fired back.

"Holy shit..." muttered Carpenter as the towering steel siding of the warehouses disappeared. She slowed immediately, throwing Petermann painfully into the HMG.

Across the road, the field opened up. It was thick with the rotting denizens of the local villages. The imposing red brick wall of the prison looked like a giant had taken a bite from it. A twenty foot section was gone completely, with

117

ragged, curved edges rising to the torn razor wire. One of the watch towers had taken a beating from the sundered masonry, listing dangerously on the three remaining legs. A grey tide surged through the opening, filling the prison.

"Sarge, ten o'clock!" called Petermann.

Glancing left, they saw what he'd found from his elevated vantage point. Undead were streaming onto the execution platform to the south, eager to get at the six men who fought desperately for survival.

"Get Matt," Holbeck said, voice hard. Climbing from the cab, he waited at the front with a set of binoculars. The time for fighting was coming. Fate was, even now, rolling the dice to see if they would succeed. The layout of the facility itself was enough of a nightmare. Getting inside, finding the civilians, and getting them out safely while fighting off thousands of decomposing cannibals added a whole new layer of trouble.

"What's up?" grumbled the burly Scot. "I thought we were getting stuck in."

"Not if I can get some more intel," Holbeck replied, ignoring the man's pain. "Who're they?" Handing over the goggles, he pointed to the platform.

Matt moved to get a better position and clear a tree from his view. Raising his arms, the crutches came with him, clattering against the blast shield. "They're nobodies."

"No gang affiliation?"

"This isn't America, lad. We don't have the Aryan Brotherhood and all that shite."

"Then they're harmless?"

"Hardly," Matt replied, handing back the glasses. "They took part in the rapes, but they weren't part of any wing bosses crew. As I said, nobodies. Scum."

"Thanks, that's all I needed to know."

Gritting his teeth, Matt hopped back into the vehicle. Holbeck jumped back inside behind him and ordered Carpenter to proceed slowly.

"Aye, Sarge."

"Ewington, I want you to stay close. We're going to try and get them down and get any information we can."

"You aren't going to save them, are you, Sergeant?" snapped Kurt. "That's not why we're here."

"I understand your anger, Kurt. What they know might give us a better chance of mission success. If you can't keep your feelings in check, it might be best to drop you here and pick you up on the way back."

Matt's arm reached out to hold Kurt back. "He'll be fine, Sergeant. Let's go."

Holbeck hesitated, staring at Kurt. Having an element who couldn't be counted on to follow orders was another potential nail in the coffin of their survival.

"Sergeant, you can count on us. It's just I've seen what those animals are capable of."

Holbeck wrestled with his misgivings. Once they broke cover it would be too late.

"Trust me," finished Kurt.

"Ok, fuck it! Roll out!"

The engines snorted, spewing black smoke from the exhaust vent.

"Carpenter, pull up below them so they can jump down. Petermann, you keep the .50 Cal on them. If they look like making a move, cut them down." Speaking over the radio, he said, "Ewington, pull up fifty yards to the south. Position yourself so Eldridge can cover the platform. Give them a shield while they climb down!"

Affirmatives came back as the lead vehicle crashed through the weak wooden railing circling the field. The men saw the commotion, and their faces lit up with relief. They screamed and hollered at the rescue party, forgetting where they were. Two of the prisoners were pulled down, the zombies tearing at the warm flesh of their prey. Blood poured through the wooden slats of the platform, soaking the frosty ground below.

"Carpenter, avoid that shit! Eldridge, fire at will!"

Gripping the handle with her left hand, she yanked the charging handle twice. Swinging up the barrel, Eldridge

119

aimed to account for the recoil and spread. If she had fired any closer, the prisoners were in danger of being hit. Firing short bursts, the jubilant zombies at the front of the pack exploded into indistinguishable hunks of meat from the power. The large calibre rounds punched through the whole group without slowing. Those at the back who were spared the initial impact were blown clear of the platform by the slug, flying away into the yard beyond. Jumping in her hands, the incredible weapon crackled with each pull.

Understanding her plan, the surviving prisoners dealt with the closest corpses. Bats and bars swung, crushing heads. The protection of the heavy machine gun was like an impenetrable shield. As soon as a new influx of decaying predators stepped out into the open, Eldridge destroyed them. Carpenter was nearly at the base of the structure when the last clip clattered into the cab.

"Magazine!" she yelled, informing the men that they were on their own for a few seconds. Tossing the box, she humped a fresh one onto the cradle. Opening the hatch, she dragged the new belt in and positioned the first bullet by the extractor. Snapping the cover shut, she charged it again. The pile of bodies was getting higher, as was the weight held by the rickety construction.

"Sarge, it's about to collapse. Holding fire."

"Roger that!" replied Holbeck over the radio. Leaning from the open door, he addressed the men. "Drop onto the rear of the Hog. If you make any move my guy doesn't like, he'll leave you in a bloody pile, do you understand."

"Yeah, man, whatever."

"No problem," added another. "Do you want us to toss the weapons?"

"No," answered Holbeck. "Now get your asses down here before the whole thing goes!"

Dropping the bats and iron bars onto the roof, they shimmied down the dark stained rope. Once safely on the roof, the first prisoner helped the others down.

"Now, hold on tight!"

Crouching down, they held on to anything they could as Carpenter accelerated away. Hearing sickly crunches, they looked back to see the undead swan diving from the platform onto the hard trodden earth below. Two dozen more forced their way onto the platform, trying to reach the strewn patches of dripping meat left of the two earlier victims. A red horror stood tall amidst the crush, unable to see through the empty eye sockets. His face was a scarlet death's head, the entirety of his skin and face missing. Both arms were gone, and one of his new family barged away from the throng, carrying the ravaged prize. Sensing warm flesh nearby, the crimson skeleton stumbled over in an attempt to eat his own arm. Lacking any coordination, he tripped over an outstretched leg and fell from the edge. Crashing headfirst into the mud, his skull caved in while the rest of his body crumpled like an accordion. Petermann watched while two of the stowaways gave up their breakfast onto the roof.

Carpenter came to a stop in the middle of the field, a good quarter mile from the site of the explosion. Holbeck and the soldiers jumped from the vehicle, training their weapons on the men. Faced with rifles, pistols, and two heavy machine guns, they slowly raised their hands and closed their eyes.

"We're not going to kill you unless we have to. Get the fuck down from my vehicle!" ordered Holbeck. "Petermann, Eldridge, watch the horde."

A few were breaking away, but at their speed they wouldn't become a threat for several minutes at the earliest.

"Do you want us to thin the herd, Sarge?"

"No, conserve your ammunition for now. You four, move away from my vehicles."

"Ok, man. Thanks for saving our asses. We've got no problem with you."

"You didn't have a problem with raping the women and kids either, did you?" Holbeck growled.

Their faces flushed with guilt and they looked at the ground.

121

"I thought so. Fucking degenerates," he spat on the soil at their feet. "You, Mr Talksalot, I want information and I want it now. Bullshit me and I'll bleed you where you stand and the zombies can finish the rest."

"Ok, man. Shit, ask your questions."

"What happened?"

"The Gypsies came for Craig and Mike. We handed them over like they asked. They were furious we couldn't give them Matt and Hombre."

"We didn't know what would happen," said his friend.

"Was I talking to you?" Holbeck snapped and the man shook his head. "Then shut your fucking mouth! Go on."

"Fred and George set up search parties to go and look for them."

"Fred and George?"

"Fowler. They were Craig's rivals, but until recently kept themselves quiet. Once Mrs Hampton showed up, everything went to shit and they made their move. They thought handing over the Arater brothers would buy us some time."

"But it didn't," said Holbeck.

"No. They blew one of the tunnels," said the man, pointing over his shoulder at the devastation.

"And where are the Gypsies now?"

"Fuck knows. They could be watching us."

The thought unsettled Holbeck, and he scanned the countryside, noting the dark patches of woodland where a whole army could be hiding. *Fuck it, it doesn't matter. We've got no fight with them, unless they want one.* He prayed they didn't.

"What can you tell me about the prison. What did you see?"

"I saw my friends getting eaten. People I've been locked up with for years, torn to bits like the dead fucks were pulling off a chicken drumstick."

"I don't give a fuck about them!" Holbeck barked and the man cowered away. "Did the undead get inside the wings? Specifically D wing?"

"I don't know. I was fighting for my fucking life."

The other prisoner slowly raised a hand, waiting to get shouted at again.

"What? Talk!"

"D wing seemed to be secure. The dead were at the door but couldn't get in. That's not to say they weren't able to get in from one of the other areas."

"Did nobody keep the inner doors locked?"

"Once we took over, we opened them all. There was no point in keeping them locked, we just had guards at each wing to keep people where they belonged."

"Did you happen to see if the rear entrance was still clear?"

"There's no reason it shouldn't be. Craig always insisted we keep the noise up to hold them along the front and sides of the prison."

It confirmed what everyone had been saying and provided the best way in.

"Ok, now fuck off," said Holbeck, moving back to the Warthog.

"Wait, you need to take us with you."

Holbeck stopped dead. His fists clenched at his sides. The sidearm was so close. Only inches from his palm.

"I suggest you turn around and disappear like good little rapists," sneered Eldridge.

"You can see we have women here. Beth, Angela, what do you think we should do with these filthy fuckers?" Petermann asked.

"If it were up to me I'd cut their balls off and watch them bleed out," said Carpenter from the driver's seat.

"Sounds like a good plan," agreed Eldridge, removing her razor sharp bayonet and holding it over the turret shield.

"Ok, ok. We'll go. You know you're killing us, don't you?" sobbed Mr Talksalot, having got his voice back.

"You've got more chance than those poor women locked up with you ever had!" roared Holbeck, rounding on them. "You've got three seconds to fuck off before I put one in each of your legs and leave you to crawl in the dirt until the zombies tear the flesh from your bones!"

Fleeing from the furious soldier, the prisoners made a beeline south towards the ocean. Their future was unknown, the dice of fate rolled and clattering in the box of life. Holbeck hoped they got snake eyes and lost everything.

Kurt turned to Matt. "I like him," he said, grinning.

"He's a regular ray of fucking sunshine," mumbled the pained Scot.

They climbed aboard, ready to head back into the fray.

CHAPTER 18

"You ready?" asked Jonesy.

"Locked and loaded, brother," replied DB.

"We're heading into a shitstorm," warned Jonesy.

DB could read his friend like a book. Their loyalties lay with the castle and their new family, not this group. "We'll call it when we break cover."

"Gotcha. Moving," said Jonesy, raising the rifle to stare down the scope.

The thin alley opened up directly into the estate. It was utter carnage.

"Jesus Christ," Jonesy spat in horror.

DB took in the scene through the crosshairs. Charred corpses huddled over freshly claimed prizes, cramming meat into blackened mouths, each bite cracking the brittle, rotten flesh. Some were still on fire, their hair and clothes engulfed in flame. Putting it out of his head, he looked for the rear of the burning store.

"We need to bring that down and plug the leak or we're fucked," said DB.

125

"We've only got two grenades left."

"The blast will bring the rest of it down. I say we use them."

"Agreed."

Shouldering the rifles, they took one of the explosives each and withdrew their blades. Ignoring shrill cries for help, the soldiers circled the green which was filled with the dead and dying, slashing at any smouldering creature that got close. A steady line of undead were filtering through the broken loading doors. The screams of the survivors nearby took their attention, sparing Jonesy and DB the initial fight. Edging along the back wall, they pulled the pins and peeled away from the brickwork. Lobbing the metal balls over the heads of the zombies, they were ignored no longer.

Ducking behind a car, the grenades exploded with twin crumps. Dust and soot surged through the open door a split second before the flat above finally gave way. Anything caught in the collapse was crushed by the burning debris and masonry. Those that had made it through safely had been swatted flat by the blast. Climbing to their feet, a pair of women who could've been twins gave chase. Their matted blonde hair was singed but unburnt from the ebbing heat of the shop. Smoke rose from their clothing. Grey skin oozed pus from freshly risen blisters.

"Double date?" asked DB.

"They're all yours, mate," Jonesy replied.

DB struck swiftly, parting skulls. Looping the strap of the machete back on his belt, he swung the rifle around and fired off single rounds into the heads of the fallen. Jonesy had his back to him, trying desperately to prioritise a suitable target. Three houses were under siege, the zombies already through the front doors. Bringing fire along with undeath, the hungry flames ate at the homes as the zombies devoured the living. Whoever had taken cover within was doomed.

"Two mags left," said DB, slapping a fresh one in the rifle.

"We don't have enough fucking bullets!" Jonesy snapped, filled with impotent rage.

"We do what we can!" DB replied, urging him on.

Snapping out of the malaise, Jonesy focused. The central green was a total loss. There were hundreds surrounding the low steel fence of the children's play area. The undead tossed themselves headfirst over the railing in numbers too high for the defenders to hold back. Even if they used all their ammunition, they wouldn't put a dent in the horde. Two cars were similarly surrounded, the glass shattered and rotting bodies already forcing themselves inside. A breaking window pulled their attention back to the houses. One of the occupants was raking a chair around the frame to clear the last shards. In his state of abject terror, he didn't seem to feel the flames engulfing his left arm. The only thing registering was escape. Flinging himself through the opening, the dead cushioned his fall. He screamed once, the pitch rising until his vocal cords ruptured. The dead consumed him gratefully.

"It's already over," Jonesy muttered.

DB pulled him forward and pointed beyond a burning van. "No! Look at that!"

Tucked out of sight behind the vehicle, a pair of men were stood within the broken sunroof of a car. They swung wildly at the gathered dead with an aluminium baseball bat and a short hatchet. Their luck was holding during the assault, the soldiers were heartened to see. Unlike the other vehicles, the glass was still intact, preventing the dead from reaching their lower legs.

"They must've backed the car up against the alley to seal the gap," Jonesy said. Dodging around the grasping arms of lone zombies, the soldiers moved towards the men. One was portly, with close cropped black hair. His face, darkly tanned, spoke of a career outside among the elements. Thick forearms and powerful hands hinted towards a manual profession. The second had longer black hair, with tattoos covering his arms all the way up to the shoulder of his vest. Jonesy could make out images of bikes

127

and quotes about "doing the ton"; a reference to bikers love for excessive speeds. Whoever they were, they fought with ferocity and purpose.

The entire back section of the saloon was a crumpled wreck, wedged tightly between the brick walls. It served its purpose as a temporary blockage perfectly. Protected by the shell of the vehicle, the tattooed man's bat rang out with hollow gongs as each skull crumpled under the blow. Seeing the two newcomers for the first time, he almost bolted. Jonesy could see the hesitation, the way he tensed and scowled.

"We're friends. Get down!"

Motioning for those behind to take cover, he slipped down into the footwell out of sight, swiftly followed by the other.

Jonesy and DB ran, putting distance between themselves and any lingering threat from the shop. Resting the rifles atop a car roof, they steadied their aim and fired single shots at the throng of undead who were beating at the now undefended windows. Puffs of skull fragment and brain splattered over the car and wall beyond. The risk of infection was high, but they were out of options.

"Magazine," said DB.

Jonesy had conserved half of the rounds from his own. Swinging around, he covered DB while he reloaded. Picking off four blackened cadavers, the crack of the shots echoed in the confines of the estate. A large portion of the playground group broke away, heading in the direction of the gunfire. DB recommended firing, and Jonesy returned his attention to the main target.

"We've got thirty seconds. No more," he said between shots, casting glances at the large group converging on their position.

"Fuck it, we've gotta move," DB shouted, leaving the car.

Inside the shell, the men heard the cry and the cessation of fire. Standing back up, they were miraculously free of most of the spilt gore. Resuming the attack, the bat and axe smashed against the skulls of the surviving zombies, crushing and cleaving.

"We've got to be quick!" Jonesy informed the crop haired man as they raced over.

"Name's Irish," he called. "I've got people back here. This is Greasy." He nodded to the biker.

"Keep swinging!" ordered DB, charging at the pack. A dozen creatures beating at the bonnet went down in a tangled heap as he hit them. Jonesy reached down to help, but DB was already pushing himself to safety. Finishing the creatures caught in the tangled heap, DB's blade struck with wet crunches.

"Come on, quickly!" Jonesy called.

Hiding out of sight, the small group of remaining survivors stood up.

"Mind the brains!" DB warned, holding out a hand.

Climbing on the rear bumper, they held out their hands. Irish pulled them forward, helping to steady their feet across the filthy muck with Greasy aiding them to reach the soldiers. DB took them one at a time, lowering them to the ground to spare a twisted or broken ankle. The children were first, three of them. Then came four women, followed by two men. None of them complained at being manhandled by the huge soldier. Even the men thanked him.

"Now both of you!"

Irish didn't take the hand, opting instead to climb out through the passenger door. Greasy simply vaulted from the roof, landing deftly on the road.

"We've got ladders set up in the eastern alleyway!" Jonesy pointed. "Get to safety!"

"We can fight! We've still got people in here!"

"It's too late! There's too many of them!" DB spat, lifting the rifle once more.

Pulling the stock in tight, he opened fire.

"But... our friends..." Irish croaked. "All our hard work and sacrifice..." He could see how hopeless it was. Leaving the others to the mercy of the dead tore his heart in two.

129

His face shifted from a mask of grief to a look of pure rage in an instant.

Jonesy saw the coiled tension of a man about to commit an act of suicide in pursuit of the impossible. He reached out and held him gently by the thick upper arm, speaking quietly. "I'm sorry, but you've got two choices. Come with us, or die. You can help us to keep these people alive."

Irish turned to the others. The children cowered behind, watching as their refuge fell. None of the adults were afraid, only distraught. They hesitated, weapons ready. Jonesy could see that if the burly man gave the order, they would charge in with him.

"I'm gonna kill 'em," he spat, pulling his arm free in disgust at himself.

"Who's *them*?" Jonesy asked, only to be ignored as Greasy led the children away towards the alley.

"Time for that later. We need to get the fuck out of here," warned DB as his last magazine ran dry.

Jonesy was down to ten rounds and urged them to make their way to safety. Irish gave the order and the adults raced after DB. Hesitating by the soldier's side, the pair stared at the ravaged sanctuary. Wincing at each cry of agony, Irish's face reddened as the rage grew. His eyes searched for something, or someone, among the carnage.

"It's time to go," said Jonesy.

"These people trusted us to keep them safe." The baseball bat hung by Irish's side, the spilled blood dripping like emerald tears.

"You've worked miracles here, never forget that. I promise we'll help you get payback."

Irish took in a deep breath and let it out with a shudder of emotion. "I guess that's all I have left now."

Turning away from the wanton destruction, they followed the others down the alleyway. Greasy remained motionless, glaring poison at the dead.

"Greasy?" called Irish.

"I'll catch you outside. I need to find her," he replied.

Before anyone could say anything, he dodged around the approaching pack and was gone into the thick of the horde.

CHAPTER 19

"How's it looking?" asked Jonesy.

"Piece of cake, but I think we'll be screwed if we have to hang around much longer," replied Braiden.

Gripping the stiles, Jonesy slipped the inside edge of his boots against the ladder and slid down smoothly.

"This is no time for showboating," grumbled DB from above.

"Sorry, mate," replied a chastened Jonesy. A sprained ankle or deep cut from a damaged ladder could mean certain death in their current circumstances. It was a stupid thing to have done.

"Who're they?" asked Sam, nodding at the newcomers.

As they all scurried down the ladder, Emma and Tara embraced them tightly. Gently pushing them away, a solid looking man reached out a calloused hand towards Sam.

"I'm Irish, I'll introduce the others when we're safe."

Looking around, he looked less than pleased to have two teenagers guarding their rear. In the distance, Winston was moving in and out of the cars, destroying the undead with heavy swipes of his battle axe. Irish's mask of consternation took on an even darker tone. Jonesy gave him a look that said *they're ok*, which went some way towards satisfying him. Returning his attention to the ladders, the children were carefully climbing down with DB giving encouragement and guidance. All in all, considering their ages ranged from around six to thirteen, they were holding up well. Tears flowed, but the usual complaints and whining of children was absent.

Jonesy caught Irish's eye and was about to mention his admiration, but the thick set man spoke up.

"We've not kept them shielded from the dead. They've had to learn to fight as best they can, you know, just in case we went down."

Jonesy nodded and thought how similar Irish's outlook was to that of Kurt's. Childhood was now limited to the few years until you could walk upright and hold a weapon. No time for cartoons, playing, exploring the fervent imagination of youth. No need to conjure monsters from the deepest parts of a developing adolescent mind. They walked among us now, and were far more dangerous than the ghouls which pursued you through hazy dreams.

"Where are you guys holed up?" asked Irish as the women started to climb down.

Braiden wasn't too keen to be sharing information with the strangers and turned away. Sam snorted, annoyed with his brother's attitude. "We took Arundel Castle."

"No shit?" exclaimed Irish with a whistle of appreciation. "Who's we?"

"Our group," Braiden replied, giving nothing away.

"How did you end up here today? Not that I'm not grateful."

"Why all the questions?" Braiden snapped.

Irish turned to the youngster and scowled. "Just trying to get a read on you."

"We're saving you, that's all you need to know," replied the teen, watching the perimeter.

"That's not all I need to know, you mouthy little shit!" Irish growled, striding towards him.

Braiden's screwdriver was in his hand before the man had taken a single step. Their eyes locked, and for a split second Sam was sure they would go for each other. Jonesy respectfully pulled the grief stricken survivor back, while Sam did the same.

"Bray, they've lost people. A lot of people. Show some compassion."

"Haven't we all?" was his reply as he stared.

Sam stepped between them, blocking their view. "I'm sorry, sir. My brother's just cautious. We've met some real bad people out in the world."

"So have we," replied Irish, his glare softening.

"Is that who you were talking about before?" asked Jonesy as the final survivor touched down.

"You mean the prisoners? Or the Gypsies?" asked Sam.

Irish frowned. "We've not met any prisoners. We did have a couple of travellers pass by on horseback, but they just traded with us and went on their way. They didn't cause this..."

"Then who?" Braiden asked.

"I'll tell you later, but for now I'm going back in to find Greasy," he replied.

"But..." DB started to say.

"We took this place together. We built this place together. If we gotta die, we'll die together fighting for our loved ones."

"At least let one of us come back with you," said one of the survivors.

"Nah, Gaz. I want you to take everyone to The Crown. Get inside and lock the doors. If I'm not there in fifteen minutes," Irish said, turning to DB. "I'd like for you to take my people home to Arundel with you. Could you do that?"

"We can do that," he agreed solemnly.

134

"I don't know if there's a God up there looking out for us, but I'm sure glad you showed up when you did. Let's hope I can buy you a beer or ten." And with that, he took the ladder two steps at a time and was gone.

"We don't have any food," warned Braiden, staring at the soldier.

"We've got what we found at the Hargis's. That'll last for now."

"Did you say the Hargis's? You know Gail and Don?" asked Gaz.

"It's why we're here," confirmed Braiden. "Christina's in the castle with us."

In spite of their anguish, a wan smile broke out on Gaz's face. "They'll be so happy to hear that. They thought she was dead."

"Hardly, she's a real fighter. She survived alone for weeks in St Richard's Hospital."

"You don't say," Gaz replied.

Winston came huffing over, waving an arm exuberantly in greeting. His double bladed axe with its dripping gore scared the children, so he tucked it out of sight behind a bin and apologised.

"This is Winston. He likes cross dressing," explained Braiden.

"I'm not sure if I like it, I haven't tried it yet," he fired back, shaking any outstretched hand. The group stared at him uncertainly.

"Private joke," said Jonesy.

"Gaz, do you want to lead the way?" suggested DB.

Casting a glance up at the top of the ladder, he hesitated.

Braiden could see the conflict on his face, the way he wanted nothing more than to join his friend. "I knew men like Irish. He'll meet us at the pub, don't worry."

Gaz paused a moment longer, listened for cries of pain, and heard nothing. Without a good reason to linger, his shoulders sagged in defeat. Enough of their blood had already been spilled. "Ok, this way."

CHAPTER 20

"What's the next move, Sergeant?" asked Kurt.

"We've only got one route in, through the rear entrance. The crater will be too deep for the Hogs to pass over, and that's even if it wasn't swarming with the dead."

"Sarge, we could take up a firing position and kill them while they fight their way in," offered Petermann.

"We don't have the ammunition, Private. There's twice as many as we fought at the farm and we've got half the rounds. Fuck!"

The weakened logistics were a necessary evil. If the numbers were to be believed, they had dozens of civilians to pull from the shit. More boxes of ammo meant less space for the people. It still left them in trouble, though.

"I might have an idea, Sergeant," said Kurt.

"I'm all ears."

"My group get out at the breach. If you can use the heavy guns to shoot a few and get their attention, we can try and pull the main horde away and kill them like we did at the castle. You'll still have a war inside, but we might be able to cut off the reinforcements."

"And what happens if you get in trouble?"

Kurt shrugged. "We're faster on foot. I'd appreciate Joan or one of the others to stay with us. To protect us from... other threats."

"You mean the Gypsies?"

"I don't even think they'll bother us. They had a reason to hate the prison. We've done nothing to them."

"Most of the time they just like to be left alone," said Joan. "But we'll be on our guard."

"I'd rather keep everyone together," said Holbeck, analysing the plan. "I don't like the idea of dividing our forces."

"It's your call," Kurt replied.

"To hell with it. Splitting our numbers means they have to split theirs. It's going to be a tight squeeze inside the prison, anyway."

"Matt can stay with you, just keep him out of sight until you're inside the walls. If we have any observers, I don't want to give them a reason to get riled."

"What happens if they find out he's hiding with you inside the castle?" asked Holbeck.

"We'll cross that bridge when we come to it."

"Ok, Carpenter, Ewington, swing up alongside the horde, a hundred yards away. Eldridge, Petermann, use a case each to thin them down and give Kurt a blockage to get started. MacLeod, you and Dougal are on fire support for the hand to hand."

"Aye, Sarge," came the replies.

Joan had slipped back into the combat role like a well worn in boot. Her heart rate was slightly elevated because of the excitement, but that was to be expected. The grip of the rifle in her hands felt natural, as if it hadn't been several years since they had last touched. Dougal grinned, his earlier worry about her suitability all but gone.

Carpenter turned the wheel and accelerated back towards the prison. A few of the more impatient corpses had given chase while they were interrogating the prisoners. Looking at Holbeck for permission, he nodded. Putting her foot down, she made a beeline for the shambling monsters. The eager, twisted faces who thought they were about to feed shattered against the slatted armour. Rot bloated bodies popped under the caterpillar tracks.

"You enjoyed that far too much," said Kurt.

Carpenter laughed and kept her eyes on the path ahead.

"Oh, that's fucking gross," said Ewington over the radio as he trundled over the crushed corpses.

Grinding to a halt on the frosty ground, the turrets whined as the gunners moved into position. Kurt left the vehicle with Matt and Louise before gathering his armoured warriors. From above, the heavy dudda dudda dudda began. Thick brass casings chimed against the roof, some falling into the dirt where they melted the ice with a hiss.

Seeing the destructive power up close, Kurt's mouth fell open. Any appendage hit by the rounds exploded, the remains sailing leisurely into the yard. Arms waved, undamaged heads rolled in confusion. More were hit in the pelvis or leg, toppling sideways like felled trees.

"Magazine!" yelled Eldridge. Swiftly followed by Petermann.

"That's enough," Holbeck yelled as they reloaded. "Move on!"

At the cry, the drivers moved north towards the rear entrance.

Kurt raised his machete and charged. "Move in!"

"We can't cover the whole horde, Kurt!" warned Dougal.

The half-moon of patiently filtering corpses was close to three hundred feet in diameter. The heavy gunfire had carved twin trenches through the tightly packed dead which pinned the central core in place for now. Bodies with missing limbs and plate sized exit wounds twitched and bled. Moving to the flanks, the mostly unharmed zombies were spreading out quickly.

"Two groups left and right! Try and hem them in!"

Without the need for designation, they seamlessly broke away. Kurt led Louise south. Peter took Jodi north. Dougal and Joan took up position to cover the hand to hand fighting. They maintained a cursory eye on the indescribable mess in the centre, just in case something had survived and crawled free of the butchery.

"No risks! Keep your distance!" Kurt yelled.

Louise started cracking skulls with her mace.

Jodi swung the baseball bat, the metallic gongs ringing out like a Sunday morning's church bell.

Kurt was more tactical. Weaving amongst the dead, he struck out with the war pick, trying to build a barrier of flesh.

Occasionally, Dougal would fire his rifle, killing any undead that looked to be a threat.

"It's working!" yelled Peter.

The crater was filling up, deeper and deeper. Starved of targets inside the prison, the zombies were trying to force their way back out to the fresh meat.

"Let's hope Holbeck keeps up his end!" replied Kurt.

Time was running out. The crush of dead would soon pour over the mound of glistening viscera. Moving with purpose, Kurt and the other fighters plugged the leaks as best they could.

"It was far easier being a plumber," he grumbled to himself.

CHAPTER 21

The tall walls passed to their left. A solitary body hung from the razor wire, the blood from his savaged body staining the brickwork a darker shade of red. People were fighting in the guard towers, but judging by the blood that sprayed against the glass, they had already lost.

"It's ironic," muttered Holbeck. "They'd hoped the prison would keep them safe and stop the civvies from escaping. All it did was ensure they couldn't escape when they needed to as well."

"If we're lucky, Sarge, the cells the civvies are locked in will keep them out of harm's way until we get down there," said Carpenter.

"Amen to that," he replied.

Passing the corner, Carpenter swung the APC wide to give them room to manoeuvre in the event of a waiting horde. As Matt had promised, the back of the facility was largely empty of the dead. Twin gates stood wide open in the wall.

"That looks wide enough for both of you to park side by side," said Holbeck over the radio.

Ewington floored it and came alongside the lead vehicle. A scattering of zombies were approaching, but they fell like wheat to a scythe under Petermann's fire. Anything left would be unable to give chase. Carpenter saw the approaching arch and had a moment's doubt.

"They'll fit," said Holbeck, noticing the reduced speed.

"Yes, Sarge."

With inches to spare, the Warthogs passed between the poorly maintained frame, stopping with the articulated rear section protruding slightly beneath the curved lintel. Signs of rot in the wood showed through the years old paint. Unlike the industrial park, these gates would have broken open at the merest nudge of the armoured vehicles.

Within, the cage was in a much better state of repair. The large emergency access gates were sealed and locked. The single personnel gate was wide open. Jumping from the cab, Holbeck checked the gaps between the Warthogs. The blast shields were nearly kissing. Nothing was getting through.

"Harkiss, Ewington, get up top and help pull Matt onto the roof. He's not gonna squeeze down the side."

"Have you seen the fucking size of him, Sarge?" Harkiss whined.

"He's a unit," agreed Ewington. The prisoners forearms were the size of his calves for fucks sake. The joys of having nothing but time and heavy weights to lift.

"Unless you want to get court-martialled for being pussies, get your asses moving!"

Scampering up the ladderlike armour, they passed Eldridge who scoffed. "Pussies."

Petermann chuckled at her jibe and got the finger from Harkiss.

"I heard what you said about me, boy," growled Matt who was already waiting outside the rear hatch.

141

Passing up the pair of crutches along with the claymore, he ignored their hands and pulled himself up without effort. Harkiss passed the second crutch to Ewington so he could help the Scot to his feet. After rising, Matt reached for the supports.

Ewington held them cautiously out of reach. "You're not going to beat us with these, are you?"

"I'd use my head and fists, pussy boy," Matt grumbled, tossing one of the aluminium versions aside and relying on the tall blade instead. "Besides, you're the ones with the guns." He left them gawping at each other, carefully navigating the equipment on top of the vehicle.

"Would bullets stop him?" asked Dougal.

Harkiss pointed at the bloodied leg. "They haven't so far."

"Will you stop jabbering and fucking help me," snapped Matt, reaching the front of the transport cab.

Bracing themselves, they helped Matt step over the cables and coupling mechanism. Dropping down to the side, he landed awkwardly in the prison grounds. "Chew ma banger, ya wee bawheed!" he ranted, the full Scottish brogue taking over in his pain.

"Matt, which way?" asked Holbeck, giving him no time to recover. They didn't have the luxury.

Ewington expected a furious response, but Matt breathed deeply and fought back the pain. "Through the veg gardens. We'll pass the gym and reach C wing. It's the closest."

"Good." He pondered leaving Eldridge and Petermann in the turrets to keep the area clear, but without knowing what was going on inside, he needed every able body. "Squad, we're going CQB. Single column. The asset forms up in the centre. Harkiss, you're on point! Ewington, your with Eldridge. Petermann, on me. Carpenter, rear guard."

Eldridge and Petermann were down in seconds, their rifles loaded and armed. Ewington formed up behind Harkiss, followed by Holbeck and Petermann. Matt moved as fast as he was able. Carpenter took position behind, the rifle at low ready.

"Move!"

They moved slowly accounting for the injured man.

"Contact front!" called Harkiss.

"Do we engage, Sarge?" asked Petermann.

Scanning left and right, the zombies were everywhere. "We need a path back. Prioritise targeting of the most mobile. Squad, halt!"

Firing while moving was a good way of laying down suppression, but against the dead it was just wasted bullets. Free to aim, the soldiers killed twenty fully intact corpses who were shambling with inhuman vigour.

"Squad, move up!"

Pausing every twenty yards or so, it gave Matt a few seconds to rest and some much needed opportunity to clear the grounds.

"Magazine!" yelled Harkiss, dropping to a knee.

Ewington moved into position to cover the reload.

"Which way, Matt?" asked Holbeck, picking off a dead nurse. The body count was rising, but their ammunition was depleting, and they weren't even in the prison yet.

"That's the gym," said Matt, pointing to a building besieged by the undead. "Around that greenhouse, we'll see the end of C block. The emergency exit should be open."

"Ok, go! Save your ammo for when we're inside."

Harkiss proceeded past the glass structure. Thinking it was a bit odd to have such a thing inside the prison, he kept the question for later. One blow with an elbow and the inmates would have razor sharp blades galore. Crazy.

"Sarge, the door's closed! They must have sealed themselves inside!" Harkiss called back.

The small metal emergency staircase leading up to the three solid doors was filled with zombies on each tier.

"Fuck! Matt, ideas?"

"That way," he said, nodding south west. "If we go around it we get to B wing. It's... open."

143

Ignoring the stutter, Holbeck acceded and Harkiss forged on. Without any renewed gunfire, the dead at the exits were unaware of the passing soldiers. All they knew in their festering minds was that meat was on the other side of the barrier and they were going to taste it. Lacking understanding of the nature of the reinforced doors, they could beat against them until the end of time and still not make a dent.

"Were they building when it all went down?" asked Holbeck as the scaffolding came into view.

"Not in the way you're thinking. That's The Gauntlet; Craig's answer to our lack of entertainment."

"I don't understand," replied Holbeck.

"You will," said Matt.

Harkiss ran for the nearest ladder and climbed onto the lower level which was only five feet from the ground. The scaffolding was built to surround the whole wing, and several walls had been removed on the outside, exposing the cells within. Petermann followed, taking up position to cover the hatch above in case anything should come staggering to investigate, and ended up falling through. Matt tossed the crutches up and hopped rung to rung.

"Which way?" asked Holbeck.

"That way," he explained, indicating the nearest hole in the block wall.

A makeshift frame had been built just inside the ragged opening, secured to the brickwork. Across the ceiling, a set of eye rings and a cable system stretched to the door.

"What the hell went on here?" demanded Holbeck, following Harkiss and Petermann.

Matt sighed, sickened at his own culpability. "We gathered and stored the dead in these rooms."

"Why would you do that?" Eldridge gasped. "Why put yourself at risk?"

"For entertainment, like I said."

Ducking through the cell door, the wing was completely deserted. Dark stains covered the floor.

"You fought zombies for fun?"

"*We* didn't," replied the Scot gruffly.

"Then who?"

"The wrong'uns. The molesters. The rapers. The paedos."

Holbeck was incredulous. "But you and your friends raped people too! How the fuck are you any better?"

Matt dropped the crutches and grabbed Holbeck by the lapels of his fatigues. Slamming him into a wall, the soldiers helmet cracked against the brickwork. "I never touched anyone. You hear me?"

Holbeck stared into the guilty eyes, while his hand ordered the troops to lower their weapons. "Ok, Matt. I believe you." The words had an authenticity because they were true. Holbeck *did* believe that the man wouldn't take someone against their will.

"I never said that we weren't hypocrites," Matt muttered, lowering the soldier until his boots touched solid ground again.

"You never put normal people inside?" asked Eldridge.

"Only the screws."

"The guards?"

"Screws."

"We should leave you here," said Eldridge, keeping the rifle trained on Matt.

"Lower your weapon, Private. That's an order."

Eldridge glared at the hulking prisoner, before slowly complying.

"We don't have time for this shit, so cut it out!" Holbeck raged. "Matt, where now?"

"Through those gates," he pointed to the other end of the wing. "That takes us to the guard station. The old seg wing is below ground."

"Ok, form up and move out."

Matt picked up the crutches and joined the column, avoiding eye contact with Eldridge. Deep down he knew the fiery soldier was right, and it hurt worse than any gunshot wound.

CHAPTER 22

"What do you want to do, Len?" asked Big John as the echoes of gunfire faded.

Lennie watched the pair of heavy armoured vehicles drive off, leaving half a dozen of their number by the shattered wall. The group was dressed ridiculously, with sections of copper attached to their clothes. He almost laughed until they waded into the dead without hesitation. Slaying them by the dozen, they fought as one unit, guarding each other in spite of their wanton slaughter. His disdain for the group disappeared. Whoever they were, they were fearless.

"We could take them all out if you wanted," he added. "There's only two soldiers. If we pick them off first?"

"And bring down the heavy guns on our heads?" Lennie replied.

Big John wasn't afraid of anything, and that sometimes made him a liability. If they attacked and the others returned and fired on the treeline with the HMGs, it was all over. The thick trunks would provide no cover. The

147

slugs would cut through them like paper. They would be torn to pieces.

"Leave them. If they want to get killed over some scumbags, so be it."

"Who are they, though?"

"Could be anybody. It's not as if we were quiet earlier."

"You don't think they're connected to the prison?"

"How the fuck do I know, John? I've been enjoying the show, just like you. They could've been on patrol, I don't know." He didn't believe it, though. They moved with purpose, as if there was something valuable within. The captives? Possibly. But that meant that the group had knowledge of the prison and its workings. It was a fact worth remembering.

"We need to tell Mrs Hampton."

"Yeah, we do. Listen, I think it'll be worth opening the caches and bringing some of the heavier stuff out of storage. A couple of dozen AKs, a few RPGs."

"You expecting a war, Len?"

"Not really. Doesn't hurt to be prepared, though."

"I guess not. Shall I send a few of the guys off to do it while we take the brothers back?"

"Yeah."

"What about them?" John asked about the four prisoners hurrying away in the distance.

"Leave them. They're as good as dead."

"Are you coming?"

"I'll be along shortly. I want to see how they get on."

CHAPTER 23

"Gaz, was it?" asked Jonesy.

"Yeah," he replied. Returning his attention to the road, he walked on.

"How far is it?"

"Not far."

Jonesy was tempted to press further, but the distress bubbling beneath the surface wouldn't take much to explode. Looking back at DB, the other soldier offered a weak smile. The survivors would have to work through their grief in their own good time. It was no different to the war-torn provinces of Afghanistan following an IED or failed mission. Numbness set in. A sense of detachment, akin to an out of body experience. The empty bunk in their quarters. The pictures of a loved one smiling that would never see the face that brought such joy again. Then anger, fury, a need for retribution. Glancing from face to face, they were currently numb. Not quite believing they had survived and wondering if they should have bothered.

DB was following up the rear with the boys. They shielded the children while the adults began the long process of acceptance. Forming a semi-circle, they broke away and destroyed any creature that presented itself. Most of the rotting locals were either at the site of the chaos, or heading that way. Fortunately, the latter hadn't crossed their path in any great number as yet.

"It's just around the corner," said Gaz, his voice flat and lifeless.

"How do you know if it's safe?" asked Jonesy.

"We secured it a while ago."

"Ok, mate."

Jonesy scanned the abandoned streets. Further down the long road, a huge Tesco store came into view. "Looks like a good place to stock up on food. Local too."

"Too many of the dead," replied Gaz. "It's not as if they want the fucking food either. They just won't leave."

"They prefer it fresher," muttered Emma.

"There it is," said Gaz.

The pub came into view. Like a fortress in its own right, the ring road surrounded the imposing structure like a black, tarmac moat. Three floors of solid Victorian construction, with high set windows, soaring chimney stacks, and THE CROWN mounted in golden letters above the front door. Metal shutters covered every window, both upstairs and down. A heavy steel gate had been bolted to the brickwork to secure the entrance. A victim of the changing tastes of society, it now provided a sanctuary, becoming useful one last time.

Gaz wandered off without saying a word. Jonesy was close to calling him back until the man knelt at a drain, lifted the grate clear, and retrieved a key from inside. He glanced around with concern on his face, searching for something. Or someone. Shaking his head in disgust when he realising caution no longer mattered, Gaz stood up and joined the group.

"What was that all about, mate? What're you looking for?"

"It doesn't matter now, anyway. They've killed us."

"Your friend Irish mentioned something along those lines. Who're you talking about?"

"He wanted to tell you. He'll be here soon."

"It's the Nowhere Man," whispered Tara.

"Men," whispered another small child.

"That's enough, both of you!" Emma scolded.

DB shrugged when Jonesy pulled a face. Childhood fantasy or stark reality? Hopefully Irish would have the answers.

Releasing the padlock, Gaz pulled the heavy steel bars away from the shuttered door. With the second key, he unlocked the mortice lock of the main doors and threw them open. Mustiness and the smell of inns across the world washed over them. Despite being teetotal, Jonesy felt comforted by the scents of their old world. Sipping on a lemonade while his friends got wasted, the feeling of community and belonging transcended the foregoing of shared inebriation. Being sober also helped to keep the more rambunctious members of his squad from getting into trouble. Namely Harkiss. The phrase "lover, not a fighter" could have been coined for him. He was far more adept at throwing cheesy chat up lines than fists. Generally a flurry of apologies was enough to defuse any trouble as they pulled him away. Failing that, a growl from DB generally ensured the peace. Except for the most drunken of patrons, whose alcohol inhibited forays into violence often caused more damage to themselves than their chosen foe.

Seeing everyone safely inside, Gaz pulled the gate shut and looped the unlatched padlock through the staple. Jonesy ushered him past into the darkness and kept watch through his scope from the shadows.

"Through here," said Gaz, leading the others around the main bar into the restaurant area.

"Shame it's not called The Winchester," said Winston.

"What?" replied Gaz, firing up two halogen lanterns.

151

"It's from a film. You know, go to The Winchester and wait for this all to blow over?"

"This isn't going to blow over, kid," Gaz snapped. "It's already over. Everyone's dead!"

Winston realised he wasn't helping the situation and retreated to a corner.

"They're fried, mate. Maybe keep the observations to yourself," DB warned amicably.

Winston sat down with a sigh. The last thing he wanted was to add to their woes with his choice witticisms. Zipping his lip, he turned the lock and handed the invisible key to the soldier.

"I'll keep it safe," said DB, pocketing the valuable in his combat fatigues.

"Does anyone want a proper drink?" asked Gaz, making himself busy in the gloom of the bar.

Surprisingly, out of those who could answer, none did. Not even a swift tipple to take the edge off of their recent encounter. Pouring himself a hefty treble of vodka, he downed the alcohol in one hefty slug. Bashing the shot glass on the polished bar, he winced at the loud crash. Looking at the two soldiers, tears formed in his eyes. Gagging once, his chest heaved. Gagging a second time, the fiery liquid gushed from pursed lips into the waiting sink.

"I'm sorry... I... I don't..."

"It's ok, mate," said Jonesy, moving to help him. "Come and sit down. Take a load off and let us keep watch, ok?"

Gaz could only nod weakly.

"What now, brother?" asked DB as the stricken man slumped in a window booth.

"We wait for Irish and Greasy."

CHAPTER 24

Irish took a long drag on his cigarette, blowing the smoke out in a thick stream. His fingers trembled as he took another puff. Whether it was from grief or hatred, Jonesy couldn't guess. He and Greasy had returned minutes ago, covered in a lot more gore, but empty handed. The biker disappeared inside and hid himself away, trying to process the loss of whatever lady he had gone in to find.

"Who did this?"

"Do you know how many people we lost securing the estate?" Irish replied, ignoring the question.

"No."

"Twenty-two. We were lucky that the dead were drawn towards the town centre where it was all kicking off. It would've been all of us if we hadn't had that day and a half to build. The night was the worst. The streetlights never came on for some reason, even though the electric was still working. With all the other houses dark, the dead could get to us before we knew they were there. We could see the orange glow from the fires raging in town, but the flames weren't strong enough to reach us. I sent out four people to turn on the lights in the empty homes. You know, to try and at least give us some vision. Only one made it back. He'd been bitten."

"I'm sorry."

Irish lit a second cigarette from the glowing tip of the first before grinding it out beneath his boot.

"We were lucky, really. We watched the TV, hoping for good news. All we saw were countries falling, going dark as the dead ate everything. I put out a call on my HAM radio. Gail and Don were on the other end. Others responded too, but they never made it to us. Things quietened down for a while and we thought the worst had passed. Yeah, the zombies were wandering around, but if we were careful we could scavenge for what we needed. We had a little community."

"Are your family here?" Jonesy asked.

"I'm divorced, no kids. The ex-wife took me to the cleaners, even though she was the one to cheat, can you believe that shit? I lost my house, half my pension, most of my savings. I was sleeping on Greasy's sofa while her new boyfriend moved in. To my fucking house! That I'd fucking built!"

"That's harsh, mate."

Irish looked at Jonesy. "She phoned me on the day it all went to shit. She was terrified. Geoff had been bitten and turned. Do you know what I did?"

Jonesy shook his head.

"I laughed and hung up."

"She'd betrayed you," offered Jonesy.

"And I killed her. Not by my own hand, but I could've gone and helped."

"You saved a whole estate full of people. Who's to say that if you'd gone off on a rescue mission, they wouldn't have all died."

"I've tried to convince myself of the same thing. It's bullshit. Truth is, I enjoyed hanging up. I took pleasure in imagining her face as Geoff came for her. It's crazy when you consider I loved the bitch at one time in my life. I think I still did, even as she died."

"We've all done bad things to survive, mate."

"I know. It's a different world now. I still can't help but feel that this is my payback. Karma looked me up and found me wanting. Badly."

"What happened at the estate?"

"They didn't want anything, that's the worst thing. They just wanted to watch people die."

"Who's *they*?"

"One of the children called him the Nowhere Man, and it stuck. She was with her mother on watch on top of one of the coaches. I know it seems rough to have children so close to the zombies, but it was our way of desensitising them to the way they looked and smelled. She made a comment about how we couldn't go near the dead, but there was nowhere the man outside couldn't go."

Jonesy frowned. "You've lost me."

"The mother thought the girl was just using her imagination. Looking where she was pointing, there were only zombies. Hundreds of them. We all agreed, figuring the poor kid was just suffering because of the horror... She wasn't. I saw the first of them in the third week. The guy was stood slap bang in the middle of a huge swarm of the dead. I could tell he was alive as he didn't have that grey, slimy look to his skin and his eyes were clear, a dark brown. He was just staring at me, totally unfazed and untouched by the corpses. He smiled at me, and it was the creepiest thing I've ever seen."

Jonesy was dumbfounded. It just wasn't possible. "How can that be? They try to tear us apart as soon as they see us. He should've been dinner."

"I know. I almost convinced myself that I was going crazy too, until he took off his baseball cap and doffed it like he was a fucking Victorian gent saying "how do you do"."

"What did he look like?"

"I'd guess about five foot ten. Same build as me. Bald, with an awful scar on the top of his head. Have you ever seen the pictures of the people who have a section of the skull removed to let the brain heal? You know, following an accident?"

Jonesy cast his mind back. "I think so. It looks all sunken in."

"Exactly! He had that stretching from here," he pointed to a spot on his forehead above the right eye, to the crown of his scalp. "to here."

"Did it look fresh? Could he have got it during the outbreak?"

"No, from what I could see it was well healed."

"An old head injury then?"

"That was my guess. How the fuck that meant he could walk among the dead is anyone's guess."

"We've got a doctor back at the castle; Gail and Don's daughter, Christina. She might be able to shed some light on it."

"The others I saw had fresher wounds."

"Others?"

"Another man, much bigger. And a woman."

"And they had the same scar?"

"Nah, it was fresh. They were all stitched up, like it had happened recently. The wounds weren't that livid, and their hair was at least a half inch long around the close shaved part near the wound itself."

Jonesy mulled the information. "On average that's about a months' worth of growth. So they were injured after the first guy?"

"Injured?" Irish shook his head. "I think they had it done *to* them. They moved freely among the zombies too. Not a single one so much as sniffed. The bigger guy even slapped one of them as if to prove the point to me."

"This is insane..." Jonesy whispered.

"We never fucked with them. I even tried offering to trade with the first guy when he came back. He just smiled again and shook his head."

"You weren't expecting the attack?"

"The first we knew the dead were inside was when the screams started. By then it was too late. They'd brought thousands with them."

"I really am sorry, mate. I can't bring your friends back, but I can keep you and the others safe. The castle's impregnable. Stone doesn't burn, and I'll gladly put a bullet through that wanker's smiling face if he ever shows up."

"I appreciate that. How do you propose we get to your home? My people haven't had much sleep with all that's happened."

"We could stay here for a couple of hours. Let you all rest and move out early-afternoon."

"Would it be better to wait for tonight? Move in the dark?"

"With the kids, I'd rather do it in the light. We can see threats coming a mile away, less chance of panic."

"Ok. Sounds good."

"What's the plan, boss?" asked Greasy, emerging with a double shot of whiskey. His eyes were red and raw, but he wouldn't show emotion in front of the others.

Irish hugged his friend, causing him to spill some of the brown liquor. "We get a few hours shuteye and move out after lunch. Even if the adults don't get much kip, I want the kids to be fully rested."

"They're pretty jazzed. Even if they get to sleep, they'll be having nightmares for weeks," Greasy replied, sipping from the glass.

Irish ruffled in his pocket, withdrawing a white medical bottle. "Grind a quarter tablet up for each of the younger ones. A half for the teenagers. It'll knock them out until we're ready to go."

"What're those?" asked Jonesy.

"Sleeping pills. I was having trouble after I split up from the missus."

"Are you sure that's a good idea? What if we need to leave in a hurry before this afternoon?"

"I didn't see the fuckers during the attack," replied Irish, lighting another cigarette.

"Or on our way back here," agreed Greasy.

"Is it worth the risk? Just laying down in the dark will help, even if they can't fall asleep. They can get a proper nights' rest once we're safely inside the castle.

Irish considered the point, then nodded. "Ok, get everyone settled and lower the lanterns. I'll keep a watch for the first half hour, then you can take over." Turning to Jonesy, he said, "Would you mind doing a watch with some of your guys?"

"That's not a problem. I'll get the boys to do a stint each after that." Jonesy looked at his watch. "That should take us to half past one."

"Where did you dig the kids up from, anyway? They don't give a fuck about the zombies. Even I keep a respectful distance unless I have to kill one."

"Their family moved across from Emsworth, through Chichester, finally to Arundel. On foot. With nothing but choppers, and a shotgun with a couple dozen shells."

"Holy shit," Irish gasped.

"Tell me about it. They're fearless."

"And a little bit crazy," said Greasy, appreciatively.

"If anyone would know crazy, it's you, mate," chuckled Irish.

"In this shit, I think we've all gone a little crazy," agreed Jonesy.

"I'm sorry how I went off to the kid. What was his name?"

"Braiden, and don't sweat it. That boy's been through Hell, and that was before the apocalypse. He's a rough diamond. A real warrior."

"Even so, when we get out of here I'll take him to one side and apologise personally."

"I know he'd like that. In spite of his gruff exterior, he has an unbreakable code that makes him a solid ally. You'll be glad to have him in your corner."

"I kinda sensed that," Irish replied. "Get some sleep, both of you."

"Wake me whenever you're ready," said Greasy, downing the Scotch.

"I'm a light sleeper," said Jonesy, moving towards the restaurant. "Any trouble, just shout and I'll be there."

"Will do. And Jonesy?"

He turned to face the burly builder.

"Thank you. I know we'd all be gone if it wasn't for you guys."

Jonesy smiled wanly, leaving the man to his mourning and cigarettes.

CHAPTER 25

"It's locked, Sarge," said Harkiss from within the gauntlet's holding area.

"Blast the lock, we don't have time to find another way around."

"Roger, Sarge." The team moved to either side of the entrance, backs to the wall. Harkiss carefully aimed at the lock housing. The first round hit, sparks flying. The second round destroyed the inner workings and the door creaked open. Holbeck held them back while he carried out a recce. Terrified prisoners were running around like headless chickens. Sets of keys could be heard jangling. They were trying to seal themselves in.

"Idiots," mumbled Matt.

"What?"

"The only keys left that open the cells and wings are locked in Craig's safe."

"How do you know they haven't got inside the safe?" asked Holbeck.

Frantic cursing from the key bearer answered for him. "They don't fucking fit!"

"Try another," said another voice.

Matt raised an eyebrow to say *you see.*

"Now we're in the lion's den. Watch your battle partner's arse like a hawk. We move unseen and use the shadows."

Taking the lead with Matt, Holbeck followed the limping prisoner. Security checkpoints were all open. Offices protected by reinforced glass were empty. Every able man was likely at the doors, trying to hold back the dead. The darkness was nearly absolute without the overhead lights working. Thin slits of high set safety glass let in a few scant slivers of winter light. Decades of budget cuts had left the panes filthy from lack of cleaning, lending the rays a murky edge.

"Down there!"

A pitch black staircase went down into the bowels of the prison. "Torches on."

The Virtus helmet LEDs lanced through the darkness, revealing nothing.

"It's clear. Rear teams hold position. Harkiss and Petermann, clear the bottom."

Staying to the right, they descended. It gave them a wider field of view of the passage as it opened up as well as allowing Holbeck and Carpenter to cover the opening from their elevated position.

"Clear!" Harkiss shouted. "There's a locked door, Sarge."

Holbeck turned to Matt. "What can we expect? What's the layout?"

"It's one small wing with ten cells to either side. Nonces on the left, normal people on the right."

"Any way out?"

"Only these steps."

"Good. Wait here, I don't expect you to hop down after us."

"I appreciate that, lad."

161

Running down the steps, Harkiss and Dougal lowered their rifles as the sergeant crossed the line of fire and moved to the door.

"Private, we may need to blow this lock too. Be ready," ordered Holbeck.

Banging on the steel with a clenched fist, he heard movement on the other side.

"Who's there? Identify yourself!"

A panicked mumbling was all he could make out.

"Identify yourself! This is the British Army!"

The mumbling changed to a sharp intake of breath.

"We're here for the civilians. Open up or we blow the fucking door!"

Expecting to be ignored despite the threat, Holbeck heard the clank of a released lock. A solitary face peered out as the door swung open, squinting at the harsh glare of the helmet torches directed at him.

"Name?"

"Perry, sir," he whispered.

"You're a con?"

"Yes... Yes, sir."

"You were keeping them locked up?" Holbeck spat, raising his gun, ready to carry out an unauthorised execution. Three others whipped up, making it four dark barrels promising eternity. The man went a paler shade of white, gulped once, then fainted. Crumpling to the ground, Perry's head connected against the door with a dull crack.

"I wasn't expecting that," Holbeck admitted, shaking his head.

Shouldering his rifle, he marched forward and grabbed the shirt collar. Pulling the man back to the foot of the stairs, Holbeck called up to Matt.

"Friend of yours?"

Matt turned and looked. "Perry. A short timer. Nice kid. Bit dense."

"Was he involved in the rapes?"

"Not that I knew of. He was as scared of the women as he was of the prisoners."

162

Holbeck called over Harkiss and Dougal. "Get him topside and roused. The cell block is empty, so Carpenter and I will handle it."

"We're saving inmates now, Sarge?"

"Only those who get Matt's ok."

The Scot nodded down in gratitude. For the first time in years he was being treated as a valued human being.

Holbeck left the others to wrestle the unconscious body up the stairs. Pulling the keys from the lock, he moved cell to cell, opening the doors. Terrified faces cowered in dark corners.

"Carpenter, explain the situation. You've got a better way with words than I do." Holbeck moved on.

"Hey, we're here to help," she assured the occupants, her voice warm.

"It's just another trick," sobbed one of the victims.

"Just leave us alone," whispered one of the children.

Carpenter moved inside and smiled, but the people shied away, terrified. If they could have achieved the feat, they would've backed through the stone and out of the world entirely.

"It's no trick. We've come to save you, but time's running out. The prison is full of the bad things." She didn't say zombies. The children had seen enough horror.

They all closed their eyes, as if not seeing Carpenter would mean she didn't exist.

"Please," she implored.

The eyes stayed screwed shut.

Holbeck was halfway down the wing. Opening the next door, a man was laid on the thin mattress, holding a woman tight. Several others took shelter beneath a blanket, as if the thin rag could keep them safe. Frowning, Holbeck started to move on.

The first cries of fear carried down from the prison wings above. They were rapidly running out of time.

Moving back to the cell, he said in a voice as soothing as he could muster, "Folks, you need to come with us. We've got somewhere safe to take you."

"We thought this place would be safe. We were wrong," said the skeletal man.

"The place I've got in mind is completely safe. There are good people there."

"There are no good people, any more," he replied, holding the trembling woman tighter.

Giving up on them, Holbeck pushed on. Unlocking the rest of the doors, he didn't waste time engaging with the prisoners within.

"Sarge, what do we do?" asked Carpenter.

"Let us out!" shouted a man from the other cells.

Despair faded as revulsion flowed through Holbeck. Children! Who does that to fucking children? They were less than human.

"I'm talking to you!"

Throwing back the viewing hatch, Holbeck aimed the rifle at the man's face. "Shut your fucking mouth or I put one through your face! Do you understand?"

The paedophile ducked out of sight.

"Sarge?" Carpenter held her arms wide, all out of ideas.

Take them out at gunpoint? Or drag them out. That was a sure fire way of ensuring mission failure. Spend a week convincing them using an as yet undiscovered psychiatrist to unpick the brutal treatment at the hands of the inmates? A week? They would need years.

Fuck!

Maybe it was useless. Maybe they were already too far gone. Would bullets be a mercy in place of teeth? Holbeck looked at the lethal weapon in his hands and counted the rounds left.

"If only we'd asked the names," he muttered.

"What do you mean, Sarge?"

"They have no reason to trust us. I didn't even think to ask their names."

"What about…" she left the last word unsaid, pointing up towards Matt.

Holbeck shook his head. Seeing one of their captors would only exacerbate the situation. "What did Jodi say the guy's name was? Jason?"

"Yeah, Jason Rechtman," agreed Carpenter. "Why don't we try and find him?"

"In this mess? There's no way," replied the sergeant.

"What did you say?" asked the man from the darkness of the fifth cell.

"Jason Rechtman. He's the guy Jodi met at the tunnel a few weeks ago. Do you know him, sir?"

"I'm Rechtman," he said, stumbling out into the passage. "Did you say you were with Jodi?"

"She's fighting outside the walls with Kurt and the others. We've come from the castle."

"The castle?" Jason staggered forward. Grabbing at Holbeck's uniform, he slumped. Helping him upright, the man weighed nothing. Holbeck could feel the protuberant ribs and lack of meat through the thin, filth encrusted shirt.

Holbeck rolled the dice on the truth. "Matt Hay helped us to find you. He's been our guide in this place. He's upstairs, wounded."

"Clarissa?" Jason croaked.

"She's fine. She's waiting for you."

The shuddering woman emerged from the cell. "They made it?"

"He nearly died getting her there, but they made it."

"Oh my God, Jason. Is this a dream?" she sobbed.

"No dream, ma'am. But we really need to move. I can have you and your daughter reunited within the hour, I promise."

"We really need your help with the others, though," explained Carpenter. "They won't move."

"My name's Sally, Sally Rechtman. We've been hurt so much. The bastards actually played a trick on us just like this, unlocking the cells and taking us out into the yard pretending we were being rescued. The prisoners all thought it was hilarious."

"Those days are over, I promise. They're getting paid back in spades."

A gurgling scream pierced the near silence.

"Good," said Sally, some life back in her voice.

Limping back to the end of the block, she cooed and cajoled those inside to move. Seconds passed and Holbeck thought she had failed. But then a child stepped out, followed by another. Soon, the civilians were all on their feet, waiting. Doing a quick head count, there were close to fifty. Holbeck almost asked about the others, considering there were meant to be nearly a hundred. He pulled Jason over and whispered it. The engineer could only shake his head.

"Please help us," whined the child molester.

Holbeck fought every urge to open fire on the door. Instead, he let out a shuddering, rage filled breath, and tossed the keyring through the small hatch.

"What do you want me to do with these?"

"Whatever the fuck you want. Let yourselves out and fight for your freedom, or stay in there and die. I don't care."

Leading the procession of pitiful humanity towards the light, Holbeck's doubts resurfaced. The people were so weak. They could barely walk after being confined in darkness for months, only to be brought out at the whims of lunatics to be abused and raped. Right there he decided that if they fell, he would fall with them. The others could go on, but he would stay until his last breath.

"That's it, come on," urged Jason, shepherding the others.

In spite of his frailty, the news of his daughter acted like a catalyst for a final burst of energy. One woman gasped at the bottom of the steps, then turned and tried to run.

"Gabby, no. Mr Hay's on our side. He was the one that saved my baby," said Sally, holding her tight.

"But he..." she started, breaking into heart rending sobs.

"He was with Craig, yes. But he was never *with* Craig," Jason explained. "He's been trying to keep you all safe for longer than you know. It was Mr Hay that removed the children from the rape list."

"It was?" asked the lady. A glint of hope sparked in her eyes, and she looked down at her little girl who saw nothing except for whatever world she was inhabiting inside her own mind.

"Folks, I'm really sorry, but we need to go. Right now," warned Holbeck as tactfully as he could.

Jason and Sally led the way, carrying a toddler each. Reaching the top of the stairs, Jason put the child down and crushed Matt in a bony embrace. The Scotsman's cheeks reddened and he stared at the floor. Sally joined Jason, kissing Matt on each blushing cheek.

"Thank you," she whispered.

Matt grumbled inarticulately, refusing to meet their gaze.

"You're a hero," said Jason, squeezing a muscular shoulder.

Grunting, he turned away lest they see his overflowing eyes.

Picking up the infants, Jason and Sally waited behind the soldiers who were watching the security wing carefully.

Holbeck climbed the steps, apologising at each bump and nudge as he moved through those waiting. What had started as men shouting commands without any kind of plan or discipline was now utter bedlam. The undead had either found a way in, or they had forced their way in. Whichever it was, the cons were falling by the score. Screams and dying moans echoed down from every cell block.

"Time to move. Matt, stay with the main group," said Holbeck. Unclipping his bayonet pouch, he attached it to Matt's belt. "Just in case," he explained. "Harkiss and Petermann, you're on point. Eldridge, you're with Carpenter now. Ewington, move up front and centre and support. I'll guard the rear. We go back exactly the way we came in."

"What if the prisoners attack us and try and take our guns, Sarge?" asked Ewington.

"Protect yourself at all times. If they follow us, fine, I don't blame them. If they try anything, drop them where they stand."

"Aye, Sarge," he replied.

"Squad, move out!"

The two man teams moved fluidly through the block, the supporting gunner's rifle aiming over the shoulder of the lead.

"Contact right!" shouted Harkiss as zombies spilled from an overrun wing.

Firing on semi-automatic, he and Petermann moved towards the threat. The open gate acted as a bottleneck of sorts, allowing them to focus their fire on the creatures who had made it through. Eldridge and Carpenter took up position on their right flank and started to pick targets.

"Magazine!" cried Petermann.

"Magazine," yelled Harkiss.

The two support gunners had conserved ammunition to cover the reload. Single shots blew out the back of skulls, covering those behind. Staggering on through the brains of their fallen, the grey skinned zombies were awash with crimson from those they had eaten. Some still chewed, the morsel too tough for their rotten teeth.

"Carpenter, Ewington, take point! Head to the gauntlet!" ordered Holbeck. "The rest of you, follow!"

Shying away from the shouts and the hellishly loud cracks of the rifles, the civilians did as instructed. Jason and Sally did their best to encourage the group, but fear was in danger of spilling over. Emptying another magazine, Holbeck saw the piled corpses were thick enough to buy them a few seconds.

"Harkiss, Petermann, disengage! Move back to the front to support! Eldridge, you're with me!"

"Holy fuck, it's the army!" shouted a prisoner, leading a group of ten men out from A wing. "Wait for us!"

"Stay back!" warned Holbeck.

"Or what?" snapped the man.

A single shot to his chest knocked the man flat. He coughed once and then lay still. The other prisoners looked around frantically. They had cannibals behind, and crazed squaddies to the front.

"Wait for us!" begged the paedophile, emerging from the segregation wing.

One of the remaining ten turned around and punched the man in the gut. Staggering backwards, a blade protruded from his stomach. It hadn't been a punch. The other kiddie fiddlers retreated back to the temporary safety of their dungeon.

"Let us come with you," begged another of the ten.

Edging backwards, Holbeck aimed at the head of the murderer and fired again. His head snapped back, and a fine red mist coated the wall to his rear. Holbeck had no love for the molesters, but he couldn't let the act go unpunished.

"Fuck! Ok, we'll leave you alone," shouted the spokesman. Wondering where to turn, he clutched his head with both hands.

"You're not coming with us, but you can follow behind and keep the dead at bay. If you make a move that I don't like, you join your friends. Understood?" Holbeck gave them a single second to mull the ultimatum. They were moving in half that time.

Yells of contact from the point guards preceded more gunfire.

"How many?" Holbeck yelled down the crowded hallway.

"Manageable, Sarge! Just a few who followed us into the gauntlet. We're clear," answered Harkiss as the guns fell silent.

"Good work! Keep moving."

Holbeck kept one eye on the open wings, and one on the entourage he'd gained. The next wing had also fallen, and a group of newly undead inmates shambled out through the security gate. Their prison uniforms were shredded, as were their limbs. Great chunks of flesh were missing from across their bodies.

Holbeck took up a firing stance.

"Leave them! We'll take care of them!" offered the prisoner.

Joining the column without answering, Holbeck watched the men work. They only had knives, with a few bats and bars thrown in. Attacking the zombies like a pack of wolves, the killing was over in short order. One of the younger men turned away, trying to hide his arm.

"Show me!" ordered the leader.

"No! I'm fine!" he replied. Sprinting away, he left drops of blood in his wake.

"That's what I thought." Turning back to the escapees, he asked, "What's your name?"

"You don't need names. Keep up your end and I'll keep up mine."

"Ok, ok. That's cool. I got no problem with you," he said, arms raised in surrender. "I'm Jezz."

"Like I give a fuck," said Holbeck.

The last few women were making their way through the gauntlet holding area. Sporadic shots came from within, but still not in great enough numbers to warrant a change of formation.

"You stay here while I get the civvies outside. I'll shout once we're in the open," ordered Holbeck.

Glancing back at the security centre, Jezz knew they had no alternative. The screams were gone. All that remained was the maddening shuffle of shoe on concrete. The undead were close.

"Go! We've got you!"

Holbeck lowered his gun to swing through the ply lined holding cell. Zombie corpses littered the floor, headwounds gaping. The captives, seemingly devoid of any fear of the undead, merely stepped over them. They might look disgusting. They might smell disgusting. But they could never look you in the eye, laughing while brutalising your most sensitive areas for their own sadistic pleasure. In some ways, the zombies were more humane than the monsters that dwelled within Ford Prison.

"Ewington, how're we looking?"

"It's fairly clear, Sarge! Kurt's group must've kept them busy!"

"Good."

Holbeck moved to address the civilians. Petermann was keeping a close eye on the prisoners at the entrance, but they weren't making any moves apart from the occasional yell and the heavy thud of a bat on skull.

"Folks, this is going to be the worst part. I need you to follow my troops and stay tight. We'll be at the vehicles and out of here in no time. Don't wander, and stay in formation. We'll kill any threat, so don't panic."

Holbeck may as well have been talking to a crowd of the zombies for all the response he got. Jason and Sally moved up and down the line, offering encouragement. Like robots, the survivors all turned as one and shambled after Ewington as he ducked through to the scaffolding.

"Is there any coming back for them, Sarge?" whispered Petermann.

"I have no idea," Holbeck replied.

Fortunately, the mental detachment still worked in their favour. Cries of *contact,* and *magazine,* coupled with the slaying of dozens more undead had no discernible effect. Wherever they had retreated to, they were safe.

"Sarge, we've got some visitors in the prisoner cage," Ewington called.

The front ends of the Warthogs were surrounded by the dead. Quite what they were hoping to reach was anyone's guess.

"It's Kurt and the others!" Ewington confirmed, spying them through the narrow gap.

The bulk of the small horde was oblivious to the soldiers approach. A few were turning, but Ewington rushed forward and slid the bolt on the gate, trapping them inside.

"Understood, Private. Kurt?"

"We're here!"

"Move away from the back. We need to clear out our new friends and I don't want anyone getting hit in the crossfire."

"Do you want us to deal with it? It won't take five minutes to cut them down from the roof."

Looking at the gathering dead to the rear, Holbeck then checked the ammunition. Most of his troops only had one or two full magazines left. The eight remaining prison crew were slowly edging towards the soldiers, caught between a rock and a hard place.

"No, we're out of time. Stand back!"

Ordering his troops into a line, they formed up as if they were a firing squad. In place of the blindfolded condemned were a gurgling throng of awfulness.

"Fire!"

Bullets punched through eyes. Scalps lifted as tops of heads were struck. Skulls crumpled and the Warthogs got a fresh green paint job. Holbeck wasn't shooting. Between each crack, he listened. Then it came. The hiss of surprise from Sally. Before she could cry out in warning, Holbeck spun around and found Jezz and the others charging forward. Spraying the men with fully automatic fire, four hit the dirt hard. The others dived for cover, expecting to be finished off.

"Clear," shouted Ewington.

"Get them inside the cage," ordered Holbeck.

Jezz was dead. One bullet had hit him in the centre of the throat, the other his heart. The other three clutched at their various wounds, wailing and bleeding.

"All you had to do was wait," said Holbeck.

"We panicked! We're sorry. Don't shoot us!"

"And now you're down to four. Poor odds with what you're facing, wouldn't you say?" said Holbeck, slowly backing towards the holding area gate.

"Don't leave us! Please!"

"There're people in the gym. The fire exit is clear," said Matt, pointing towards the clear door.

"And what if they won't let us in? We could be dead fucks for all they know!"

Holbeck closed the gate and locked it. "Then you can wait there until we're gone." The undead were closing in fast, they would be forced to flee. If they had simply followed orders, he would have allowed them to take refuge in the cage while they loaded up. They hadn't, and now it was too late.

"Please!"

Holbeck's barrel directed them back to the gym. Cursing his black heart, they dodged the zombies and raced for the door. The three wounded prisoners gave their lives so their friends could get away. Slowly. Agonisingly. Holbeck looked away.

Carpenter was already reversing the Warthog. Colliding with the second vehicle, the metalwork squealed in protest.

"Sorry, Sarge," she called.

Ewington grimaced at the contact. When she was clear, he swung the articulated vehicle out wide to give everyone room.

"How was it?" asked Kurt.

"If we'd been an hour later, we'd have never got inside. The zombies had a few distractions." The faltering gurgles of the shot prisoners emphasised his point. "How was it outside?"

"Tough. We all need a wash." The gore dripped from his clothing, armour, and weapon. He was a walking infection.

Jason stepped towards the fearsome group. "Jodi?"

She saw him, but the sunken features thwarted her efforts to recognise him for a second. "Jason?" she blurted when it clicked.

"I'd hug you," he laugh sobbed. "But you're a little messy."

"You can do that later. I told you we'd be back for you."

"I'm sorry it took all this time, mate," said Kurt.

"It would've been suicide with the walls still standing. I guess in some ways, the Gypsies did us all a favour."

The four men beating at the sealed fire exit were finally surrounded and taken down. Their screams of pain washed off Holbeck like water from a duck's back. "Not everyone."

"Any sign of our friends?" asked Holbeck.

"If they were there, they didn't bother us. I couldn't see anyone," replied Kurt.

"Are they dead?" demanded Peter.

Holbeck scowled at the man. "Are *who* dead?"

"Mike and Craig. The Araters. Mike killed my... my friend."

"They're not inside," answered Jason. "The Gypsies took them earlier."

"So they're still alive?" Peter raged. Running into the cage, he started to butcher the dead reaching through the steel. Paige was still unavenged. The theft of their burgeoning love unanswered. His normally mild manner was gone. His hate burned like the core of the sun.

Holbeck looked to Kurt, bewildered by the outburst.

"We lost someone special. It was Mike's fault. Peter needed closure."

"Peter?" Jason said, joining the furious man.

"What?" he snapped, completely out of breath.

"If it helps, I don't think they will have a good time of it. The travellers killed a whole prison in retaliation."

"It doesn't help," he growled. "I wanted to see them die. I *needed* to."

Kurt walked over, smiling at the engineer to thank him for his intervention. Grabbing Peter in a bearhug, he whispered, "They're as good as dead. We've got a new group of people to take care of and I need you. Are you with us?"

"I'm with you. It's just I still see her face. Every night."

"Knowing who she was, do you think she would approve of your vengeance? Or would she smile and ask you to forgive them?"

Peter looked at his boots. "Probably not."

"Probably not what?"

"She wouldn't like it," he muttered.

"Exactly. Remember her. Be a better person *for* her. Paige is all that was good in this world. I think keeping her memory alive is more fitting than enjoying death, don't you?"

"I guess," Peter lied.

Holbeck was almost finished with the seating arrangements. As with the holiday park, the children were sequestered in the safety of the transport cabs. Most of the adults sat atop the vehicle. Harkiss had tied ropes and looped them from side to side through the slatted armour. It gave them something to hold on to. In their starved condition, he wouldn't have been surprised to see them float away on the growing wind.

"Looks like we're on foot," said Kurt.

"You guys are tired. Take the lead and my drivers will keep pace with you. Don't force it, we may still have to fight."

Kurt took one last look at the inside of the prison. Fires had started in some of the wings, the flames burning behind the barred windows. The gymnasium was surrounded, dooming the prisoners inside to a slow death or a reckless attempt to break free through an overrun facility. As he watched, dozens more zombies arrived, adding another layer to the undead.

"Let's get home, Sergeant. I need a cuppa."

175

CHAPTER 26

Winston stretched in the shadows, trying to pull loose the knots in his arms and shoulders. The previous night's activity had left him aching more than expected. Wielding the battle axe was exciting, and if he was honest with himself, a tiny bit arousing. He felt powerful, unstoppable.

"Ouch, you bastard," he winced as pain flared in his rotator cuff.

So much for being unstoppable. He felt eighty. The weapon would be returned to the display case as soon as he arrived back at Arundel, to spend the remainder of its days as a source of medieval history. Until Winston couldn't ignore the allure any longer and brought it back into action. It would be a few days, at least. Long enough for the memory of the aches to fade.

"No pain, no gain," he whispered, bending back each painful finger.

The crippling pain in his hands was unexpected, until he considered how tight he'd been holding both weapons, and the sheer number of undead that fell to his blows. The jarring impacts against bone, as well as the accidental contact with harder surfaces added to the damage. Yawning, he leaned back and reached for the ceiling. It felt wonderful. Falling asleep had been easy. On three occasions, DB nudged him awake for snoring or talking in his sleep. The conversations, it transpired, were somewhat... intimate. Involving a certain young lady from back at the castle. What made it worse was that Winston had no recollection of the actual dream that generated the rude mumblings.

"Just my luck."

Moving to the bar, he took a glass and pressed it to the optic dispenser of the half full bottle of Jack Daniels. Returning to the doorway, he swirled the shallow measure of alcohol. Sipping at the whiskey, he gagged and spat it on the floor.

"Eugh. That's awful."

How on earth did the people in movies drink that stuff? They looked so sophisticated, arranging million dollar deals, or relaxing after a game-changing legal case. It tasted like arse. Winston would never join the upper echelons of polite society, that was a certainty. Tipping the dregs down the drain, he returned the glass and picked a bottle of cola instead.

"I'm lower class, but I'm happy," he said, savouring the fizzy sweetness.

Time passed slowly on watch. After twenty minutes of inactivity, the cold was finding its way through his thick clothing. Doing star jumps, he tried to keep the noise down to heavy breathing and the scuff of trainer on time worn carpet. After a minute he was sweating. After two it was running down his face. Pausing, he used a dry bar towel to dab at the moisture. Almost immediately his heartrate slowed and his breathing returned to normal. *I really am getting fitter*, he thought happily. The extended loop of his belt flopped down towards his knees. The original, widely stretched holes in the leather were eight notches away from his present size. The fact that he could even see the belt as it hung was a miracle, unimaginable in the old world. Pea had suggested he replace it for a new one she'd found in the castle. Politely declining, Winston liked to keep it on as a reminder of his efforts. The world had died, and he had been reborn. It seemed a sick joke that he was thriving when billions were rotting on their feet.

The wind picked up, changing direction to an easterly breeze that carried the last traces of smoke from the scene of battle. Winston tried his best to ignore the tang that accompanied the fumes. The fresh, and not so fresh, accompaniment of burned meat. The growing force of the gusts chilled the sweat on his face, so Winston moved away from the doors and peered through a tiny crack in the steel shutters. Nothing moved on the empty streets except for a paper coffee cup that rattled past until it wedged beneath a car's flat tyre.

A lone zombie shuffled into view in the distance. Winston couldn't make out how badly he was wounded. None of the clothing seemed to bear the hallmarks of an attack. No brown crust, no fresh red blood from the recent attack. He might've been bitten on a finger and succumbed, Winston had seen that before. Instead of wandering off, the creature stopped in the middle of the road. If Winston didn't know better, he could've sworn that it was actually searching for something. Narrowing his eyes to firm up his weak vision, the zombie wasn't a zombie at all. It was a man.

"Holy shit!" Winston gasped. "Guys, we've got a survivor! Wake up!"

Hurrying out into the crisp daylight, Winston was forced to shield his eyes from the sudden change in brightness.

"Over here!" he called, waving to the individual.

"What did you say?" demanded Jonesy, joining him.

"It's a survivor! Look!" He pointed towards the unmoving man.

Jonesy's inner alarm bell was screaming. Lifting his arm, the individual waved back, moving the arm slowly back and forth like an upturned clock pendulum. Counting down, down, down. "I don't think that's a survivor." Racing back inside to get his rifle, Irish was nearly bowled over as he emerged from the pub.

"What's going on?" he asked, sluggishly.

"Is he one of your people?" Winston asked with trepidation, slowly backing up.

Irish squinted in much the same way as Winston had moments earlier. Seeing the man, the colour drained from Irish's face for a split second, before blooming with red rage. "That's the fucker who *killed* my people!"

"Sir! Wait!" Winston called as he charged off like an enraged bull.

"How the hell did they find us?" demanded Jonesy.

"I'm sorry, Jonesy. I saw him and I thought he was a survivor. I came running out like a complete idiot and called out to him."

"It's not your fault, mate. I should've explained the situation better," he replied to the crestfallen youth.

Irish was still running at full pelt towards the Nowhere Man. Jonesy took several steps to the left to clear his sightline. The crosshairs of his scope pulled the grinning face in tight. Lowering his arm, the man slipped two fingers between his lips and blew. The shrill whistle ended as Jonesy pulled the trigger. The firing pin clacked, but no bullet erupted from the barrel.

"No, no, no! Not now!"

Winston turned back to the man, whose smile widened further. He didn't seem fearful of the firearm at all, shrugging apologetically at Winston and Jonesy who was frantically trying to clear the dud round. Irish was about a hundred yards from his position when the swarm of undead poured from the side street. The zombies were filled with confusion for a second as the source of the summons was absent. Irish came to a grinding halt, nearly faceplanting as he rapidly slowed. Upon seeing him, the corpses groaned with relish.

The crack of the rifle caused Winston to drop his machete in fright. Snapping back to the Nowhere Man, Winston couldn't see him through the growing throng.

"Did you hit him?"

"I think so. I can't be sure, though."

Peering through the scope, dead, hungry faces stared back. Salivating at the nearby meal, black drool spilled from gnashing mouths. A sea of glistening grey, filled with eyes, white like pearls. A flash of colour. Crimson amongst the insipid blandness of the dead. A single brown eye, filled with hate, staring over a ravaged shoulder. The top of a living, damaged ear, hanging from the bloodied cartilage. Firing again, the bullet hit with a puff of brain and emerald gore.

"Fuck!" Jonesy raged as the villain disappeared completely.

"Get everyone moving!" Irish yelled, sprinting back towards them.

The children filtered from the shadowed doorway, closely followed by DB and the adults. His instinct that all was not well had proven correct, and they were suited and booted, their meagre belongings secured in bags.

"Which way?" called DB. "You know the area."

"That way, past Tesco!"

The empty road beckoned. Jonesy took one last look through the scope as the others fled the approaching horde. If the monster was within the swarm, Jonesy couldn't see him. Stowing the rifle, he turned from the zombies and looked at the dud round. It was almost unheard of. Whatever had gone wrong had ramifications far in excess of a faulty primer. Instead of severing the head of a snake, he'd only pissed it off. Their list of mortal enemies was only going in one direction. Up.

CHAPTER 27

"If you've got a plan, I'd love to hear it," gasped Irish as he jogged alongside Jonesy.

"The first part is you need to give up smoking, mate."

"I hear that," Irish puffed.

Their pace was set by the children's slow progress, but even that was proving difficult for the nicotine addict. In a stand-up fight, the builder's bulk gave him an advantage. In a tactical retreat from a foe that never tired, not so much.

"DB, can you and the others check any large vehicle for keys?" Jonesy shouted. "A van, a bus, I don't give a fuck."

"You got it!" he replied.

Jonesy turned, running slowly backwards. The undead were lost from sight which was a positive. If they could slip away down a side street, they might be able to extend the distance and throw them off completely. The bigger problem was that the mindless corpses were the least of their worries. The Nowhere Men could search using human cunning. There were at least three according to the survivors. Who was to say there weren't more. The dark windows and shadowy nooks took on a feeling of brooding menace. Eyes could be watching right now, and they would have no idea. They could slip and slide, twist and double back, hide and conceal, only to have a scarred enemy summon the festering dead with a whistle.

"Here's one!" called DB.

The minibus in question had collided with a vehicle racing in the other direction. Skid marks stretched from the scene of impact to a burned out house where the speeding car had embedded itself before exploding.

"It's only been sideswiped by the look of it."

"Ok, try it!" Jonesy replied, watching the rear. The groaning tumult of the dead was close.

"Keep the kids back," DB warned as he approached the open driver's door.

Peering inside, it was like someone had opened a temporary abattoir. The seats were caked with dried blood. Chunks of rotten meat were laden with the unhatched maggot eggs made dormant by the winter. As soon as the temperatures climbed, the cab would be thick with black flies.

"No good. It's too dirty!" DB called.

Emma joined him and wrinkled her nose. "Dirty's a nice way of putting it."

"Sanitising it for the kids, ma'am. They don't need to hear about all the gore."

"I appreciate that."

"Ok, move on! Keep your eyes peeled."

With the vast number of abandoned vehicles on the roads and on driveways, none were suitable to ferry the whole group. Cars passed, doors open, no keys. No more vans, no more minibuses, nothing. Greasy ducked inside a large estate car. It would be enough for the children at least. Fumbling at the empty ignition, he cursed and kicked at the bodywork.

"Did they think someone would steal it when they were running from the zombies?" asked Greasy, dumbfounded. "Why take the keys with them?"

"Panic is a strange force," DB replied.

"Do you think we should start heading south? There's only another village the way we're going."

"You think there'll be more undead?"

"More homes normally means more zombies."

DB stopped, allowing Irish and Jonesy to join the main group.

"What's up?"

"Why did... we stop?" gasped Irish, reaching for his cigarettes.

"We need a new plan. Greasy says there's another village down that road. Not only does that mean more chance of running across the dead, but it means we're moving further from the castle. Greasy thinks we should head south, and I'm inclined to agree."

"One problem with that," said Jonesy.

"Such as?"

"We're going to slow to a crawl. The kids won't be able to jog across the fields and woodland, no way. The zombies can't see us at the moment, but if we get caught out in the open, we'll never shake them."

"Better ideas?"

Jonesy mulled it for a second. The wails of the dead were growing, reinforcing the relentlessness of their enemy. Hiding somewhere was no longer an option with human faculties thrown into the mix. Winston's mistake aside, one wrong move ensured they would be surrounded and either burned out or devoured. The faces of the children looked at him, exhaustion evident in their dark, sunken eyes and constant yawns. If he was honest, Jonesy was beyond impressed at how well they were holding it together in the circumstances.

"What do you think?" he asked them.

"We'll keep up," said Tara.

"We have to," said a young boy. "Or the monsters get us."

"We won't let that happen, Tommy. I promise," said Greasy, ruffling his hair.

"That's what my dad said," he replied, burying his face in Greasy's trousers.

Jonesy looked at Irish who nodded to confirm Tommy's father was among the fallen. Gaining a new level of respect for their resilience, Jonesy promised the same. "Once we get to the castle, we can hold a small ceremony. We did the same for our own people."

"I'd like that," replied Irish. Pointing the glowing tip of his cigarette back the way they had come, he said, "Clock's ticking."

"Cross country it is. If the kids start to tire, we'll carry them," DB declared.

Jonesy raised an eyebrow. The one thing not being discussed was the exposure of their fortress to the Nowhere Men if they couldn't outpace the invisible threat. Craig Arater and his henchmen were a big enough concern, and they were governed by the same rules as everyone else. Go out in the open, get eaten. The new enemy could walk right up to the gate and knock, rendering their meat shield redundant. The rescue mission could have consequences that endangered everyone. Knowing there was little alternative, he agreed. "Ok, we move south. We'll try and use the forests to our advantage."

"We can share them with piggybacks when the going gets tough," suggested Braiden.

"I can toss this if need be," said Winston, holding out the axe. Instantly regretting his selfless offer, he hugged the beloved weapon close.

"Let's go," said Irish, tossing the half-smoked butt.

"You realise those thing's kill you," Jonesy warned.

"I'll take my chances with cancer over the zombies," chuckled Irish.

"If you can't keep up, the undead will do for you faster than abnormal cells."

"Your friend will just have to carry me too."

"He's strong, but even DB has his limits," chuckled Jonesy.

A piercing whistle to their rear put a stop to their discussion and breathed fresh life into tired limbs.

"It's like they're herding them," Irish grumbled.

"That's exactly what they're doing. Pick up the pace!"

CHAPTER 28

"Mr DB? My feet are really sore," said Tara.

"Ok, sweetheart. Let's take a quick break."

"Are you sure it's safe?" asked Emma.

"Nothing's safe anymore," DB replied. "But it'll get a whole lot more dangerous if we can't move."

Kneeling in the gloom, the twigs and brush crunched under his weight. Undoing Tara's laces, he gently removed the tiny shoe. The small child hissed in pain.

"I'm sorry."

"It's ok," she replied, smiling through a yawn.

DB lifted the thin leg to inspect Tara's foot. Seeing the damage, his heart ached. The once white sock was saturated from sweat, and worse. A darker, orange tinge stained the cotton at the heel and toes from the mixture of blood and pus. Carefully removing the sock, the skin of the burst blisters had already come away, leaving the raw, suppurating wound fully exposed.

"I've got a first aid kit," offered Braiden, shucking off his pack.

Handing over the plastic container, DB took it gratefully and unpacked a small patch of gauze.

"What's up?" asked Jonesy as he reached the stationary group.

"We've got to think of another plan, brother," he replied, dressing the injury. "I say we both head back and lead the dead away from here. The boys can get everyone back from here safely if they follow the train tracks."

"Train tracks?" asked Winston, looking around at the impenetrable woodland.

"You can't miss them. We checked the maps before we set out after you. If you head due south, you'll hit them. Follow them and you'll reach the castle by mid-afternoon."

"Kurt's going to kill me," moaned Winston. "Do you think we could still blag it?"

"You're already in the shit," admitted Jonesy.

"What do you mean?"

"We didn't want to say anything, but Kurt already knows."

"No, no, no!" Winston wailed.

"Don't panic," said Jonesy. "He's got bigger fish to fry."

Sam jumped in. "Is he ok? Is Mum?"

"They're fine. They're better than fine, in fact. Some of our buddies from Thorney showed up while you were gallivanting across the countryside. They brought us a resupply of ammunition and some heavy weaponry. There's a shitstorm coming that we'll all need to pull together to get past." He kept the prison assault secret, to save them worrying.

Sam sighed with relief. Winston wondered what part Kurt would work on first.

Something cracked nearby.

"We've got movement," snapped Jonesy, hearing the whisper of disturbed foliage.

DB's massive arm swept the children to cover behind the adults. Jonesy aimed the rifle at the source of the noise.

187

The bushes rustled, the branches swayed. Stepping from cover, someone emerged wearing a full ghillie suit.

"Please, forgive my sudden appearance. I'm a friend, I promise," said the man, hands raised.

"Who are you? What do you want?" demanded DB, moving to the side, ready to attack.

"Pull off the hood! Now!" ordered Jonesy.

"You got it, dude. Just chill on the trigger, ok," he replied. Pulling the covering off, his long brown hair fell past his shoulders. A thick beard hung down to his chest. Trimmed short at the cheeks, it looked like a forgotten goatee. Twigs and dried brush had been threaded through the hair on top of the camouflage. He smiled disarmingly. A golden incisor glinted in the afternoon light that made its way through the tree cover.

"Ok, good," Jonesy said, relaxing slightly.

"Let me guess. You were looking for a shorter haircut? With maybe a scar?"

"You know them? Are you one of them?" Jonesy's finger slipped the guard and curled on the trigger.

"Fuck no, dude! But I know *of* them."

"What does that mean?"

"I see a lot of things, while not being seen. I've been keeping an eye on their movements for a while."

"You know who they are, then?"

"I've never got close enough to talk to them. Listen, dude, we don't have time for that right now. I can take you somewhere safe. Somewhere to ride it out until the swarm moves away."

"How do we know you're on the level?" Irish grumbled.

"I could've stayed still, let you pass, and then bolted before the zombies even get close. I chose to expose myself as you seem like good people. People in trouble. The choice is yours," he shrugged.

"Ok, I'm Jonesy," said the soldier, lowering the rifle. "The big man's DB."

"I'm Ian. Ian Thomas. Give me the girl." He tucked the camo hat away in his belt and reached for Tara.

Emma was hesitant, but the young girl returned his beaming grin. Taking her beneath the arms, he flipped her around and on to his shoulders in one fluid movement. She giggled as the dried leaves tickled her skin.

"I like your beard. It's like Father Christmas. Except his is white. And not full of stuff," she said.

"Why, thank you. I like yours too."

Tara giggled. "I don't have a beard, silly."

"Are you sure?" he teased. "Keep your head down, ok? This is going to be a bumpy ride."

"I don't have anything to hold on to."

"Use my hair if you have to. I need my hands free."

"Are you sure? Won't it hurt?"

"I'm tough. I can take it," he replied, reaching up to pat her knee.

"I like your tattoo," said Tara, pointing at the small blue lizard on his left hand.

"I like yours too."

"I don't have any tattoos. I'm too small, silly."

"You're not twenty-one?"

"I'm six. I'll be seven in forty nine days."

"That's a great memory you have there," Ian praised. "Is everyone ready? We've got about half a mile of rough terrain to cover. I suggest the smaller kids go on shoulders too."

"What if we come across some zombies? We'll need our hands free," said Winston.

"I'll take care of any we find. I keep my forest clear for the most part," he replied, unsheathing a pair of combat knives.

"Until now," said DB.

"Yeah, dude. Until now. I need a sign that says; 'Trespassers Will Be Shot'."

"The dead won't pay much attention to that."

"No, but humans might," Ian said, frowning at the ragtag group. "Let's move."

CHAPTER 29

"Here we are," said Ian, lifting Tara from his shoulders before gently sitting her down.

"Where's *here*?" asked DB. "It looks exactly the same as the last mile of woods we've run through."

Ian smiled. "That's the entire point, dude. Watch."

Moving to an unexceptional patch of dead bracken, he crouched down and retrieved a short section of rope. Pulling on the cord, a camouflaged trap door opened up.

"Ta-da!"

"A bunker? That's where you live?" marvelled Winston.

"Hardly a bunker. More a hole in the ground. But it does the job, now follow me."

Scooping up the small child, he hurried down the steps and disappeared. Jonesy looked to DB. Irish looked at Greasy. Lots of questions flowed without words. Irish finally shrugged and reached for the crumpled pack of cigarettes.

"Maybe it's time to quit," said Greasy, snatching them from his hand.

"Whoa! What's gotten into you?"

"The smell can carry for half a mile. You might as well leave a sign pointing down to let them know where dinner is."

Irish tensed, looking like he would attack his friend for the stolen prize. Letting out a deep sigh, his shoulders dropped and all aggression fled. "I'm sorry, mate, I don't want to put anyone in danger. I'll try and find some gum when we hit the next pharmacy."

"And until then?"

"I'll do my best to not kill everyone."

"Good man," said Greasy, patting him on the back as he descended.

The darkness below was nearly absolute. Once Jonesy moved beyond the entrance, he had to feel with his hands. Ian was foraging in the back with much rustling and clanking of goods. Suddenly, a light bloomed to life from an old halogen lantern. He set it low, barely strong enough to illuminate more than the faintest outlines of the shivering occupants, but it was enough. Hurrying back to the hatch, he pulled on the other end of the rope and it snapped shut. DB winced, expecting a heavy clap to announce their position. Instead, it hit home with the dullest of thuds.

"Rubber washers, dude. It kills the sound."

"How can you be sure they won't find us?" asked Irish, already grumpy from the lack of nicotine.

"You saw the hatch. I made sure to set it within a thick hawthorn bush to deter wanderers happening across my little hidey hole."

"How could you do this on your own? It's amazing," praised Jonesy as his eyes adjusted.

The "room" itself was about twelve foot long and seven wide. Carefully shaped logs were used to support the weight of soil above, much like a mine support system. Rather than being damp, it was relatively dry. Two cot beds

191

had been installed down the left-hand side, with a few chairs formed from stubby sections of thick tree trunk.

"I didn't do it on my own, dude," he replied. Reaching beneath the nearest bed, he pulled out a waterproof locker. Releasing the catches, he removed a handful of blankets and handed them around. "Get warm while you can. The kids can have a nap if they feel like it, we'll be here for a bit."

"Thank you," said Emma, taking one of the thick covers. Helping Tara to hobble to the camp bed, she laid the blanket over the small child. Within seconds, her eyes had closed and she was breathing evenly from sleep.

"You said you didn't do this alone. How many of you are there?" asked DB.

"No offence, but I don't know you well enough to share life stories. Let's just keep it as a friendly face came along at just the right time."

"No offence taken. These are dark times. Thanks again for risking yourself for us, mate. I know you could've left us out there alone."

"My pleasure, dude. Don't get me wrong, I get a good vibe from you, especially knowing you're army. It just takes me a while to trust."

"Even so, thanks," finished DB.

They settled in as best they could, grateful to be out of the wind above. With the timber insulation and over a dozen bodies, the temperature climbed steadily to a bearable level.

"If I didn't know better, I'd say you'd been in the forces," said Greasy.

"*Was* being the operative word, dude. I did my four years like a good soldier, but it wasn't for me. I'm just not cut out for taking orders."

DB turned to Greasy. "How could you tell? Did you serve?"

"Many years ago in another life, my friend," Greasy replied, saying no more. There was something painful in his past, that much was plain from the look on his face.

"Shh!" whispered Ian urgently.

"What can you hear?" whispered DB.

"Nothing. I can feel them. They're close."

One hand was on the rough bark of the nearest vertical support. Ian closed his eyes, deep in concentration. Raising a finger to his lips, he urged silence. Jonesy pointed to the lantern and Ian nodded. Twisting the dial, the meagre light faded, plunging them into utter darkness. It dawned on Jonesy that the move might frighten the children to the point they cried out for comfort. Expecting to turn it back on, his fingers hovered near the invisible dial.

Nothing. Not a single whimper.

Irish and the others had worked miracles.

Locked in unending blackness, their ears picked out the faintest sounds. The faint creak of canvas as Tara moved in her sleep. A rattle with each breath from Irish's smoke damaged lungs. Then the first traces of the rustle shuffle of dragged feet. Growing. Getting closer. Closer. A pause. Frustrated cursing. Wailing dead. A piercing whistle. The clomp of thousands of feet moving away. Fading. Fading. Gone.

"Told you," whispered Ian.

"If they were a decent tracker, they might've seen through our efforts to cover our movements," said Greasy. "How could you be so sure they weren't?"

"I'm a good judge of people, dude. Plus I kinda prepared a few fake trails in case they weren't complete morons. Luckily for us, those fuckers are nuts, but that's about it." Remembering there were children present, he apologised for the language. "I normally swear like a... erm, a pee'd up squaddie."

"In the current climate, I think bad language is acceptable. It's not as if it ever killed anyone."

Jonesy turned the lamp back on to the lowest setting, sending the shadows fleeing back into the nooks. Irish made a quick check of everyone to keep himself occupied.

"How long should we wait? We need to be getting back to the castle."

193

"They're moving north-east now which will take them out of the forest in about fifteen minutes. I'll take you the fastest route to get you back to Arundel."

Jonesy clapped him on the back. "Ian?"

"Sup, dude?"

"Thank you, mate. Truly. We were in the shit there."

Ian stared at the soldier hard, as if he was boring into his very soul. Long seconds passed in awkward silence. Jonesy was close to breaking the impasse when Ian snorted in frustration.

"Fuck!" he blurted.

Jonesy took a cautious pace to the rear.

"Sorry, I needed to get that out. What the hell is wrong with me?"

"Huh?" Jonesy was perplexed.

"I'm going to break my first and most important rule and I'm not sure how I really feel about that."

"You don't have to. You can just get us out of here," offered Jonesy.

"What's your first rule?" asked Winston, crashing in like a bull in a china shop.

"I'm very cautious about new people. Very cautious," he emphasised. "And I never tell them about us during the first meet."

"You still don't have to. You've done enough," Irish replied.

"Stop being so..." Ian blurted. "So... decent. This is the fucking apocalypse!"

"You're funny," giggled Tara who'd awoken during the exchange.

Ian psyched himself up. "Fuck it, I'm doing it! We've got two dozen of these shelters littered around the forest and wider area. You can tell where they are by the trees around them. We lopped off the two lowest branches but left them six inches too long."

"You sound like an arborist," said Sam.

"I'm fully qualified as a tree surgeon. I was part of a team that maintained the forest for the Council and the

194

Duke of Norfolk estate, plus some other posh fuckers. Once I left the army, I wanted to be away from people for a while. This job was a dream for me. Peace and quiet. Guys that didn't talk too much. I started to take outdoor survival courses, the ones where you stay away from civilisation with no amenities. It was easier than I imagined."

"And your people move from shelter to shelter?" asked DB.

"No. These're our emergency stops. If we're out and about and it gets too dark or too many of the dead catch wind of us, we lay low for a few hours."

"How many of you are there?" wondered Winston.

"Seventy-four. People that I came across in the wilderness. Lost and alone, looking for help. I've always heavily vetted them... before today."

"Did you say these were only for emergencies?" Jonesy probed.

"Yeah." Ian hesitated, searching the faces of the group for any threat. All he saw was good people trying their best to survive. That they had risked everything to keep the children alive when others simply discarded their burden sealed the deal. "Our home is deep within the forest. And I mean *deep*. It was an old warehouse where we kept all the equipment for the day to day. Quads, diggers, chainsaws, you name it. A garage pit to carry out repairs if they were needed. Plus a pair of underground tanks for petrol and diesel that was filled once a year. We'd only just been topped up."

"How do you feed them all?"

Ian chortled. "Food's the easy part, dude. Even if I couldn't pick the local stores clean of all their goodies, the forest has all we need. I can forage and trap with the best of them."

"What about the zombies?" asked Braiden.

"We've made it as difficult as possible for them. The terrain works in our favour as we're tucked away near a hundred foot precipice. The rise itself is quite a climb, and they seem to follow the path of least resistance when the going gets tough. It also means we only have to defend on three sides."

"Cool," Winston exclaimed, picturing towering Transylvanian castles perched on cliffs. Impregnable to the enemy. Mysterious and filled with secrets.

"If you don't mind me asking, how far is it? You really don't have to tell us, though," Jonesy explained.

"It's about a mile if you're a bird. One and a half if you've got legs, dude. Why?"

"I'm going to ask a massive favour. Tell me to get fucked if I'm overstepping. We've got troubles at the castle of a human variety. I was going to take Irish and his people back with us, but I can't guarantee they'll be one hundred percent safe there."

"The "Nowhere Men"? Was that what you called them?"

"No. The lunatics at Ford Prison. We had a run in with the brother of the psycho in charge. They've been gunning for us ever since."

"I see," replied Ian. "We've seen them around but kept a respectable distance. Except for one incident a few nights ago."

"What happened? Have they attacked you too?"

"No, they have no idea we're even there. Three of my people found a man wounded in a stream. He'd been shot in the leg."

"Matt Hay!"

"You know him? I tore them a new arsehole for being so stupid. We'd seen what they do at the prison."

"We saw the platform too, mate," said Jonesy. The images of the guard would forever be burned into his mind.

"Exactly! But my people rushed in, dragged him out and patched him up. It was only when they took off his soaking jumper they found the prison gear."

"Matt's one of the good ones. He risked everything to get a young girl away from those monsters."

Ian's scowl softened at the news. "Really?"

196

"Yeah, he was in a bad way. It was touch and go. If we didn't have a doctor he'd have died."

"Looks like they got lucky in the fuck-up then. I'll let them know that I overreacted."

"That brings me on to my favour," began Jonesy. "Your home sounds like a much safer haven for these folks than we can provide at the moment. Would you have space for them?"

Irish stepped forward. "Don't I get a say in this?"

"Of course. Listen, mate, we've got a war coming," said Jonesy. Briefly explaining the mission to secure the failing garrison on the Chiltern Mountains as well as the fight to retake Portsmouth, Irish started to come round. The boys listened in silence, accepting the news with resolve.

"Ok, I see what you mean."

Jonesy looked at Ian. "So, how about it?"

"We can always use people who aren't afraid of a hard day's work. We have a few kids with us too. I hope I don't regret this."

"We'll earn our keep, don't you worry," declared Irish.

"But only if you're sure," added Jonesy.

"I'm sure. Time's up!" Ian exclaimed. "Let's get moving."

"Can you point us in the right direction before you leave? I don't want to follow the compass and end up in a dead end," explained DB.

Pushing the hatch clear, Ian turned around. "I'll do better than that. I'll take you to the edge of the woods closest to the castle while one of my people collect your friends."

"How will they know?"

"I'll light a fire and send smoke signals."

"Really?" Winston was excited to see the practice in person.

"Of course not, dude," Ian chuckled, retrieving a radio from his suit. Turning it on, the speaker crackled. Transmitting, he said, "Base, this is Ian. Come in, over.

"This is base. Go ahead, over."

"Jas, we've got some folks out at number six. They need collecting asap. Over."

"Anything we should know? Over."

"Yeah, stay quiet. The free walkers have been out causing trouble. Keep your eyes peeled. Over."

"Will do. We can be there in under half an hour. Over."

"Thanks, dude. Over and out."

Turning the radio off, he turned to the small, huddled group of estate survivors. "Get back below and rest a bit more. You'll need your strength. There's food and water under the second bed. I'd normally leave it alone for a more dire emergency, but you'll need some energy."

"Thank you both," said Greasy, shaking hands with Ian and Jonesy. "We owe you everything."

"I'm sorry we couldn't do more, mate," commiserated DB.

"You did more than you needed to. I'll never forget that."

Irish was hovering uncertainly. A man who was unused to showing emotion, he choked down the newly formed lump in his throat. "Thanks. I didn't think anyone good was left. I was wrong."

Saying their farewells, the survivors hid themselves away and Ian closed the hatch. Braiden, Sam, and Winston were stretching, ready for the next leg of the journey.

"What do we do with the food?" asked DB.

"I think we can offer it as a down payment towards their hospitality. Ian, there's a Merc parked by the train gates at Hardham. There's a few bags of healthy goods in the boot. It'll help offset the food your new members eat."

"Are you sure you can spare it?" said Ian, gratefully.

"We'll sort something. We've got some heavy artillery back at the castle that we can use to raid a local store."

"Ok. Follow me." Ian slipped the hood on, becoming one with the woods once more.

CHAPTER 30

The return journey from the outskirts of Arundel had taken only fifteen minutes. Ian was back before the search party could find them, and now led them to a point where they would intersect with his people.

"She's asleep," whispered Emma.

Ian had felt the young child lolling as the pressure on his hair diminished but didn't realise she had drifted off completely. Sheathing the knives, he carefully lowered her from his shoulder and cradled Tara in his free arms. She mumbled once, then tucked herself in tighter to the crook of his arm, unheeding of the twigs and leaves.

"You've kept yourself hidden all this time?" asked Irish.

"When the apocalypse hits, not everyone out there is going to be friendly, dude. Hence your bald friends back there."

"We never hurt anyone. We kept to ourselves. Why?"

Ian shrugged. "Evil has always been around. It's just free to roam now."

"I'm going to kill them all."

"Worry about your people for now, dude. Revenge can wait for later."

"That's if there is a later."

"You'll be safe at my camp, I promise."

"How the hell did you build a camp in the woods?"

"The compound was already there. We just... secured it after the shit hit the fan."

"Care to tell me about it?"

Ian could see he wasn't really interested in the tale, he just wanted an excuse to think of anything else other than nicotine withdrawals and loss.

He began.

Ian checked over the final work schedule for the coming fortnight. Everyone would be busy, that was a certainty. Managing the estate and public areas was always frantic between March and September. The fact that they were coming to the end of the season had no impact on the visitor numbers.

Adding fresh grounds to the coffee maker, he set the machine to brew. As the heated water started to percolate, he turned his attention to the schedule once again. Ian Thomas Sr had been a stickler for the adage, check, check, and check again. The old man would likely be on the sun lounger on the Royal Caribbean cruise ship, alongside his mum right now, soaking up the Jamaican rays near Montego Bay. Time and time again he promised to accompany them one day, but he wouldn't. Trapped on board a floating petri dish with thousands of strangers was Ian's idea of Hell.

"No thanks," he shuddered inwardly.

They weren't due back in port for another ten days, but Ian checked the reminder on his phone for the eighth time, just in case.

"Docking at eleven thirty. Disembarking by twelve thirty."

He would be in the carpark at twelve on the dot.

Ian looked out of the warehouse window on the unbroken treeline surrounding their remote compound. The dark clouds in the grey sky were swelling, spoiling the view somewhat. But this was his Heaven. Empty, still, quiet. A rabbit hopped out from cover and seemed to stare directly up at him. Ian gave the furry critter a wave. The rabbit responded with a wrinkle of the nose before bouncing away.

Heaven.

"Ian, are you there?" asked Jasper over the radio.

"Here, Jas. What's up, dude?"

"We've got some shady shit going down here. Are you still coming over?"

"I've just put the coffee on for break. What's up?"

"Just get down here. And turn on the car radio."

"Will do. See you in ten."

"And Ian?"

"Yeah, Jas?"

"Bring some of the axes."

"Ok, dude. But why?" Ian let go of the transmit button and waited.

Jasper didn't answer.

The team were on a maintenance job in the grounds of Wiggonholt Manor, one of the three stately homes that fell under their forestry contract. The lady of the house had complained that the bougainvillea in two of the public displays were dying. Ian thought she was full of shit, but when the boss calls, you answer. Soil samples were fine. It was just a few of the blooms were being lost to an unknown rot. The flower beds were still stunning. But for now, they would extract the dying flowers and plant fresh to tidy it up. Once the grounds closed in a few weeks, they would get to the bottom of the issue.

Leaving the pot gurgling, Ian left their small office and headed to the tool lockup.

"Why axes?" Ian muttered, taking four felling axes from the brackets.

Leaving through the roller shutter, he ignored the quad and headed directly for the Land Rover. The exhilaration of hammering cross country on the machine would have to wait. Jasper was one of the most laid back people he knew, and Ian was the master. The edge in his friend's voice was unmistakeable, and unheard of before the last transmission.

"Jas, I'm on my way, dude."

The in car radio system remained silent, so Ian tried again on the handheld. Nothing.

"Piece of fucking shit!" Ian spat, tossing the radio. It was decades out of date, but requests for a newer system were ignored. One of the senior managers had the temerity to send a snarky email telling him they should be willing to use their personal mobiles to stay in touch. Ian had sent a snarky email back in response explaining the concept of phone signal coverage in an area of woodland covering seven thousand acres with no local masts. The expletives hadn't helped, resulting in a formal warning. Ian thought they were well placed and necessary.

Turning the dial on the stereo, a local station came on playing banal pop music for mindless drones.

"Give me The Fratellis any day," he grumbled.

Searching for another source, the one note caterwaul of Katy Perry gave way to a half hourly news broadcast.

"A breaking news story is just coming to us from the local police commissioner. It appears large pockets of civil unrest are being reported across the country. Intelligence from GCHQ suggest this is not being orchestrated by any particular group or via an organised campaign on social media. Authorities have asked that all people return to their homes and stay off the streets. Remain indoors unless it is absolutely necessary. Police leave has been suspended while they bring the outbreak under control. The Prime Minister is currently chairing an emergency session of COBRA in Westminster. We'll have more as we receive updates."

Is that what Jas was worried about? People kicking off? If anyone was threatening his crew, they would get the beating of their fucking life.

Pressing the accelerator a little harder, the old vehicle picked up speed. The rutted tracks were unforgiving on the solid suspension, and Ian found himself bouncing around inside like a jack-in-the-box. Hitting a particularly deep divot, he bounced so high his head connected with the steel roof.

"Fucking wanker!" he spat, massaging the growing lump on his scalp.

Easing back on the throttle, he realised getting there in one piece was more important than gaining a few seconds and possibly wrapping himself around a tree trunk. Or completely flattening the top of his skull.

Wild horses bolted as he sped past. Birds took to the skies. The unbroken forest passed in a green blur.

"Jas, speak to me!"

Silence from the radio.

The song on the stereo cut away mid chorus.

"We've just had word that the government has declared a state of emergency. All non-essential travel is now forbidden. Public transport, as well as domestic and international flights have been suspended. Take shelter where you can. Churches and public buildings have been deemed safe havens. The armed forces are being mobilised to support the eventual evacuation of population centres and aid the relief effort once the situation is brought under control. The government stresses that the decision to deploy the army has not been taken lightly. Their only concern is for the wellbeing of the public, and our frontline services. We've also got this short clip of the Chief Inspector of the Metropolitan Police."

"Initial reports we were receiving from our officers were of people unwilling to comply with orders. They refused treatment by the ambulance services, even once restrained. Subsequent rumours of the rioters being... I don't know how to say this without it sounding ridiculous... the rioters being dead, are, of course, completely false. Furthermore, the spread of this false information across social media will be fully investigated. Do not approach the rioters, who are nothing more than criminals who will face the full force of the law."

"That's all we have currently," finished the presenter.

"Ian? Where are you?" crackled Jasper's fraught voice.

"Jas? I'm nearly there, dude. The southeast trail. Hold on!"

Ian gunned it, holding on to the steering wheel for dear life. The Land Rover rattled and complained from every rivet, but the sturdy work horse held together. Bursting through the open gate into the wide field, the ground improved dramatically, sparing his jarred bones from further discomfort. Half a mile away, the stunning manor house stood, steadfast and timeless.

"Oh, fuck!" Ian hissed.

The home was ablaze in the western wing. Is that what the axes were for? To break down doors and save those within?

Ian floored it, diverting from the well-worn path, making a beeline straight across the meadow.

As if in answer to the flames belching from a dozen windows, the heavens opened. The clear landscape disappeared into a hazy, liquescent meld of green, grey and orange. Switching the wipers on, they couldn't cope against the sudden deluge. The scene opened up, then closed, then opened, flickering through the snapshots of growing devastation like an old slide projector.

The already damp soil took on the rainfall and quickly became a quagmire that stole all traction from the Land Rover. Fishtailing, Ian wrestled to keep it in line. A boggy patch spun him a full one eighty and the engine coughed, then died. Twisting the ignition, it turned over and he shifted back into first. The wheels spun, churning deeper ruts, going nowhere.

"Fuck you, you fucking fuck!" Ian yelled, punching the steering wheel.

Jumping from the vehicle, the rain plastered his hair down in an instant. Thankfully, the ponytail held it in place, or he would be fighting the elements and his dripping, unruly locks. Grabbing the axes, he slammed the door, kicked the rear tyre in frustration, then started to forge towards the growing shouts at the back of the home.

Two more windows exploded outwards, sucking in fresh oxygen like a drowning man.

By the time Ian rounded the exquisitely pruned privet hedge, the whole west wing was a lost cause. Flames licked from beneath the tiles of the roof which would soon be collapsing inwards to add to the destruction. Ian's boots were little more than clods of mud, and the water was running down through the neck of his raincoat, saturating him inside and out. He ran even harder, losing hunks of the soggy brown anchors to the path.

The rear gardens were made up of four square flower beds set around the central fountain. Twin seasonal marquees were erected and joined to the east wing. One tied directly to the kitchen to provide a limited menu and a place to get out of the sun. The other was separated into six hubs with activities for the children ranging from colouring, to digging for fossils in sand. Jogging past the plastic coated fabric of the huge tent, Ian could just make out muffled fighting and cries of pain over the seething hiss of rain on the roof.

"Jas? Where are you?"

"Ian? I'm round here!"

Ian came out into the gardens proper. People were hunkered over supine bodies, seeming to give first aid. Whatever had happened indoors had spilled outside. He looked around for the team, only seeing their three small tractors and the caged trailers for tools and cuttings.

"Over here!"

Jasper was crouching within the opposing oleander bushes, mostly hidden from sight. His unkempt grey hair was plastered to his head. The weathered age of his face had accelerated remarkably. From a rough looking fifties, he now looked eighty.

"What the fuck's going on, Jas?"

"Hell, Ian. It's Hell come to take us," replied Jasper, terror stricken.

"Snap out of it, Jas!" Ian ordered, tossing the weapons and dragging his friend from cover. "Where are the others?"

"They ran inside when the first demons came. I got cut off. I hid."

"Demons? What the fuck are you talking about, dude?"

"Them..." Jasper pointed at the visitors assisting the injured.

"They're helping, Jas!"

"They're... eating," Jas shuddered, trying to back into the shrubbery.

Ian held tight to his collar, but looked more closely at the gathered Samaritans. Rain, thick and unrelenting, washed over their hair and faces. One of the helpers rose from her crouched position, and Ian could see the clotted crimson before the fat droplets sluiced it away, dripping from her chin. She dove back in eagerly.

"No..."

"Yes," confirmed Jasper.

He pulled free of Ian, but not to hide this time. "We have to help them." Picking up one of the axes, Jasper wiped the handle as best he could to get a grip.

"What are they?" gasped Ian as the half-eaten victim sat upright. The rain drenched gluttons lost interest now that their meal had become one of them. Standing up, they groaned and started to lumber towards the two men. The partially completed replanting in the flowerbeds was destroyed as they shambled onward. Pink blooms, already beaten under the ferocious rain, stood no chance against the ill-timed, awkward steps of the demons.

"Be careful, Jas," warned Ian as they drew near.

"Die, demon" Jasper cried, burying his axe in the nearest woman's chest.

Ribs parted and her breasts bounced as she hit the floor, freed from her torn blouse by the blow. Jasper looked on in horror as she tried to sit up. The handle was too long and each time she moved, the wood hit the sopping mud and pushed her back down. Giving up, she rolled sideways, driving the blade deeper. Still, she ignored the awful wound.

"Jas, keep moving, dude! They're slow, we can outrun them."

Ian tossed him a second axe and started to jab at the monsters, utilising their lack of equilibrium to knock them over. In the distance, people and frantically revving engines screamed in unison as the visitors tried to flee from the public car park. Bulges appeared in the coated canvas of the marquees from the people fighting within. Blood streamed from below the pegged liner, giving the answer to who was victorious.

"Are Melv and Norm definitely inside there?" Ian asked, clubbing another demon away with the blunt wedge of the axe. He wasn't afraid. It was way past that. He was terrified, and wanted to be certain of their goal before committing. Getting trapped between a wall of fire and the cannibals wasn't a good idea.

"They wanted to help. They could see people at the windows."

Jasper pointed at the blackened openings which spewed dark smoke and tongues of soaring flame.

"I don't think they can be helped, dude. We need to get the others and get out of here."

"I'm ready," said Jasper.

Ian caught sight of the activities tent and turned away immediately. His mind couldn't process the partly devoured children pushing through the door flaps, leaving small, bloody handprints on the glossy white. The adults were bad enough.

A trio of demons met them at the food marquee entrance, midway through the hanging fabric. Ian held the axe sideways and barrelled forward, knocking them over like bowling pins. Dodging to the side to avoid their arms, Jasper followed suit. It was good to be out of the rain, but the concealing patter was weaker inside, and the sounds of tearing flesh and gurgling deaths were all around.

"Dear God," Jasper muttered.

As an atheist, it was weird for him to talk of God and demons. Looking at the scene before them, Hell was the only explanation. Bloated, decomposing corpses slopped around, falling wetly onto whatever poor victim the more agile monsters held down. A mad painter had been let loose, his palette consisting only of varying shades of scarlet. The stench of rot, blood, and faeces fought with the clotted cream scones, winning decisively. A woman, bitten on the shoulder, stabbed desperately at the rear wall with a butter knife. Managing to puncture the strong material, she sawed fruitlessly at it with the blunt utensil until either exhaustion or shock caused her to collapse. The other demons were too consumed in their feasting to pay her any attention.

"We can't help them," warned Ian. "Just stay out of their reach."

Moving rapidly between the human feasts, they headed around the trestle tables towards the tunnel that would lead them to the Manor's kitchen.

"She's ok!" spat Jasper, coming to a halt. He looked at the thrashing bodies, trying to find a route to the woman who had stood back up.

"She's not," said Ian. Her eyes were white. The wound had stopped bleeding. She was one of them now.

"Fiddlesticks," muttered Jasper.

It was the worst expletive Jasper would utter, which showed his level of distress.

"Come on, dude. We need to find the others."

The servers were nowhere to be seen, most likely somewhere within the house. The cash register stood wide open, hundreds of pounds ripe for the taking. Ian closed it as he hurried past.

Why did you do that, for fuck's sake? he questioned. It was simple. Duty. Right and wrong. Even in the demon apocalypse.

Steam and smoke eddied against the low ceiling of the joining tunnel, making them crouch lower to avoid the choking heat. Emerging into the kitchen, one of the chefs lumbered towards them, his hat still in place, his face missing. The lower half of the hygienic head covering was saturated with spilled blood, giving it a dipped, two tone effect.

Ian considered leaping over the stainless steel counter, but the scattered food would probably cause him to slip. One mistake and the hefty cook would be eating again. Raising the axe overhead, he swung down, embedding the remaining pristine white of the hat into the top of his skull. As the man fell, the crimson leakage banished the last traces of white. Wrenching the weapon free, the chef stayed down.

"I guess head wounds work?" Jasper suggested.

"Idiot!" Ian snapped.

"What did I do?" Jasper moaned, pained by the insult.

"Not you, dude. Me! What monsters can only be killed by destroying the brain?"

Jasper stared at him through streaming eyes. The smoke was getting thicker by the second. "How should I know?" Jas was a wanderer, like Ian. His interest in movies and fiction in general was non-existent. He preferred the wilderness and his own thoughts to the excitement of a car chase, or the shooting of guns. A slowly trickling stream in a deserted field, miles from human habitation, held far more allure than the ripe bosom of a mid-twenties starlet. His was a simple life.

"Zombies, dude!"

"Like from those films?" Jasper asked, following Ian out of the kitchen into the dining hall. He remembered seeing a poster in the eighties, something about the dead walking the earth. A half head, injured, like the rising sun. He was on shrooms at the time and it freaked him right out.

"Just like the films," confirmed Ian. He wasn't a massive movie buff either, but he scanned his memory for the pertinent details. "Kill the brain. Don't get bitten. Find somewhere to hole up."

"Kill the brain. Don't get bitten. Hide," Jasper repeated.

One of the four doors in the room was heavily charred, the grains of the wood issuing a fine stream of smoke from the fires raging in the adjoining room. The dining room would soon be an inferno.

"We've got to be quick."

"I don't know where they might've gone," said Jasper, coughing into his sleeve.

"We go where the fire isn't, it's all we can do, dude," replied Ian, ducking low and heading for the only exit that wasn't about to explode.

Pushing through, the lobby was filled with smoke which poured through the tall front doors. Being a vast, open space, the fire was struggling to gain a foothold. The ceiling high above was a different matter. Patches of the burning lathe and plaster were breaking away and hitting the marble floor, sending embers flying in all directions. As they looked through the thick smog at the upper landing, the fire moved with purpose, bubbling the years of stain before igniting the flammable coating in an unending chain that quickly consumed the whole area.

"Fuck!"

Anyone upstairs was now cut off. They would have to try and find another way down.

209

"Which way?" asked Jasper, taking deep breaths of the mildly fresher air. The height of the doorframe worked in their favour, expelling most of the smoke before it could settle lower.

"East wing! It's the only part that's not on fire yet!"

"Ian?" came a cry from outside.

"Norm?" he yelled back.

"We're out here!" Norman shouted.

Appearing at the open doorway, Melv was by his side, covered in blood and grime.

"Is anyone else inside?"

"No, we got them all out."

"Good man! Jas, go!"

Ian glanced up just in time, and pushed Jas forward as a huge chunk of the weakened ceiling collapsed. Leaping back using the force of the thrust, Ian cleared the danger zone. The debris burst from the thick black cloud like a meteor, catching Jasper on the outstretched leg. A split second's hesitation on Ian's part would have seen them both crushed.

"Son of a tinker!" Jas yelled, dragging himself away from the blazing wreckage, still clutching the axe.

Ian took him by the unladen arm and pulled him across the glossy floor. Already stick thin, the years of polish eased the man's passage so that Ian hardly had to struggle at all.

Another blazing object fell from above, this time hitting the marble with a wet squelch. Two more followed, landing in a blazing heap. Before Ian wrestled Jasper through the door, the objects started to move. Through the flames, white eyes stared as they blackened.

"Holy moly!" Jas blurted through the pain.

"Is it broken?" Norm asked.

"I don't know," Ian replied. Kneeling by his friend, he said, *"Jas, I'm just going to take a look, dude. If it's broken, we'll need to splint it before we move or the bone could sever an artery."*

Rolling up the trouser leg, the calf muscle was raw, bloodied, and already going purple.

"I think it just clipped your muscle as it fell. Look at the scuff down the skin."

The others looked at the wound.

"If you say so, Ian. What now?" asked Norm. He was as wide as Jas was thin, with a cheerful disposition. Normally. Today his heavy jowls and overhanging belly were covered in unmentionable filth.

"Were either of you bitten?" Ian demanded, pulling Jasper away from them.

"No. This is from... other people," replied Norm, tugging at the too tight t-shirt with the wet stains.

"Ok, good. We need to get round the back and get the ride-ons. I'll need you to pull the Rover out of the mud and I'll follow you back to the lockup."

"Ian," said Norm, grabbing him by the arm, "I... I don't want to go back round there."

Melv stared silently, but his face told the same story.

"Ok, we leave them, but we need some sort of plan."

"A plan for what?"

Ian handed both axes over to Norm and Melv, before helping Jasper to stand and looping an arm around his midsection.

"A plan for this," he motioned with his head at the carnage all around them.

They moved away from the house as quickly as possible. More windows exploded as the fire spread, sending waves of intense heat out after them as if the inferno was furious to lose its prize.

"What's this?" pushed Norm.

"You're really going to make me say it?"

Melv nodded. Norm waited.

"Fuck! It's some sort of zombie fucking apocalypse! Are you happy?"

Melv snorted derisively until a sight to their rear caused him to let out a cry of fear. The human candles had grown in number to seven. Moving sluggishly as their juices burned, they couldn't see, but still made directly for the forestry workers.

"Fuck this shit," Ian moaned, carrying Jasper for the most part.

Melv hurried behind them, pulling on Norman as if to ask; Is he for real?

"You saw the same as I did, mate," Norman confirmed to his mute friend. *"Burning people don't generally walk around like that."* He pointed at the figures who were starting to collapse from the intolerable damage.

Melv gave them the finger.

"Yeah, dude. Fuck 'em," said Ian.

They staggered across the wet meadow, slipping and sliding onto their rumps more than once.

"I'll need you both to give me a nudge," said Ian as he drew near the trapped vehicle.

Helping Jasper aboard the Land Rover, Ian gently lifted the damaged leg and lowered it in the footwell. Norman and Melv moved around the back, ready to push. Ian reached the driver's door, jumped in, and started the engine in one motion.

"Ok, now!" called Ian, gently pressing the accelerator.

The tyres chewed into the slop, going nowhere.

"Fucking fuckers!" he yelled, spying the staggering creatures that were moving in their direction. They would never get Jasper to safety on foot. *"Again!"*

Norm and Melv grunted with exertion, their feet sinking into the quagmire. The tyres spun uselessly, spraying them with mud. They were completely bogged in.

"I'm going to skull fuck this fucking rain!" Ian roared, trying to think of a way to get free. If they had time, they could gather some scrub and branches and pack the tyres to give traction. The nearest zombie would be on them in less than two minutes.

"What now?" gasped Norman, wiping sweat and rain from his round face.

"We're going to have to run," replied Ian.

Norm scowled as if to say he'd rather take his chances with the undead. Melv pointed frantically as three cars burst through the low hedge lining the driveway. Racing across the pristine lawn, they didn't have a destination in mind, but upon seeing the workers, spun in their direction. Skidding to a halt, a terrified woman in the lead car tried to soothe the screaming children as she wound down the window.

"Is there another way out of here? The road is filled with those... things."

"There's a rear entrance but the gate will be locked. I can show you a path in the forest if you wouldn't mind giving us a nudge?"

The woman looked at the approaching ghouls, then at her gleaming BMW, then back at the creatures. Giving him a nod, she showed great awareness and gently coaxed the vehicle around in a wide circle to the rear of the Land Rover. Ian got Norm and Melv safely aboard before jumping in. Opening his own window, he waved the lady forward. Using the camber of the field, she barely accelerated at all. The resounding crunch of bumper against the towing eye sounded as if she hit the rear end at thirty.

"Great! Follow me!" he called as the impact pushed the vehicle clear of the sodden trap.

The two other cars pulled in behind them, trusting that they knew a route to safety. As Ian watched in horror, the entire roof of the west wing collapsed into the blazing ruins. It wouldn't be long before the rest joined it. Centuries of history, gone in less than an hour.

The four workers stared through the windshield numbly. Their entire view of what was normal had crumbled as surely as the stately home that spewed clouds of dark smoke into the rainswept sky. Ian nearly forgot about his entourage and their own journey. Skidding to a halt at the muddy intersection, he jumped from the vehicle and hurried to the BMWs open window.

"If you follow that for about half a mile, you'll come to a wooden gate. It'll be locked, I'm afraid."

"She's already taken a good knock," she replied, rubbing the dash fondly. "What's a bit more paint on a respray?"

"Take the lanes slowly, they're not designed for high end motors like that. If you find yourself stuck, or the road is too dangerous, we've got a compound about a mile that way." Ian pointed forward. "Once you get to the end of this track, it veers off but you'll be able to see the roof."

The woman reached out a hand. "Thanks..."

Ian took it and gave it a firm shake. It was trembling. "Ian."

"I'm Anna."

213

"Take care, Anna. And remember my offer. This thing is going to get much worse."

"I need to get back to my family," she said apologetically.

Behind her eyes was an acceptance that her mission was doomed to failure. She gave him a final, lingering smile, then closed the window. Ian stepped back into the brush, and she led the other two cars around the bend. Faces peered out at him like wraiths as they passed, the flowing water giving their features a nebulous quality.

Ian watched them until they disappeared from view. By the time he sat back in the Land Rover, the rain had even crept into the crack of his arse.

"What now?" asked Norm.

"We need to think about getting your families," he replied.

Sitting in the track with the engine idling, he looked in the mirror at his friends. They had the same look as the woman. The previously ignored radio broke through their frenzied thoughts.

"The World Health Organisation has declared a worldwide pandemic of unknown origin. At this time they can't state the source of the unknown disease, or if the pathogen that causes the aberrant behaviour is airborne. The order to remain indoors has just been confirmed by the Prime Minister declaring martial law. The army has set up evacuation stations outside key cities. They will be sending in search and rescue missions to find you, so stay inside, and stay safe. More news will follow when the Prime Minister addresses the nation in twenty minutes."

"Well fuck me," Ian gasped.

"Crikey," muttered Jasper.

"My kids," Norm groaned.

Melv gave the radio the middle finger.

"Christ, it sounds like you had a hard time of it too," said Irish.

"That was just the beginning, dude. We're nearly there. Just around this copse."

As the camp came into view, the survivors gasped in awe at the sight.

"Whoa," exclaimed Tara in his arms, fresh from her sleep.

"You ain't seen nothing yet, kiddo," Ian winked.

CHAPTER 31

Stephanie removed her glasses and stifled a yawn. The lesson plans on the desk were boring, but necessary. The castle contained a veritable bounty of books and encyclopaedia that shamed her state comprehensive. First editions of the Encyclopaedia Britannica. The classic works of Dickens in leather bound hardback. Even an original Shakespeare. Macbeth, no less, locked in a safe that Alina had opened. The education of the children would be world class, she would ensure it. Gone would be the enforced whims of the government of the day. Useless, politically driven criteria that added nothing to their life skills, only serving as indoctrination of the current fad.

In the apocalypse, could studying the old words of long dead scholars keep the zombies at bay? Not likely. But once the zombies returned to the earth, her charges would have a love and appreciation for everything beautiful, whether it be exquisite prose penned by quill, or the artwork that lined every wall inside the castle. By throwing herself into the work, she was able to ignore some of the awful grief that plagued her dreams. In the waking world, planning, structuring, and delivering the lessons kept the ghosts at bay. Once her eyes closed, the faces of her husband and children called to her. It was the same, night after night. They would scream and plead without making a sound. Their skin would pale, their eyes glazing with the milky hue of the undead. Then their flesh would slough, peeling away and melting as decomposition stole their innocence. The shrieking skulls would crumble, the dust blowing away on the wind.

"That's quite enough of that," she said, standing abruptly.

Striding from the room, Stephanie closed the door with a bit too much force and the boom echoed away down the cold passages of the castle keep.

"Are you ok, Miss Lunsford?" asked Toby.

She smiled warmly and ignored the question, moving like quicksilver, left, then right, trying to escape the memories. The loss of her family had been crippling in the early days. Stephanie wasn't ashamed to admit that she had climbed between the crenulations of the tallest watchtower on three occasions. Each time she had stood tall on the lower embrasure, refusing to hold onto the merlons for support. The wind had been like a living beast, caressing her, knowing her. Begging the unseen Gods for release; Amun, Fūjin, Vayu, whichever deity would answer, she had waited for their gentle kiss to push her from the edge. Instead, a gust out of nowhere sent her reeling back into the tower. Following the third failure on the third night, Stephanie had lain on the frigid stone, promising herself she would go on. Staring up at the star kissed sky, an avowed atheist became a true believer. It comforted her to think of her children, Sebastian and Mia, driving the wind under the watchful eye of Anthony, her husband. Their spirits comforting her always. Except in her dreams.

"Are you ok, dear?" gasped Gloria as she came close to being knocked flat.

"I'm sorry. I'm fine. I just need some air," Stephanie babbled, hurrying away.

The matronly elder had been a rock since her arrival, even though her own faith was wavering. She never turned the younger teacher away when she sought solace. Deep down, Stephanie felt her instincts about her saviours were in some way comforting to Gloria. She would smile wistfully, stealing glances at the cross when she thought Stephanie was lost in prayer.

Emerging into the daylight from the keep, the courtyard was alive with activity. The children were running back and forth with wheelbarrows full of ammunition. A dozen greetings were dismissed with a smile and a wave. Feeling guilty that she wasn't helping, Stephanie moved away from the human chain. Moving below the bailey gate, she found most of the others gathered on a portion of wall overlooking the south east. News of the prison attack had reached her, but she wasn't in the mood for idle gossip and fearmongering. A calming walk along the wall, enjoying the sights of Arundel town and the surrounding countryside would be enough.

Spying the foam archery targets, she had a change of heart. Sending a couple of dozen arrows downrange might help to soothe her mood better than a solitary activity that left more than ample time to dwell on the past. The trestle table was topped with a selection of the finest weapons brought back from the local archery store. A sleek black recurve bow called out to her. Typically a compound type of girl, the Tongtu bow just had... something. That je ne sais quoi. The contours of the grip seemed to be moulded perfectly for her hand. The draw, although heavier, was getting easier by the day.

Taking a fresh target which, ironically, was of a zombie, she moved to the foam pads and carefully removed the previous card. Pinning hers in place, she moved back thirty yards to the table and slipped on the brown glove. The new leather was still being broken in, but it protected her fingers far better than the cheaper tabs.

Artemis, goddess of the hunt, she'd named the bow. But only to herself. The others might have made fun of her if they'd known.

Taking the weapon and a selection of thirty-inch arrows, she moved into position. Laying the projectile on the rest, she got into firing stance and took a split finger grip on the string. Three under had never felt comfortable to her, no matter how hard she tried. Her accuracy didn't seem to suffer either, so she left it alone.

Drawing back her arm, she looked down the shaft and released in one smooth motion. The string snapped taut, and the arrow sailed downrange, piercing the green throat of the cardboard monster.

"No good."

Taking another arrow, this one hit the creature in the nose.

"For goodness sake."

On the next attempt, Stephanie pulled the string further to give it a little more oomph. The arrow struck in the bullseye, dead centre of the rotting forehead.

"Better."

She put four more into the small ring, before moving back five yards and doing the same. By the sixteenth shot her arms and hands were aching and the painful memory had been put back in the box, ready to be brought out when her conscious defences failed through slumber.

Returning the bow and glove, Stephanie moved towards the steps of the Bevis Tower. The walk around the wall would now be enjoyable, of that she was certain. Interlocking her fingers, she bent them over and stretched out the aching tendons. Repetition was reducing the pain, but the task was strenuous by its very nature. Still, she had to be prepared to fight.

Peering over the wall, the emptied moat was a sea of green instead of blue. Reading one of the castle journals, the source, Swanbourne Lake, had been sealed off hundreds of years ago. Given the opportunity, it could prove useful to reinstate the ancient protection. Especially considering the undead had some inexplicable fear of the water. Pausing by a dying brazier, Stephanie added a few logs and stoked the embers. The radiating heat was a welcome change from the winter's chill. In the distance, she could hear the faint patter of automatic weapons. Praying for their safe return, she resumed her journey. Coming to the next brazier, she frowned and added more fuel. She wasn't one for telling tales normally, but the dereliction of guard duty through the excitement would need addressing. They could be attacked and no one would know.

"Shut the fuck up!" came a seething whisper from below the wall.

Stephanie fell still, like a statue, rooted to the spot in terror.

"They're all on the other section. If we stay quiet, we can be up and over before they have a clue. Dumb cunts," gloated another.

"Get the ladders up there, now!" growled a third voice. It had a level of menace unheard in the others, however vulgar they were.

Fixated on the battlements, unable to draw breath, Stephanie watched. With much grunting, the top stiles clattered against the nearest section only a few feet away, the aluminium fresh as if they'd just stolen the ladders. A second set joined the first on the next embrasure. Then another. Paralyzed by fear, she watched the metal strain as someone climbed on, grinding against the stone with each step.

"Will someone foot this fucking thing? It's moving all over the place."

Without knowing how, Stephanie found herself by the brazier. Clutching the legs, which thankfully weren't hot enough to burn her, she tipped it over. The top of the circular frame clanged into the stone, spilling the red hot embers from the fire pit itself over the rim. A sharp intake of breath preceded a hellish scream and the sounds of falling.

"What the fuck just happened?" roared the toxic voice.

"Get up there! Now!" yelled a second, with the same poisonous authority.

Stealthy ascension gave way to frenzied climbing as whoever was on the other side raced up the massive ladders.

"What's happening?" called Sarah from the other side of the castle.

Picking up a flaring log that hadn't dropped, Stephanie ignored her and moved to the wall. A face came into view, twisted with hate. Jabbing the fire into his eyes, the man screamed and fell backwards, knocking the others from the ladder as he fell.

"Steph? What is it?" yelled Denise, who was running around the perimeter for all she was worth.

"Attack! It's the prisoners I think!" she finally managed to call back.

"Knock, knock, baby," chuckled the earlier voice from below. "You're going to pay for what you did."

"Sarah, get everyone inside! Now!" ordered Denise. Seeing the first man to breach the wall, she stopped and took on a shooter's stance. The convict was too preoccupied with revenge and the fresh meat to notice the gun pointed at him. Two pops saw a twin crimson bloom appear on his chest. The tidy red flowers spread quickly as his life force flowed from the torn arteries. He fell.

"Steph, move!"

Picking up another log, she felt her skin burning. The last ladder was full, the obese prisoner in the process of stepping over. Launching the fiery timber, he yelped and ducked away just in time.

"You're dead!" he snarled, earning a bullet through the ear for his troubles.

Slumping in death, his huge girth sealed the gap and those behind cursed their misfortune.

"I'm getting those!" she called, pointing at the neatly laid out bows. They would need everything at their disposal to fight.

221

"I'll cover the wall. The next bastard to show me a face gets the same treatment," Denise cried. It was an empty threat, designed only to buy time. Her gun was empty, the last of the ammunition spent. She hadn't had time to check the calibres in the supply crates, but the ones she had noticed were for the rifles, not her pistol.

"What do we do?" asked Sarah.

"Get the kids, and help Steph with those bows. We're going to need to hold the fort until Kurt and the others get back."

"Use the fucking shooter!" growled the leader.

Denise saw the shotgun barrel lift over the stone and point in their direction. The muzzle flashed, followed by the crack of the cartridge. They were miles off.

"You should take cover!" called Sarah.

Denise shook her head and held the gun steady. Obviously the threat was still working, otherwise they would be pouring into the castle.

"Just another minute. Please," Sarah begged. It was all they needed to be safely locked inside.

The top of a bald head peeked over the top and she swung in his direction. Dropping out of sight, they were slowly getting a bead on her. The shotgun appeared again, firing off another round. The pellets tore into the stone ten feet from where she stood.

"Pea, Holly, everyone, grab what you can as fast as you can and get inside the castle!" said Sarah, desperately.

Another head appeared and stared at Denise. They were getting braver by the second. A shit eating grin appeared on his face, suddenly disappearing as his eyes bugged. A crack to Denise's side would have made any normal person leap out of their skin, but she wasn't any ordinary lady. Gloria's carefully aimed shot peppered his face with tiny pellets, but didn't kill him. Made of sterner stuff than the others, he didn't yell out in pain, just ducked out of sight, clutching at the damage.

"The other cartridges are indoors. I think we should probably go now, dear," said Gloria.

222

"We're good!" shouted Sarah as the group ran past, their arms full. "Go!"

Disregarding the last boxes of ammunition, the group fled back to the living quarters. Sarah glanced back before ducking through the bailey gatehouse. Six men were already over, one of them wearing a mask of blood.

"Kurt, we need you," she whimpered.

All that work. All that sacrifice. Undone by an impossible series of consequences.

CHAPTER 32

Slamming the oak door, Stephanie locked it and slid the bolts home.

"We need a plan," Denise declared. "They're armed. It won't take long to get through that door."

"We're armed too," said Sarah.

Gloria looked at the boxes all around their feet. "Does anyone know how to use this?"

"There's nothing to use, love," said Bert, the old soldier who'd assisted in taking the castle. "The mortars are useless indoors for obvious reasons. The rounds aren't for the guns you have. About the only useful gear is this," he said, kneeling slowly at a green wooden box.

"Let me get that, sir," said Holly, helping the man lift it.

"Thanks, love. These grenades are about the only thing worth bothering with. Lethal at five meters, casualties guaranteed up to fifteen. I'd still keep my head down once they're thrown. I saw a friend take a sliver in his thigh. Lots of blood."

"Ok, we take them with us. Can we hold the Baron's Hall?" asked Sarah.

"I wouldn't," replied Bert.

"He's right. There's only one area that's defensible until Kurt gets back with the others," muttered Denise. In terms of the time of year, it was the worst place to be. They had no choice. "The old keep. The watchtower."

"There's no roof. We'll freeze to death," complained Zack, one of the holdovers from Jasmine's group.

"He has a point," said Sarah before recriminations could fly.

"We don't have a choice," explained Denise. "It's got water and only one access up a steep flight of steps. The old dungeon will keep us out of the worst of the weather. If we need to huddle for warmth, so be it."

"What about ladders? Can't they just climb up again."

"No, the walls are too tall and the banks way too steep to even walk up easily. It's our safest bet."

Sarah was convinced. They needed to buy time for the big guns to return. "Clarissa, go with Stephanie and the other kids. Holly, take the grenades and as much of the archery equipment as possible. Zack, go to the kitchen with your friends and grab as much of the cleaned food as you can carry. Grab Christina on your way. I'll go with Denise, Gloria, and the others to the Hall and pick up as many blankets as we can."

"What about firewood?" asked Zack.

Muffled shouts carried through the dense door. Their blood was up. They were hunting.

"We don't have time. Whatever's left up there will have to last."

Expecting an argument, he nodded instead and ran off with the others in hot pursuit. Stephanie led the youngsters away, their goods clattering.

"I can't help thinking we're missing something," said Sarah.

225

"I think you've covered all the bases, love," said Bert. "Shall we get a wriggle on? I'm not the fastest on my feet, and the fellas out back don't sound like the friendliest sort."

The portraits of long dead aristocrats scowled down as they passed, as if they disapproved of the hoi polloi sullying their home. Denise had always found the idea of an upper class to be positively ridiculous. At least in America you were judged solely on your merits. Your station wasn't dictated by some arbitrary network of families and birth rights, only on the effort you put in. *Let's see how you like the new arrivals,* she thought. They'd probably burn the paintings to keep warm. Or just for the sheer hell of it.

"Grab the thickest blankets you can find. I'll see if I can find a sack to carry a few more," said Sarah.

Bert reached beneath his bed and pulled out a holdall. "Use this, love."

"Thanks, Bert."

"I'm here to help."

"Well isn't this cosy," chuckled a new voice.

Spinning round, Denise pulled her empty revolver.

"I wouldn't," he warned, aiming a rifle directly at her chest.

The filth on his clothes and skin was nothing compared to the brown teeth. His wide face and heavy jowls lent him a friendly, friar tuck look. The jolliness of his dirty smile wasn't mirrored in the rapidly blinking, desperate eyes.

"How the hell did you get in here?" demanded Sarah.

"I fucking flew. How do you think I got in, you silly tart? I climbed the walls."

"That's impossible. You were only just in the courtyard."

"I didn't come in that way. There are two groups. You weren't expecting that, were you?"

Gloria groaned in pain. Staggering forward, she clutched at her chest. "Help me. It hurts. My heart."

"Stay back," he growled, keeping the gun on Denise.

"I need my tablets," she complained, in obvious discomfort. "My heart. I can't take it."

"Do I look like I give a fuck about your heart, you dozy old bitch?" he snorted. The decrepit bint was too old to rape anyway. Best she just go toes up and leave the fresher meat for him.

"Please, won't you help," she croaked, reaching out a gnarled hand.

"Just die already," he sneered, ignoring the frail woman.

"You first, dear," she said from her stooped position. Coming up under the barrel, she buried the knife between his ribs.

Pulling the trigger in spasm, the bullet spanged from the stone walls, passing dangerously close to Bert's head. The prisoner gaped down in shock at the stainless handle of the kitchen utensil. Survival instinct kicked in and he backhanded Gloria who went sprawling over a nearby chair. Cocking the rifle, the spent shell tinkled as it hit the limestone. Summoning the last ounces of will to kill his killer, he sighted the murderous old bitch. Hit like a truck, Honey hung from his arm, tearing at the flesh beneath. The second round embedded harmlessly into the carved wooden ceiling. Whipping her head back and forth, something ripped. It might have been his clothing, but it had a wet quality more akin to skin. His punctured heart gave up and he fell face forward, nose and brown teeth breaking against the unforgiving floor. Extracting the blade, Gloria forced it up through the soft spot at the base of his skull.

"They'll be coming! We need to go."

"We're already here, darlin'," said a new voice, thick with a scouse accent.

Before Gloria could snatch up the dropped rifle, a pair of double barrelled shotguns were levelled at her head. The man stepped over the threshold between the gunmen and nodded appreciatively at the setup. Mid-fifties, with black, slicked back hair. So dark was the bottled colour it seemed to absorb the light. Greying brows confirmed the dye job. Brown, emotionless eyes glared from below a protuberant brow. Tattoos encircled his neck like a colourful, patchwork scarf. The top of both meaty hands were similarly decorated through the gore. Menace emanated from every pore.

Honey growled, ready to attack. Gloria pulled her back before she got hurt.

"I think I'm gonna like it here," he said, surveying the exquisite room.

"Looks like they got Ron," said one of the gunmen.

"Gobshite should've waited like I told him," grumbled the Liverpudlian.

"Who are you? What do you want?" snapped Denise.

"A Yank? Well isn't this a small world?" he chuckled mirthlessly. "I'm Fred Fowler. You'll get to know me really well."

"She can yank my pole any time she wants," sneered one of the subordinates.

Denise held his gaze, wishing the gun was loaded so she could obliterate the smirking features.

Gloria backed away slowly towards her friends, one hand raised while the other coaxed the dog to retreat. She could feel the thick blood trickling down her forearm. It didn't go unnoticed.

"You did Ron? Well fuck me sideways," Fred exclaimed. "I think we're gonna get on real well. I like a bird with balls."

The other prisoners filed in, appraising their new home. Tossing the belongings of the castle group around, they searched for any valuables.

Fred was warming himself by one of the huge fireplaces, rubbing at the green blood with someone's shirt. Rounding on his men, he barked, "Cut that shit out! Dean, Cob, Jeff, wait here and keep an eye on them. The rest of you, follow me. We're gonna round up the others and find George."

"Yes, boss."

Kneeling down by Ron's corpse, he pulled the knife out with a sickly grating of metal on bone. Laughing to himself, he looked back to Gloria and laid the weapon down reverentially on a small cabinet as if it was a gift. Taking a hand rolled cigarette from behind his ear, he placed it between thick lips, unlit.

"Move," he ordered the men.

Leaving the room, the three remaining guards instantly began ransacking the hall again. Smashing cups and glasses against the stone walls, they then turned their attention to the antique furniture, breaking it apart and tossing it onto the flames.

Bert could see the anger growing. He knew what was coming next. When the fun of destroying the inanimate could no longer satiate the rage, they would turn their attention to the women.

"Right you hooligans!" he barked, hobbling forward. "That's enough of that!"

"Shut the fuck up old timer," warned Dean, a red headed con in his late thirties.

"Bert, keep quiet. We need to think how to get out of here," whispered Sarah.

Smiling warmly, he winked at her and turned away, continuing to advance on the prisoners.

"So you're billy big bollocks, eh?" mocked Bert.

"Do you want to get hurt, you old cunt?" he snarled, picking up his metal bar.

"You're a big man with a weapon, aren't you. Ginger prick," Bert spat.

"You think I need a tool?" Dean demanded, wielding the thick bar.

"What's the matter? You making up for a deficiency somewhere else? Little dick."

"I'm getting sick of your shit, old man. Now fuck off before I hurt you."

"Did you get bullied at school? Was that it? Poor ginger prick," Bert mocked, nearing the trio.

229

Denise held Sarah back when she tried to pursue the stooped gent. She had seen the same escalation coming. They were whipping each other into a frenzy. Until Bert had poured cold water on the raging inferno. The fire, though quenched, was flourishing again at the shocking antagonism. Denise knew Bert didn't have a mean bone in his body, the insults were solely to get a rise. But to what end? He couldn't take a bar and two shotguns with invective.

"I've had enough of you," Dean exploded, tossing the black iron.

Charging at the old man, Dean wound up a right hook and swung it at the wrinkled face. Bert ducked the telegraphed blow easily and snapped out a quick left right which sent Dean staggering backwards.

"Two time Army middleweight champion, you ginger prick. Let's see what you've got."

Faced with the suddenly sprightly septuagenarian, Dean hesitated. His head was still swimming from the combination. Blood trickled from a split lip.

Bert was bouncing on his toes as much as the arthritis would allow. He wouldn't admit it, but the punches had been agony, the needles of pain radiating up to his shoulders.

"Bert, come back here!" Gloria cried as the two other men surrounded him.

"Get back, love. Get back!" he replied, adding weight to the last two words.

Denise picked up the hint and seized the two women by their arms, pulling them away.

"What's he doing?" Sarah sobbed. Any moment now they would rush him.

"No! He's mine!" Dean warned, shaking away the daze.

Charging in, he bent at the waist, aiming to rugby tackle the old codger. Bert took a step back and whipped an uppercut straight into the downturned face. The momentum carried Dean forward and they went down heavily. Cob and Jeff jumped in, stamping and kicking at the pinned senior.

Sarah screamed as she heard brittle bones crack under the onslaught. Dean had recovered from the blow and knelt atop Bert, raining punches down.

"Leave him alone!" Gloria shrieked.

Amidst the brutal attack, Denise heard the twang of metal. Laughing through broken, bloodied teeth, Bert raised his shaking hands. Held in the twisted fingers were two innocent looking pins.

"What the fuck are you laughing at?" growled Dean, raising his fist again.

"Five meters, sonny," Bert chuckled, coughing up a torrent of blood.

"Get down," Denise yelled, tackling the two women and the yellow hound. They fell sideways behind an antique dresser.

Secreted in Bert's favourite pullover, the two stolen grenades detonated. Dean became several individual pieces that painted the walls and ceiling with claret. Cob and Jeff were shredded by the razor sharp slivers, their tattered bodies blown against the stonework. Deafened by the explosion, the cowering ladies couldn't hear the tinkle of shattered glass as every window disintegrated. The blast wave surged up both chimneys. As the void refilled with air, smoke and soot were forcefully dragged down, gushing into the room like the mouths of dragons preceding ignition. Instead of a twin inferno, the expelled logs and embers in the black wave sat atop the rugs, starting smaller blazes of their own.

"We need to go!" shouted Denise, feeling the vibrations of her words but not the sound.

Gloria stared up in mute shock.

Honey shook her head, turning around in a circle.

Sarah jumped to her feet, shrugging free of Denise's restraining hand. Jumping over the debris, she fell to her knees at Bert's body. Torn in two, she ignored the horrendous damage and stroked his cheek. Even in death his lips formed a half smile.

Pulling Sarah to her feet, the retired police officer yelled in her face. "We've got to go!"

Sarah heard nothing, only ringing.

Together, united in grief and soot, they ran.

Honey licked Bert's face once, whined, then followed.

CHAPTER 33

Holding tightly to Bert's full hold all, Sarah followed close behind Denise. Most of the blankets had been abandoned as soon as their hearing returned slightly and the furious shouts of Fred got closer. Running up the main staircase, the second floor put them one below that of the entrance arch to the old keep. Enraged cries seemed to come from every direction. The rest of the prisoners were inside, searching. Doors slammed. Antiques smashed. Manic laughter haunted their every step.

"We're nearly there!"

Passing the looted castle store, they raced down the passageway. A prisoner stepped into view from one of the other staircases. Denise's gun sent him scurrying back out of sight. As they passed the dark stairwell, the man had tripped over his own feet. Tumbling down, the solid treads broke bones. Amusement at his injuries were short lived at the realisation they were out of time. The men had swarmed through the castle like a virus.

Reaching The Lady's Chamber, the mannequin in her luxurious dress stared at them in her mirror. A spiral staircase led both up and down, tight and steep. It had been designed to favour the defenders, curving in a clockwise direction so the attackers had to do battle left-handed. Opening up, the arch led directly out into the necessary passage from the original castle.

"Check everyone's safe," ordered Gloria, covering the gloomy tunnel with the shotgun. Satisfied they were alone for the moment, she snapped open the gun and slipped the red cartridge into the chamber. Four remained, and she would make them count.

Sarah bolted out into the light. The massive steps leading up to the imposing structure were empty. "Who's up there?"

Stephanie moved out from cover and waved down.

"Is everyone with you?"

"Only some of the children," she called.

"What do you mean *some* of the children?" demanded Sarah.

"Holly refused to stay. She went back with Clarissa to look for you. I'm so sorry."

"How could you let this happen?" Sarah shrieked. "You were supposed to watch them!"

Stephanie's face crumbled and she started to cry.

"She's learned to be headstrong from us. You can't blame Stephanie."

"They're going to be caught by those animals. Can you imagine what they'll do to Holly? I've got to go and find them!" Sarah was frantic.

"Where are Zack and Alina's group?" called Denise.

"They haven't made it either," she sobbed.

"I'll go with you," said Denise.

"No."

"Then I'll come, dear," offered Gloria.

"No. I need both of you up there with the others. If the worst should happen, keep the kids safe until Kurt gets back."

"But..." spluttered Gloria.

"Promise me?"

"I promise."

Denise nodded sadly.

"Thank you. Now go!"

Honey started to follow her mistress back into the castle.

"You go with them too, girl. You've done enough fighting for today." Sarah scratched behind her ears, a spot she adored. "I love you, you furry beast. Go! Find Gloria!"

Whipping her head back, she saw the teacher halfway up the soaring staircase. Bolting after her in pursuit, Honey was alongside the older lady in seconds.

"Good girl," whispered Sarah, heading back into the fallen sanctuary.

CHAPTER 34

"What happened to Sarah?" asked Pea.

"She went back in to look for Clarissa and Holly," explained Denise.

"I told them not to go," she replied, wiping away fresh tears.

"They did what they thought was right. We just need to wait a few minutes and hope they find each other."

"Denise, what do you want to do with the doors?" asked Stephanie.

Giving Pea a quick hug, Denise left her with the other children. "How do you mean, sweetheart?"

"They've been fixed open to stop the tourists messing around with them."

Two thick brackets were bolted through the stone, holding them securely open. Gloria remained watchful on the battlements above, and Denise could make out her shadow on the steps below from the afternoon sun. Rust and time had weakened the metal, but it was still solid enough to stop any movement. Checking the thick hinges themselves, they were in a better state of repair, but only marginally. Tucked below the guard post above, the rain had never touched the doors. Moisture in the air was another matter, as testified by the orange flecks around the sturdy pin.

"Pea, can you and the others see if we have anything strong enough to break this?" asked Denise.

The blonde girl ran over, took one look to ascertain the tool required, then ran off. There was very little to search in the ancient watchtower. The fifty yard wide lookout had lost its roof centuries ago. The original stone floor had crumbled, leaving only mud to walk on. Below in the dungeons, the castle stored non-essential items. The dank, black cells were nothing more than three stone walls now, the doors crumbling to dust long ago. Lighting equipment and cables were neatly stored in waterproof boxes, ready to be hung for any festivities. Ladders and other equipment filled another. As Pea surveyed the goods, the torch caused shadows to loom and dance. Afraid, alone in the gloom, she imagined they were the ghosts of the long dead prisoners. A pair of cages in the floor itself were covered with safety grates.

"They're oubliettes," explained Stephanie, causing her to start.

Shining the torch at the teacher, she returned the beam to the vertical shaft at her feet. "Oobly what, miss?"

"Oubliettes. Horrible things. You needn't worry yourself. How's the search coming along?"

"I found these?" said Pea, holding out a pair of tripods. The central metal pole was fairly robust. Trying to bend it over her knee, it moved not an inch but sent a stabbing pain up her leg.

"These might just work," said the teacher.

"What were they used for, miss?" asked Pauline, aiming the torch down through the steel.

"Do you really want to know? It's quite graphic."

Pea's face pleaded. It would help keep her mind off of Winston and their current woes.

237

"This type were designed to be some of the worst," said Stephanie, joining her. "The word derives from the French word to forget."

"They kept people down there?"

The smooth sided stone shaft stretched down about fifty feet. "They *forgot* about people down there. It's only wide enough to stand in. You couldn't kneel. You couldn't sit. You could only sleep when exhaustion made it possible to ignore the discomfort of being wedged tightly between the stone."

Pea was horrified. "When would they be let out?"

"For exercise you mean?"

"Yeah. Or to use the toilet."

"They went to the toilet down there, there was no being let out. People would die in filthy squalor in the darkness. Sometimes you were thrown in one where there was already a dead body. Can you imagine? Trying not to stand on the rotting body. Surrounded by flies. In the darkness."

Stephanie was loving playing the teacher, even if the content was a little ghoulish.

"Any luck?" called Denise down the steps.

"I think so!" Stephanie replied. "Pea found something we might be able to lever them open with."

"Ok, great!"

Pea was enthralled by the vile torture devices. "I want to put those men down there. They deserve it."

"Let's hope we get the chance, darling. Now let's try your tripods, shall we?"

"We've got company!" called Gloria from atop the wall.

Stephanie and Pea came at a run, the solid iron tripods in hand.

"Sarah and the others?" Denise asked.

"Not unless she's grown a beard, dear," said Gloria.

"Stay down, Gloria. We know they have rifles."

"Hiding as we speak," she replied.

The mood dropped and the fear spiked amongst the survivors in the tower. Denise took up position with her back to the guardhouse door. Stephanie and Pea snapped off the plastic brackets and the support legs, leaving the thick pole intact.

"Do we have time?" whispered Stephanie.

"We'll make time."

Snatching a glimpse through the archway, the two men were moving slowly.

"Where're our friends?" demanded Denise.

"Safe!" replied one of the men. "Now come on down and you'll be safe too."

"Fred and George don't want anyone hurt. You have our word."

"Forgive me if I tell you to go and fuck yourself," Denise shouted in response.

Pea inserted the steel and was yanking on the strut for all her worth. The L shaped bracket started to loosen, until the rusted bolts came away completely. Little remained of the shank that had been buried in the stone but rust.

"Try the door," said Denise, darting across the opening to take cover on the other side. Neither of the men were armed with guns, only knives. She didn't want to chance a sniper was keeping a watch from the dark niches behind the creeping intruders.

Straining against the aged oak, nothing happened.

"Shit! Gloria, would you mind giving them a warning shot? But keep your head down."

"I'll go one better than that, dear," she said from above.

Denise heard both men gasp before the crack of the shotgun shattered the day. The gasps were replaced by thudding as someone topsy-turveyed down the stone steps. Then came the cries of the wounded prisoner.

"I said to keep your head down!" Denise shouted.

"Desperate times and all that," came the reply.

There was no one watching or they would have taken a shot back at the crazy teacher. Looking around through the arch, the man on the right had taken the buckshot in his shoulder. The fall had broken his good arm and one of his legs. Fearing another shot, the uninjured man took the steps two at a time, leaving his friend to wail and gibber. *No honour among thieves,* she thought.

"Steph, get the others and try to close that door. Pea, come over here, sweetheart. Break that bracket just like you did on that one. Stay low."

"Ok," replied the teenager, ducking and scurrying across the opening. The angle of the steep steps gave her cover, but there was no point taking any chances.

Nearly the whole class crammed around the seized door. Taking hold of anything they could, they grunted and pulled. With an awful grinding squeal, the hinges gave way. Slamming it shut, Stephanie pulled them all back out of harm's way.

"Nearly... there!" groaned Pea, straining against the slightly stronger metal of the second hinge.

Denise slipped the empty gun in her waistband and added her own weight. The pole started to bend, then folded in two.

"Damnit! Pass me the other one," said the youngster.

Stephanie held it at arm's length, and it was just as well she did. A bullet tore through the wood an inch above her limb, sending slivers flying. One loose shard stuck in her forearm, causing her to drop the bar.

Seeing blood, Denise feared the worst. "Were you hit?"

"A splinter, that's all," she hissed.

Pea carefully retrieved the fallen pole and commenced working again.

"Gloria, can you keep your head down now, sweetheart? They've brought their big boy toys."

Denise took the half folded second tripod and added her weight to the task. With both of them straining, the stone cracked and the bolts and fixings both came away.

"Good work!"

Stephanie turned to the students. "Crawl across as low as you can. They can't hit you."

"Ok, miss," said Anthony, leading the way.

Joining Denise and Pea, they wrestled with the second door. In comparison to the first, the hinges gave up with little fight and they carefully closed it against the stone jamb, mindful of the watching gun. No shot came, which either meant the gunman was out of bullets, or he had an appreciable level of discipline to not waste shots. If it was the latter, that was a whole new level of threat to anyone watching the approach.

"Anthony, can you get the bolts?" asked Stephanie.

The teenager was almost scraping his belly as he shuffled across the ground. Denise couldn't blame him for his caution. The heavy duty sliding bolt dropped into the holes in the floor, securing the oak doors.

"It's good, but it's not good enough," said Denise, spying the three levels of wrought iron brackets set into the stone. Slipping the pole across the eight foot opening, she let it fall into the central pair. A solid length of timber would have been better, but beggars couldn't be choosers.

"The rest of you, can you go and see if there's something we can drop into the other brackets? If the bolts give, it will buy us some time."

The students eagerly complied, crawling below the line of fire and heading off on another search.

"They'll need to be occupied," warned Stephanie. "It was hard enough on them when we were safe and it was only the dead to contend with."

"Can I count on you to come up with something, sweetheart?"

Stephanie gently touched her arm. "Of course. Leave it with me."

Denise surveyed the gatehouse and decided it was secure enough. The twin doors opened into a narrow, left handed alcove, designed to force any attackers into a bottleneck of sorts. In the event of a breach, they would face swords and arrows in the confines before making it into the old keep.

It was better than nothing.

Climbing the stone steps, Denise joined Gloria who had already fashioned a looking glass of sorts with the use of a pocket mirror and the kitchen knife.

Crouching behind the battlements, she asked, "Any movement?"

"Only our injured friend writhing on the ground. No one seems in a hurry to come and help him."

The shrill cries had faded to inarticulate groans. Taking the mirror, Denise angled the glass to look. Blood saturated the four lower steps, dark and wet.

"I think you hit his artery."

"I think so too," said Gloria, quietly.

Her conscience was weighing heavily. The lives she had taken were necessary, of that she was in no doubt. The whole of her family might have, even now, been suffering under the whims of the prisoners. Beaten. Raped. Killed. She had no choice. Quite how that excuse would play at the pearly gates, only time and passing over from the mortal realm would tell.

"Can you see our shooty friend?" asked Gloria.

Denise moved from the archway at the foot of the stairs, to each window. Several were open, which wasn't helpful. A muzzle flashed, swiftly followed by the crack of the shot. It missed the mirror, gouging a chunk of masonry from the angled embrasure.

"First floor, second window."

It confirmed her opinion about the shooter. He was watchful and skilled, if not a bit rusty. The bullet's impact was only three inches off, which would have still meant a fatal wound if he had been aiming centre mass on a living person.

"Shall I fire back? It might spook him?"

"Don't waste the shell. It wouldn't do any damage, and if my hunch is right, he'll be moving position now anyway. He knows I saw him."

"Is he trained?"

"Possibly. Or he might just have common sense and experience from watching movies. The target was fairly big, and the distance only about eighty yards. It wasn't a difficult shot."

"A skilled amateur?"

"That would be my guess."

"What do we do now?"

"I'd give anything to have a portcullis like the main castle," Denise complained.

The housing level above their head was empty, the thousand-year-old barrier long since returned to dust. Runner notches sat within the thick stone walls, ending at an eight-inch-wide letterbox opening where the reinforced portcullis would have dropped through.

Staring down through the slit, Denise had an idea.

CHAPTER 35

"Thank you for joining us," said Fred.

The Baron's Hall was freezing. Chill winds whistled through the fragments of glass held in place by the twisted, patterns of window lead. The small fires from the explosion had been extinguished, but the stench of blood, shit, and burned fabric pervaded the frigid air. Their home. Their sanctuary. The place they had fought and bled for, was gone. Sarah struggled against the men that painfully gripped her arms.

"It seems we underestimated you again," he said, kicking gently at Bert's remains.

"You get your filthy foot off of him!" she screamed, wrestling free.

The men were as shocked as Fred at her strength. Wailing like a banshee, she charged. Three men stepped between Sarah and the target of her hatred, one of them rugby tackling her mid-flight. Twisting to the side, they slammed her onto the floor. Her fury was all consuming.

Writhing beneath the weight, three full grown men, powerful in their own right, struggled to contain the hellcat.

"Calm down or I'll kill your friends," Fred warned.

One of his men levelled a rifle at the group of people she hadn't noticed. Zack, Alina and the food collection team were bloodied and bruised, cowering in a corner. Trying to see if Clarissa and Holly were among them, her head was pressed hard into the floor. The thin rug did nothing to ease the compression, and she started to buck and kick again.

"Let her up," said another Liverpudlian.

Twisting her head, the fabric abraded her skin and a few strands of hair tore free of the scalp. One glance told her all she needed to know. He looked too similar to the other man to be anything but a brother. His greying hair was untouched by chemical attempts to conceal the unrelenting ticking of the clock. Unlike Fred, he had few tattoos.

"She wants to kill me, George," Fred chuckled.

"And I don't blame her. You'll have to forgive my brother, he's the hot head. I wanted this to go as smoothly as possible."

"My husband will be back soon. Then you'll find out the true meaning of hot head," Sarah snapped as she was hauled upright.

"You know as well as I do that when he sees a knife to your throat on top of the wall, he'll do fuck all," George replied, losing patience.

Sarah fell silent as the truth hit her.

"Now I want you to point out any other hiding places in this place. After that, we're going to pay a visit to the tower so that we can bring the others down safely. We don't want to hurt any of you."

"Like I believe that. Is that what you told the people you raped inside the prison, you fucking animal?"

"We didn't make the rules in there," he replied. The cruel smirk and glint in his eye said that he hadn't been averse to complying with the regulations, however. Purely to be a good inmate, of course.

245

"I won't do anything you ask."

"Kill one of them," said George.

"Kill them all," Sarah fired back defiantly. "Then rape and kill me. If you think I'd ever put those children in your hands, you're stupider than you look. And your brother thinks that Grecian 2000 bottle is fooling people? What a wanker."

Fred ran a hand self-consciously through the impossibly dark locks.

"I told you to leave it be," George agreed.

"Fuck off. I look good."

"Does he?" George asked Sarah.

She slowly shook her head, staring venom. "Like a toilet brush dipped in shit."

"That's mostly brown, but I get your point," said George.

"What does she know? She's just a gash."

"Please, Fred. Let's de-escalate the situation. I'm sure we can come to an understanding."

"Let us go, and I'll help you. The castle's yours. I just want to get my people out of here."

"We know it is. But why would we let the new meat go?" Fred asked. "Me and the boys need our entertainment."

"Anyone who touches me will lose their tiny dick," Sarah snapped.

"We're keeping you safe from all the dead fucks outside. I think a little compensation is the least we can ask for."

"Your compensation comes from having a fortress for a home. Let me and my people go, and we won't retaliate."

Fred roared with laughter. "Retaliate. Check out the balls on this gash."

Sarah crossed her arms disdainfully, looking Fred up and down. "What did you do when the dead rose? You hid in your cell behind your walls, that's what. When you were sticking your dick in the poor people who tried to shelter with you, we were fighting the undead across the south

246

coast. We've killed thousands. Tens of thousands. And at the end of it all, we took this fucking castle bare handed. What have you done? Raped a few women. Real big men. Not even strong enough to take over from the Araters. Always scared. Always hiding."

Fred's face was bright scarlet, ready to blow. He took a step towards her, fists clenched. "I'm going to bash your fucking teeth out. Then I'm going to destroy every hole in that fine body. Then I might just kill you for the hell of it."

"Go on then!" spat Sarah, matching him pace for pace. "But know this. Kurt and my friends will retake the castle, I guarantee it. You won't know which direction they'll come from. You won't ever be able to sleep. Every moment you'll be looking over your shoulder. They could be waiting around any corner. And when he gets you, I promise you'll die slow and painfully. You'll beg to be given to the zombies to eat. You think Craig had inventive ways to dispose of people? You haven't seen anything yet."

They were face to face. No one had ever spoken to him like that before. What made it worse, was that deep down her words chilled him to the marrow. He actually *feared* this woman and her threats. It was an unaccustomed feeling and he didn't like it one bit. Fred drew back his arm, ready to pummel the pretty face. A heavy hand grasped his meaty fist, stilling the blow. Sarah didn't even blink.

"That's enough. Fred, take the others and lock our guests in one of the bedrooms. Then search this place from top to bottom."

"What are you going to do?" Fred seethed.

"I'm going to have a little chat with..." George intoned the word, waiting.

"Sarah Taylor."

"With Sarah here."

"What about?"

"The arts. Politics. The existential dread that is the human condition."

Fred turned to face his brother, still furious. "Don't treat me like a mug. Don't speak down to me."

247

"We're going to talk about the future, dear brother. Don't be so emotional," replied George, placating his younger sibling.

"She's mine later," Fred declared.

"Fine. Whatever," said George dismissively.

Grunting, Fred gave Sarah one last glare, then sulked off. A couple of the other inmates smirked as he passed. George stared at them and their faces dropped.

"Come on! Fucking move!" Fred snapped, dragging Zack and the others away with more force than was necessary. They were already terrified.

"Now, where were we," said George, smiling.

CHAPTER 36

Denise knew something was coming. Her hunch had been tingling for more than half an hour, and it never let her down. She watched the shadowy archway below, before turning her attention to the windows which were all now open.

"Clever, aren't you?" she muttered.

The shooter needn't have bothered. The shotgun was not a lethal threat at his range. If they had been slug shells it would've been a different story, but they weren't. The buckshot might wound, or even take out an eye if Gloria was lucky. With only a few left, the shells were far more valuable as a close combat last resort. The empty Glock in her waistband might have been worth a damn if she had ammunition, but the magazines were empty. At best she could use it to pistol whip their enemies to death. The boxes of armaments in the castle were achingly close. They may as well have been on the moon.

"Do you see anything, dear?" asked Gloria.

"It's all quiet. Too quiet."

"Like the calm before the storm?"

"Exactly."

"Do you really think they'll try and get up here? Can they be that foolish?"

"They've got the others, and I'd imagine by now they've extracted information about our numbers. And *ages*," Denise replied.

"I still feel quite sprightly, I'll have you know."

"*I* know that you are, but all they'll know is there are a couple of... middle aged ladies, a bunch of school children and teenagers, and a few adults. And there are dozens of them. And they're armed. I'd say it's guaranteed."

"What do you think our chances are?" asked Gloria. It was the first time in their time together that Denise had seen her shaken. The repeated glances down into the watch tower grounds and the gathered youngsters told her that it wasn't her own safety she feared, but that of her children.

"Honestly? I don't know."

"That's not exactly encouraging, dear," chuckled Gloria, the laugh carrying a nervous edge.

Denise smiled at her, attempting to portray strength and self-belief that she wasn't entirely convinced of. Their fates were a coin, mid toss. The tumbling quarter would land in their favour, or it wouldn't. They had everything in their favour in terms of position. Nowhere in the castle or wider area could provide a fire position to suppress them provided they didn't stand. The imposing fortress within a fortress was only accessible by a single steep, stone staircase. The oaken doors were inches thick, and well secured now that additional struts had been wedged in place. They had enough water to last forever. The meagre pile of wood was troubling, but she had already decided to move the brazier and fuel into one of the dungeon cells below. The warmth would be trapped, instead of dissipating immediately to the outside air. The walls themselves would absorb the radiant heat and give more thermal comfort. Those not on watch could shelter out of the cold.

The food, though...

Pea had found a secret stash squirreled away in between the stored equipment. Denise thanked the Lord for the selfish bastard who had stolen the goods, buying them at least a day before the stomach lining started to eat itself. She had no doubt it was one of Jasmine's group, but all that was past them now. Tomorrow night, the last of the stale crackers and tinned peaches would be gone. The attack would come long before that, though. It had to. Both her tingling cop senses and the ticking clock of Kurt's return would ensure it.

There! Movement in the archway. A shadow moving in shadows.

"It's time," said Denise.

Gloria took a steadying breath and changed position, ready to open fire if the need arose.

Denise waved down to the students. They came waddling in pairs, careful not to spill anything of the contents they were laden with.

Stephanie waited for them to return, before forming them into three rows with their chosen bow. Arrows sprouted from the mud at their feet.

Thank God for Kurt, thought Denise. His decision to harden the castle inhabitants might be what would save them. The faces below were fearful, but determined. Even the adults such as Freya and Nick who had initially failed during combat, were now ready. Anja stood beside Stephanie, a standard recurve bow in hand.

"You, in the tower!" called a rough, scouse voice.

"Hey, you, not in the tower!"

"You're a funny gash, aren't you? We'll see who's laughing when we're alone later."

Denise peered across to Gloria with a frown. "Gash?"

"I think he's talking about the female anatomy, dear."

"Ooh." Denise replied.

"This is your last chance to give up, or we're coming for you. I promise, you won't like it if we have to force our way in."

"If you hadn't been so rude, I might've taken you up on the offer. As it stands, this gash says; Fuck you, pencil dick!"

"I was hoping you'd say that!" he shouted back.

Furtive movement could be seen just inside the archway. If her eyesight wasn't failing, Denise estimated around two dozen people crowded in the passage. More would undoubtedly be just out of sight in the gloom. The question was, would their new friend launch everyone at the problem, or send waves?

A war cry from below carried out over Arundel and the surrounding countryside, the first in many centuries. Six men charged out wielding one of the many sturdy antique benches that lined the long corridors of the castle. Their mad flight came to a grinding halt when they reached the steps. Humping the awkward battering ram, they saved their breath for the laboured ascent. Twenty more followed, holding up shields made from broken doors, tables, anything that provided cover from the feared buckshot. Their pace was dictated by the men with the bench, and by the tenth step they were all shouting complaints about how they were exposed.

"You fucking carry it then!" snapped one of the men.

"Just move for fuck's sake. I don't want to get shot!"

"It's alright for you fuckers! You've got protection!"

"We'll be under that roof soon. Stop fucking whining!"

Gloria whispered over to Denise. "Shall I let them have it?"

"No, stay down, sweetheart." Even if Gloria raised the gun and fired without exposing herself, the kick would likely break her fingers.

Listening to the bickering coming from outside, Denise's fear scaled back a notch. They were still in danger, of that there was no doubt, but the enemy was fractured, undisciplined. With each unhindered step, their confidence grew and the squabbling ceased. They felt they were invincible, infallible, guaranteed victory based on the fact they were men. Men going up against women and a few kids. She had seen it all before. The arrogance of a perp when confronted by a female officer. Quickly turning to humiliation when she would take them down and cuff them. It was a strong card, as long as she played it right.

"Now, dear? They're getting rather close."

"Save the shells for if they breach the gate."

"Will do," said Gloria merrily.

"How's it going fellas? You sound a bit tired," Denise teased.

"Fuck you, cunt!"

"Cunt. Gash? What is it with you boys? I need to have stern words with your mothers about how to speak to ladies."

"Keep on chatting shit," huffed the lead man. "You won't be laughing when Fred and George get their hands on you."

"So you are just little boys doing as the big boys say. Good to know. And where, by chance is Mr Fred or Mr George?"

"Shut your mouth!" barked the man.

"So they're hiding below?" she shouted loud enough to be heard at the archway. "I figured them for cowards. I shit better men than them."

"I'll show you a fucking coward!" roared Fred, leaving the safety of the passage.

Like a bull out of a gate, he charged up after his men. For the first fifteen steps.

"Bit out of shape there, honey?" Denise mocked as she listened to the footfalls slow and the breathing intensify.

"Dead... You're dead..." he gasped.

"By the sounds of it, you'll be having a cardiac arrest before you get through to us."

"Fucking... gash..."

"Might I suggest quitting smoking and some light jogging?"

"Cunt..." he wheezed.

"Is that such a wise idea? I mean, if they get through?" whispered Gloria.

"I want them mad. I want them not thinking straight," Denise replied.

"I trust you, dear."

"Thank you. Can you imagine where we would be if you and your family hadn't turned up?" Denise said, bringing up a subject she thought long overdue.

"You'd all be fine. You and your wonderful friend, Patricia, would've taken charge at some point."

"I'm not so sure," Denise replied, ignoring the growing clamour from below. She had to say her piece. "We were only two. Louise and some of the others might have joined us, but what good would it have done? We were trapped and unarmed. If Fred and George had found us like that, we'd already be dead. Or worse. You amazing folks saved our lives then, and you're doing it again now, and I love you for it."

"You're too kind, dear. You forget that it was you that saved *our* lives on that dark day."

Denise reached out a hand and took Gloria's. "I guess God had a plan for us, after all."

"If we survive the next hour, I might give Him another chance."

"Let's pray that we do then."

The source of the voices moved directly below their position beneath the gatehouse. Denise nodded to Gloria. "Here we go."

A cry of *heave* preceded the first heavy clash of wood on wood. The deafening impact was swiftly followed by cries of pain and another crash as the bench was hastily dropped.

"Careful of the vibrations, lads," laughed Denise.

"Shut up, you whore!" roared Fred. "Pick it up, you fucking muppets!"

"A good manager knows how to treat their workers!" called Gloria.

The two ladies could hear the growing agitation amongst the prisoners. A few thwacks of fist on flesh carried up through the portcullis slot. The gates rang with another heavy thud of contact, and this time they didn't drop the ram. Again they struck.

"Ready?" asked Gloria.

"Ready."

Denise stayed in a kneeling position to avoid any gunfire as she moved into position. Gloria placed the shotgun down and did the same. Eight metal pails of near boiling water steamed in the frosty air, the liquid drawn from the ancient tower well and heated by the braziers. The ice crystals formed on the moist stone had receded from the ambient warmth of the liquid in the containers. Denise had a moment of doubt at what they were going to do.

"I want those kids!" Fred leered to his men. "I bet the girls are ripe."

Fearing the shotgun, the men were all crowded in the alcove before the gate. It made swinging at the door difficult, but at least they were covered. If anyone had looked up, they would have seen the four chutes that terminated directly over their heads. They also might have questioned why the tower needed so many gutters and why they would be designed to saturate anyone coming or going during heavy rainfall. They didn't look up, and therefore had no idea of their true purpose.

"Now!" whispered Denise, all doubt erased by the vile grunts of the excited men at the thought of tender, young meat.

Pushing the buckets over with the aid of a cloth wrapped hand, the metal clanked against the stone. Water poured into the funnels that once would have carried red hot sand. The effect was the same. Boiling liquid erupted from the murder holes, soaking the first two rows of sheltering men. Denise heard the splash and the sharp intake of breath as a million nerve endings were seared. The screams that tore through the afternoon were barely human. If the lives of the children hadn't been on the line, she might not have carried out the next step.

"Get back!" cried the prisoners who had only been mildly scalded.

Above, Denise and Gloria tipped the last four buckets towards the portcullis cavity.

Driven back by the heat and pain, those that could flee did so. Straight into the scorching torrent of the newly formed waterfall from above. All courage and dreams of rape vanished as the men scrambled for safety, their skin bubbling. Those hit by the worst of the boiling deluge lay on the ground amongst the cooling water, making small sobbing noises as their bodies shut down from the unendurable agony. Several were unhurt judging by their quick, but careful descent down the steps.

"Stephanie, now!"

In the courtyard, the archers nocked their arrows. The teacher took the lead, raising the bow to forty-five degrees at the same time as drawing the bowstring. Everyone complied silently, without the shouted orders. They wanted to give the brutes no warning. The twang of multiple releases rebounded from the concave tower walls. Denise craned her neck as the colourful arrows soared overhead like a flock of thin, brightly coloured birds.

"Look out!" shouted the hidden sniper.

Too late.

Instead of heeding the warning, human nature ensured that people almost always had to look at the *what*. To see the danger they were trying to avoid, and why. This time was no different. Only two of the projectiles found their target, which was fortuitous in itself considering Stephanie and her team were firing blind. The living, breathing men weren't immune to the damage in the same way as the zombies during the first attack with Kurt. One struck a thigh, and the second a shoulder, with the others rattling harmlessly against the stonework. Pierced by the shafts, the wounds were bad, if not life threatening. The real damage came from the momentary paralysis of shock from the impact, and the inevitable loss of balance. Tumbling backwards, two bodies became ten. Bones broke, skulls cracked, men howled in torment.

Denise held up a hand, then dropped it. A second volley of arrows whistled past. The prisoners at the foot of the steps would have been incapable of avoiding the arrows, but the angle was off anyway. In some small way, she was relieved as the tips plinked harmlessly against the cold stone. The scale of suffering meted out in the past two minutes was on a scale akin to war. Stephanie waited for another signal. Denise waved her off and the archers lowered their weapons. Cradling a grenade, she considered tossing it down the chute or down the steps to finish the job. Realising she didn't have the heart to do it, she slipped the ball back into a pocket.

"We did it," said Gloria.

"We did," replied Denise. "We really did."

Gloria spoke of victory. Denise of something else. Something intangible. Something dark, and impossible to undo. A stain, forever on her soul.

Below, men whined for their mothers.

CHAPTER 37

"What is there to talk about? I've got nothing else to say."

George motioned for her to join him at the newly lit fire. With the air temperature in the room barely above freezing, the comforting zone of warmth was hard to resist. Why stand defiantly in discomfort when her point had already been made. Glowering, she approached the hiss and crackle of the fire. The furniture had been brushed down, which only served to smear the ash and soot into the upholstery. Ignoring the grime, she sat down and faced him.

He eyed her with amusement.

"I know you think we're monsters, and we are. Neither Fred or myself are innocent. We've stolen. We've raped. We've murdered."

"What do you want? A chufty badge? A fucking gold star to stick to your special criminal chart?"

"A little respect for what we could do to you," George growled, "but haven't. Yet."

"Until your brother gets back, that is."

258

"Fred will do as he's told. You have my word."

"Is this a *'comply with my demands and we'll be oh so reasonable and treat you well'* speech? If so, save your breath. There's nothing you can do to make me give up my friends and those children."

"You must know that we'll get them eventually?"

"Not a chance."

"We know they have no food. We caught your friends trying to sneak it up there."

"So what?"

"So they'll starve," George replied, wondering if the crazed woman was the full ticket.

"They'll be three or four days ahead of you, that's all. Have you seen how little we have? And none of you look like the type to accept rationing. But you'll be dead long before they starve, anyway."

"And how do you figure that?"

"Because you have no water, my scouse friend," she laughed.

"What? That's bollocks. And even if it wasn't, they'll be dehydrated too."

"Wrong again! They're trapped in the only part of the whole castle that has water. There's a pretty little well in the watchtower, filled to the brim with glorious H2O."

"There's bound to be stuff in tanks and pipes."

"All gone!"

"It'll rain."

"Not a drop for days. Are you willing to risk your life on British weather?"

"I don't believe you."

"It doesn't matter what you believe. When they're suffering from terrible stomach cramps in four days' time, we'll all be dead."

"I'll just send a few boys out to bring back some bottles."

"Knowing how many zombies are out there, good luck getting volunteers. And that doesn't include them dodging bullets when Kurt and my friends get back. If they don't get eaten, they'll get shot or caught."

"A few executions might focus their mind," replied George. He was fast losing patience and considering letting Fred loose on the woman. Their plan had been formed out of desperation. South would have taken them towards the coastal habitations. Scouting teams had given up on them long ago. They were crawling with the dead. East would have seen them enter the territory of Mrs Hampton and the gypsies. The west was uncharted, but they knew about the castle. They also knew it was lightly defended thanks to Pesci's reconnaissance. It was a crying shame Craig sacrificed the prisoner on the doomed gate crashing. Pesci was a nutter, with barely any human emotions, but he was dependable.

"If you try that, you know full well Kurt will storm this place. We *know* the castle far better than you ever will."

"You think a dozen people on foot would stand a chance? Don't be fucking ridiculous."

They don't know about the soldiers, Sarah realised. Whatever route had brought them to the castle, it hadn't been the main roads. Before he could pick up on her surprise, she masked it with a laugh. "You don't know my people. Our dozen would cut through your fifty in a heartbeat."

"More like eighty, darlin'." George looked at the grenade shredded men, then considered those lost at the wall. "Ok, closer to seventy. You fuckers really did a number on us."

"And that was without our best fighters." She let the words hang in the air. The Liverpudlian was obviously a violent and dangerous man with a history checkered with offences. In a world with laws, it would elevate him among the general population and his peers. In a world where only warriors survived, he was average at best. Considering his months of being locked away, Sarah would even go so far as to say he was below average. Weak, even. The prison had insulated them from the hell that was southern England.

"You can still salvage this situation," she offered.

"And how would we do that?"

"Give up and leave. As long as you behave, I might even see if we can help you secure another home. On the obvious understanding that we never cross paths again."

"That's not going to happen. I think we'll be nice and comfortable here for quite a while."

Sarah sat back and folded her arms. "Then we're done here. Do what you want, but know that this is going to end badly for you. You have no idea what's coming."

"A warm meal and comfy bed is all that's coming, sweetheart."

Sarah said no more, fixing him with her steely gaze.

George looked away first.

CHAPTER 38

"You've murdered my friends!" Fred bellowed. He probed gingerly at his face and scalp. The pus inside the growing blisters gave under the pressure, feeling like a roll of human bubble wrap. Except for the pain. It was like a second, pliant skin covered his face and upper body. One that was made of fire.

"We didn't start this!" called the gash.

Cowering within the safety of the passage, he could just about see up to the gatehouse of the watchtower. Steam from the scalding water was gone, the bitterly cold stone leeching the heat. In an hour, it would be an icy death-trap. Bodies lay where they had fallen, burned far worse than he himself. A few of his men, injured but alive, watched the murder holes with dread, awaiting the torrent that would finish them off. Arrows littered the steps, a warning of what awaited them if they should try and scramble for the safety of the castle.

Those amongst the pile of broken men at the foot of the stairs who could move, had done so. The rest lay dead.

Benny's neck was twisted at a funny angle. The arrow in Archie's shoulder had pierced an artery and he'd bled out. Fitzy's skull was laid open, the grey brain slowly leaking from the ruptured cavity.

"What now?" shouted Fred.

The watchtower was silent.

"I said, what now?"

"Are you going to attack again?" replied the gash.

"With what?" Fred shouted, defeated. "You've done in half my men."

"And I repeat, we didn't start this!"

"You've certainly finished it," whispered Fred. How could things go to shit so quickly? A matter of hours ago they had controlled the prison and everyone in it. Then the Gypsies decided retribution was more important than diplomacy. Against all odds, the castle had fallen, but Fred had never imagined in a million years the defenders would be so tenacious. Undone by a suicidal pensioner and a few gallons of water. Unbelievable. Fred felt dead on his feet, a combination of the pain and the series of crushing defeats.

"Is everyone still alive down there?" called the woman. Fred no longer thought of her in the previous derogatory terms. She'd fucked him as hard as anyone he'd ever raped.

"They're all ok, yeah," he replied.

"Including Christina?"

"Who's Christina?"

"Pretty blonde lady. The doctor."

"I think so!"

"You *think*? You'd better be damned certain!"

Fred thought quickly, scanning the faces in his memory. She was one of the few who weren't in the least afraid of their assault.

"She's fine! I'm sure."

"Then you have my permission to get your wounded clear, but in the meantime you need to put your friends down before they rise again."

"Are you kidding? As soon as I set foot outside this passage, you'll shoot us full of arrows. Or you'll wait until we're up there under cover and you'll boil us alive again."

"You have my word, you'll be safe."

"And your word is worth what?"

"More than yours, Fred. Far more."

"Fuck!" Fred grumbled.

"Time's running out! Get them quickly and I know she'll help you as best she can. We don't have much medicine, but it wouldn't be right if we didn't try. But you've got to hurry."

"What do we do, boss?" groaned Travis, the one with a colourful insert in his upper thigh and a newly shattered arm from the fall.

"They're done for. Fuck 'em."

"You can't mean that," he said, grimacing through the wave of pain.

The others looked on with barely concealed hatred.

"If you want to risk your arses, go ahead. I'm going to find George and tell him what happened."

"Tell him how you fucked up, you mean?" sneered one of the prisoners.

Twenty four hours ago, it would've meant a savage beating or worse. Probably death. Fred met his eyes, and then looked away. They knew he was weak, diminished, losing his grip on power. Hawk-like eyes watched as he slinked past, weighing their options, considering their own rump on the throne.

It's over, he thought, miserably.

Travis watched as his former wing boss skulked away. His former friend. All respect was now lost, and he could tell by the faces that the other inmates felt the same. Holding out his good arm, Joey C moved to help him stand. Hopping to the archway, the jarring landings sent lances of agony through his arm and pierced leg.

"Did you mean what you said?" he called.

"Who's that? Where's Fred?"

"Fred's gone. I'm Travis, one of the ones you shot," he replied, no malice in the words.

"Are you a rapist too, Travis? Were you looking forward to the *ripe children*?"

"My mum would cut my dick off if I ever mistreated a lady like that, much less a child," he groaned. The pain was increasing by the second.

A long silence followed and he assumed their conversation was over.

"Travis?"

"Yeah?"

"I'm going to trust you. You'll need to be even quicker than that putz, Fred. Your friends will be coming back any moment now."

Travis looked at the dead bodies at the foot of the huge steps. The stone had done for some of them, caving in skulls as they fell. Groans from above could be heard, but it was hard to tell if they were the wounded or newly risen.

"I don't think we have time!" he called.

"No, you don't!" Denise cried, frantically. "Tell your gunman to back off and we can save your injured friends!"

"Whoever's got the rifle, hold your fire!" Travis yelled.

No answer was forthcoming. He could hear the curses from the lady above.

"If he shoots me, I'm going to be mighty pissed. You hear me?"

"I hear you," Travis replied. "Don't shoot! She's trying to help."

He could almost hear the mind of the shooter. *After she killed us in the first place, why shouldn't I fire?.*

The moans below the gatehouse turned to a weak cry of pain. Whoever was being eaten was in so much agony, they barely registered the slight increase to their suffering.

The gates swung open, and a pair of women moved swiftly towards the newly reanimated zombie, stabbing him in the brain. The wounded prisoner who had been bitten was gently dispatched as well.

Travis waited for the crack of rifle fire, but nothing came. Either the man had fled, or he was watching their act of mercy and feeling as conflicted as Travis.

They stepped between the fallen, carrying out triage. Eight more times he heard the faint crunch of knife piercing through skull.

"Ok, that's all of them. You have seven men who need medical attention. They're hurt bad, but they might pull through. I suggest that you keep a close watch on them, and I mean don't take your eye off them for one second. We had an outbreak of a single zombie and it cost us."

He caught a fleeting glimpse of them as they disappeared back into the watchtower before the gates slammed shut.

"You won't hurt us anymore?"

"I told your idiot boss, Fred. We didn't start this. We didn't want this. Do you think I'd have risked catching a bullet if I wasn't on the level?"

"You can trust us, dear," said another lady.

"Ok, we're coming up."

Travis nodded to the others to proceed. For a moment, it appeared they would ignore the order. One quenching with boiling water was enough to fracture the hardiest spirit. Their reflections turned to the wounded at the top of the steps and, with some reluctance, they started to climb. Faces peered skyward, expecting to see the incoming flash of colour that would precede their impalement. The skies remained clear. Reaching the edge of the gatehouse, the portcullis slot and murder holes still

266

dripped with the now chilled water. It was all too easy to imagine stepping beneath the grey stone and hearing the rush of impending doom. Watching in dread fascination as the clear, innocent looking water poured forth. The memory of that steaming torrent would haunt what short time they had left. Even if time was kind, and memory faded, mirrors would be a constant reminder of their undoing. The scars impossible to erase.

"Hurry! Don't forget to watch them. If they go limp, check for a pulse."

The echoing warning carried down the chutes and portcullis housing, making the men jump in surprise.

"Don't try anything!" one of the men called back, his voice shrill.

"For the hundredth time, you started this!"

"Well, ok. But please don't do anything," he replied.

"We won't need to," chuckled the hidden lady.

"What do you mean?"

"Hear that?"

Over the moans, the rumble of powerful engines steadily grew.

"What's that?"

"Our friends. It might be time to consider surrendering before they get here," she laughed.

"Fuck that! This is our place now!" he yelled, manhandling his friends onto their feet.

He tried to ignore the dead faces. He tried to ignore the slick of crimson that slowly washed away the water. He tried to ignore the pain of the burns up his left arm and shoulder. He tried to ignore the throaty roar of the approaching fighters.

He failed.

CHAPTER 39

"Are you ready for the last push, mate?" Holbeck asked Kurt.

Arundel Castle loomed in the distance, just over the bridge. A quarter mile of looping through the cobbled streets and they would be at the breach in the hedgerows. Then they would need to work out how on earth to get the people over the walls. None of them would have the strength to climb, that was a certainty. Rope harnesses and brute strength would be the order of the day. Half of them were asleep, being cradled by the others. Kurt marvelled at how they'd managed to drift off with all the bumping and noise. After considering their previous situation, it might have been the first time in months they had actually felt safe enough to let their guard down. It didn't seem so outlandish in hindsight.

"Kurt?" Holbeck pushed.

The promise of a steaming mug of tea beckoned.

"Let's do it. Move slowly so we don't get bogged down. Don't use the cannons unless absolutely necessary.

We don't want the whole town to come and see what all the fuss is about."

"And if we get overwhelmed, we go to plan B?" asked the sergeant.

"Yeah. Get them to safety, and we'll fall back to the pub to the south. If they follow us, we'll just keep circling until you can swing back and get us."

"Roger," said Holbeck, pulling the passenger door partly closed, leaving enough of an opening for communication.

"Everyone ready?" Kurt called to the melee fighters. Jodi and Peter took the lead, and the others, though tired, fell in behind and prepared.

Kurt banged on the armour with his war pick, and Carpenter rumbled forward, skirting the vehicles knocked aside during the lorry assault.

"It's a bit quiet," said Kurt.

"They might've followed us and got lost?" suggested Holbeck, leaning forward to get a better view of the streets.

When they had rolled out, the streets were teeming with rotters. Only a quarter as many remained, if that. The battle they had been expecting on the journey home was going to be a boring affair following the prison.

"I doubt it. We'd have crossed their path on the way back."

"Lucky then? At least we don't have to fight to keep those poor people on top out of harm's way."

"Maybe..."

The convoy wormed its way through the scattered dead, passing the ancient homes of Arundel. All tall chimneys and squat doors. The latticed windows on most ground floors were broken in. All eyes turned to the Black Dog pub and hotel. Soldiers and recent captives both found themselves yearning for a sneaky pint and a comfy stool. Unfortunately, the current proprietor and patrons would be an unwelcoming bunch. Far more interested in cannibalism than customer service.

Kurt and the others formed a ring of steel around the Warthogs. The undead attacked in dribs and drabs, low numbers that were easily dealt with. Sensing they were in danger again, the freed captives were all awake, watching the fighters below. Having endured physical and emotional torture beyond imagining, each blow of Kurt's war pick chipped away at their fear. They were a long way from coming to terms with their ordeal, but knowing good still existed was like sunlight searing away the fog of their despair.

By the time the fighters were navigating the crushed brush to the south of the castle grounds, Kurt and the others were dripping with blood and gore once more. The thought of a warm bath was closely beating the hot cuppa.

"This isn't right," said Kurt, drawing the group to a stop.

Hundreds of the dead had taken up position by the gore smeared walls where they had exited. No faces peered down from above, waiting for their return. The throaty grumble of the Warthogs could be heard from a mile away on the southern tower. Someone should have been on watch. The braziers along the wall were dead, only the dying embers left glowing as the wind flowed past. The ropes were missing too.

"Where is everyone?"

Kurt's anger was dampened by an inkling that things were completely off.

"What brought the zombies round here from the town?" asked Peter. "They should have followed us, if anything."

"Kurt, what's your gut?" asked Holbeck.

"This is all wrong. We loop around to the north and try the second way in."

"What about them?" Holbeck nodded at the gathered horde.

"If we double back, we can take the Duke's access road to the northern gate we sealed. It'll screen us and the noise from our rotting friends over there."

Carefully exiting back onto the main road, the remnants of Arundel town were trying to give chase, but as with all major swarms, the most damaged got left behind. They crawled and slopped, making little progress in their pursuit. Passing through the dead security gates, the unpowered steel screeched as the APCs forced their way through. Kurt turned back, closing them up and wrapping a short length of cord thrown by Eldridge around the struts. With enough weight brought to bear it would give way, but they would hopefully be safe and warm by that time.

"Kurt, can you climb up here quickly?" asked Eldridge.

Her tone and demeanour told Kurt that his hunch was one hundred percent correct. The dread washed over her face as he hoisted himself carefully atop the slowly moving Warthog.

"See that?" she pointed.

Hanging on to the turret shield, he followed her finger.

"Is that where I think it is?"

Kurt's heart started to palpitate. Eldridge saw him start to sway, and reached out just in time to stop him falling as he dropped to his knees.

"What was that?" called Ewington from the driver's seat.

"It was Kurt. Keep going," she shouted down. "Sarge, be aware we've got a problem. Be on alert."

The radio came alive at once. "What problem. Be more specific."

Kurt was slumped against the turret, unable to look away, even when the treeline became choked and he couldn't see. Still, he saw. The image painted indelibly on his retinas.

"The windows of the big hall we were in are all blown out. I only noticed because most of the stained glass is gone, along with all the colour."

"What do you mean blown out?"

"Take a look, Sarge," replied Eldridge.

271

Petermann dropped through the turret hatch and Holbeck appeared in his place. Scanning the main castle over the wall, he quickly found the hall. The glint of glass was gone, only the darkness of the room beyond was now visible.

"What the hell did that? Do you think they had an accident with the ammunition?"

"I can't see it, Sarge. They don't seem daft enough to play with the grenades or mortar rounds."

"We aren't," said Kurt, weakly.

"What's going on?" asked Matt, overhearing the exchange.

"Explosion in your hall," said Holbeck.

"The Gypsies?"

"What about them?" asked Peter. "You ok, mate?" He saw Kurt slumped against the turret, white as a ghost.

Everyone had left their positions and walked alongside the second Warthog. Holbeck swapped places with Petermann again, before jumping from the APC.

"I don't like this one bit. Is there anywhere we can stow the civilians while we get a better lay of the land?"

"The canal boat is just through those trees," offered Jodi.

"Yeah, we can fit everyone. Just about," said Peter. "It'll be a bit of a squeeze."

"Ok, Jodi, was it?" Holbeck asked.

"Yes, Sergeant."

"Would you be able to take your team and see these folks to safety without our help? I don't want to waste any time."

"Kurt, careful," gasped Eldridge as he stood on unsteady legs.

"I'm ok," he lied. He'd left his wife alone, thinking she was safe behind the walls. Whatever was going on, she was in grave danger, he could just feel it. He seemed to slide down the armour as if made of jelly.

Jodi and Peter opened each of the rear hatches on the transport sections, urging the people to exit and follow.

Several were lapsing back into catatonia, but Jason and some of the others helped and in less than a minute a small procession was heading away from the vehicles. Louise and Jodi hesitated momentarily, desperate to know what was happening inside their home. Kurt waved them away.

"Shall I go with them, just in case?" asked Joan. "I don't like the idea of them being armed with only bats and a bad attitude."

Holbeck agreed.

"They'll be fine, mate, I know it," declared Peter, squeezing Kurt's shoulder.

"We'll see," he replied, as if any confidence on his part would trigger some cruel god to steal them away out of spite.

"Quick magazine check and we move. Eldridge, Petermann, you keep your eyes on the wall at all times."

"Aye, Sarge." The turrets whined as the long, dark barrels of the HMG lined up with the ramparts.

The soldiers had spent a portion of the journey injecting rounds into the empty magazines. Each combat vest had five which were fully replenished, plus the one in their rifle. They were as prepared as they could be.

"Kurt, jump in my seat. Let's see what's going on."

Kurt floated across the ground, weightless. It was as if it was all a bad dream, and any moment he would wake to Sarah's gentle rapping on his locked bedroom door.

Holbeck climbed aboard and slammed the door, startling Kurt.

This was no dream.

The convoy rumbled on, deeper into the waking nightmare.

CHAPTER 40

"What the hell happened to you?" George blurted when Fred entered the great hall.

The recently returned castle prisoners grimaced at his awful wounds as he glowered at them. Livid blisters were only getting worse as the minutes passed. Fred wanted to scratch at the fierce burning, but he would only end up peeling the top layers of skin from his entire upper body.

"*Her* people happened to me!" he snarled, making straight for Sarah.

"Leave her be!" George warned, stepping between them and offering a bottle of gin in consolation. "I said, what happened?"

"We tried to take the tower. The bitches killed twenty of us, probably more by now."

Fred swigged from the bottle until George yanked it from his grasp, chipping one of his front teeth.

"What the fuck are you talking about?" roared George. "I told you to lock the people away, not attack!"

"I made a call." Fred tried to grab for the bottle, missed, and sulkily probed at his damaged tooth instead.

"You *made a call*?"

"Yeah."

"And how did that turn out?" George growled through gritted, undamaged teeth.

"Not too well by the sounds of it," snorted Sarah.

George shot her a glance that was part warning, part pleading.

"We... lost... twenty... men," Fred repeated snidely.

"We already lost three fucking hundred, you cunt!" George drew back his massive fist and Fred tried his best not to shy away. The anger bled out in an instant when he realised the implication. "Why? We were already weak, and you've made us weaker."

"If this group can hold the castle, we don't need everyone. We've still got just as many people."

"It isn't just *this* group. Their fighters are at the prison, trying to help," George lied. "These are the women, and the children. And look what *they've* done to us. Imagine what happens when the men get back."

"Whoa, hold on there Mr Sexist." Sarah couldn't help herself.

George raised his hands in supplication. "I know you women are fighters too. And so do a great deal of my dead men by the look of it. It wasn't meant like it came out."

Fred was growing red with rage. "Why the fuck are you explaining yourself to that gash? I think..."

"Because that gash and her friends have fucked us!" George rounded on him. "Don't you see?"

"No, I don't see," Fred muttered.

"Ok, brother of mine, tell me this. Did you send the nobodies to attack the tower? The people who don't matter a fuck in the big scheme of things? You didn't send the hardcases in, did you? Tell me!"

Fred's face drained of colour.

"You, absolute, fucking, bell end." George emphasised the insult with pauses as he slumped back into a deep, leather chair. He was a beaten man, that much was obvious. He turned away from his pale sibling to stare at the flames, seeing their future burn away as surely as the pages of the expensive book which sat atop the crackling logs.

"George, we can salvage this," Fred tried to say, kneeling by George's side. The wounded started to filter into the room, ending the nonstarter conversation before it began. George was away somewhere else at the moment.

The groans and cries of the blistered and broken echoed weirdly in the hall from the damaged windows. The other prisoners shied away, trying to ignore the damage. Sarah stood up and took George by his meaty paw.

"Help me get these chairs out of the way. Your people are going to need the warmth for the shock."

"Ok, Sarah," he said absently, allowing himself to be led away.

"Where's Christina?" begged one of the men as he hobbled in with an arrow sticking out of his leg. "Where's the doctor?"

Fred marched towards the injured. "Travis, what the fuck are you doing?"

"What you should've done, Fred. Help our friends."

The burly scouse prisoner took a menacing step towards the limping figure, but four uninjured bruisers interceded. The look on their faces told him if he made a move he was going to be crippled.

"Doc?" Travis pleaded, searching the room.

Sarah met the hidden doctor's eyes and understating passed between them. Christina stood up from her place among the castle captives, and carefully stepped over the crouching forms.

"Please, help us," he begged.

She moved towards the arrow, but he gently shooed her away with his unbroken arm. "No, these guys need help first. I'll be fine."

She moved from man to man, inspecting the damage. "These are deep dermal burns. There's no way I can guarantee their treatment will work with what I have here," she said, honestly.

"Can you do what you can? If you're desperate for medicines and stuff, I know some of us will go out and get it."

Most of the men looked away, but a stoic few nodded grimly.

"We're going to need beds, and water. Lots of water. And as many towels as you can find. And any clingfilm or plastic wrap. We need to stop them getting infected."

"And how the fuck do we get water when it's all locked away in your tower?"

Sarah ignored Fred's outburst and spoke directly to the men who had dragged the wounded back to safety. "Tell Denise that we need as much water as she can provide. If she argues, come and get me and I'll confirm it."

"They'll open the gates to us?" asked one of the prisoners.

"Not a chance," replied Sarah, tossing a small spool of washing line cord they had left over from the criss-cross of clothes drying wire in the hallways. "They can lower it to you."

"It'll take too long," said Travis, trying to put a brave face on his injury.

"It's all you'll get," Sarah replied, busying herself by moving cots closer to the fire, but not close enough that Christina warned her off. They needed to be warm, not hot.

When ten were set up in a neat semi-circle, she quickly moved to the second extinguished fire. Hastily piling some kindling atop some old paper, she struck a match and lit the fire. As she knelt, blowing on the flickering flame, a man came running into the hall.

"We've got company! It's the fucking army!"

"The what?" demanded George, returning from the fugue state.

"The army. They've got machine guns on the tanks. Or maybe they aren't tanks, but they're definitely army."

"Why didn't you tell me?" George asked, angry and disappointed.

"You didn't ask nicely," Sarah replied, smiling menacingly.

Two of the prisoners seized her, but without the earlier force. George led the way, leaving Fred in charge of a room in which both sides increasingly hated his guts.

CHAPTER 41

"What the hell?" asked Holbeck as he spied a ladder hastily disappearing over the wall.

"Did you see it too?" said Kurt.

"There are men up there, Sarge," said Petermann, the HMG trained on their position.

"Our men?" asked Kurt. It was a silly question. The soldiers had little time for introductions, much less an opportunity to memorise the faces of the castle dwellers.

"No idea," Petermann confirmed Kurt's suspicion.

"There are bodies," Carpenter pointed out.

Two forms lay still at the base of the wall as a handful of zombies feasted.

"Take them out," ordered Holbeck.

Petermann opened fire and the crouched figures exploded. Nothing was left of the meal except green and red smears. The parts that still twitched were no threat.

"Carpenter, pull up a good distance away from the wall. I want to see what's going on before we approach."

"Roger, Sarge," she replied, steering away from the fortress.

279

A bullet ricocheted from Petermann's turret shield, whining as it rocketed away. Another crack of a gunshot followed, completely missing.

"Petermann, report!"

"The people on the wall are firing. Shall I engage?"

"Give them a short burst. Make them think twice before trying it again," replied Holbeck.

Petermann fired off three bursts, blowing hefty chunks from the thousand-year-old limestone. The heavy dudda, dudda, dudda, of the gunfire carried across the surrounding fields, summoning anything within earshot. Time was now against them.

"Hold your fire!" cried a voice from the wall.

Holbeck pulled Petermann back into the vehicle and climbed through the turret hatch.

"You fired on us! Identify yourself!"

"I'm George Fowler, and the castle's now mine!"

Holbeck couldn't believe what he was hearing. "You were at the prison?"

"We were. And now we're here."

Kurt opened the door and jumped from the Warthog.

"Kurt, get the hell back inside!" shouted Holbeck.

Kurt ignored the order, marching towards the wall.

"Where are my family?"

"They're safe. How long they stay that way is up to you."

"I want to see them or I'll bring this whole fucking place down on your heads!" Kurt yelled. The fear for his family's wellbeing filled him with a white hot rage.

"Want me to shoot him, boss?" asked another man.

"No!" George snapped. His own fear was evident in the words.

Something had happened inside to fill the convict with doubt. The explosion?

"Where are my fucking family?" Kurt screamed.

"Kurt, I'm here," called Sarah. "We're ok."

"What happened?"

"They took us by surprise. I'm so sorry."

"What about the Baron's Hall? What happened."

Sarah began to talk but her words were instantly muffled by a hand.

"One of your old timers really did a number on us," replied George. "Now you've seen your wife, you can leave. If not, I start killing your people one by one, starting with her."

The words lacked conviction. Considering their strong position, Kurt expected unassailable arrogance and contempt. George was... fearful.

"Let my family and friends go, and I promise I won't kill you," Kurt replied with his own offer.

"Did you not fucking hear me? Get the fuck out of here before I start slitting throats!"

Sarah appeared between the battlements, a man hiding behind her with a knife to her soft neck. A trickle of blood ran from the blade, incensing Kurt. He ran for the wall, withdrawing his war pick and hammer. Spinning the claw hammer around, he slammed the teeth into the mortar, beginning to ascend like a climber with an ice axe.

"Get down or she dies!" George shouted from above.

Kurt climbed.

A rifle appeared over the wall. The barrel blazed, the bullet missing Kurt by several feet. Petermann fired at the man, using the large calibre bullets as a warning rather than with lethal intent because of Sarah's proximity. It worked and he ducked back out of sight.

Kurt climbed.

"Fuck! Will you tell him to behave!" George pleaded.

"Kurt, you can't make it. Please climb down," said Sarah, calmly.

Hanging from the embedded weapons, toes wedged in any nook he could find, Kurt hesitated ten feet from the ground. The soldiers looked on in awe. The prisoners down in trepidation. The man was a lunatic.

"Babe?" said Kurt.

"Please, love. Don't do anything silly," replied Sarah, filled with love.

Pushing away at the same time as he pulled the weapons, Kurt dropped back to the blood-soaked mud. He felt his weakened ankle twist painfully, but stayed upright.

"Let them go, and you can leave in peace," he warned.

"You're not in position to be making demands, Kurt. Just get the fuck out of here, and no one will get hurt."

"Is that what you told the people you had locked away in the prison?"

George faltered, unable to reply.

"If you harm one hair on their heads, I'll torture each and every one of you to death. It'll last days. If you... touch them, I'll rape you to death with red hot pokers. You'll beg for the Hell I'll send you to."

"Kurt, we need to go. We've got no move here," whispered Holbeck who had snuck up behind him.

"Please, just go," called George, his voice tremulous. Kurt's words had gotten through.

"I'll see you soon, babe, I promise. Tell everyone to stay strong," said Kurt as he allowed Holbeck to lead him back to the APC.

"We've got one hell of a problem, Kurt. We can't just sit and wait on the canal boat with the civilians. Our whole plan relies on having the castle as a defensive position while we attack the horde moving on our troops in The Chilterns. That's all shot to shit now."

"There's a way in that they might not know about. An escape passage that takes you into the Duke's suite."

"Sir! Look!" cried Petermann.

Holbeck and Kurt's heads snapped back to the castle. A solitary arrow peaked in the air, the black ribbon fluttering from the shaft as it fell back to earth. A second followed.

"Where did it come from?" Kurt demanded.

"That massive round building in the middle of the grounds," Petermann replied, pointing.

"The watchtower. Some of them must be hiding inside."

"If we can get close enough, we might be able to infiltrate the castle from there too. Attack from two angles."

"Possibly. But before we decide, we can wait until dark, sneak up the hill, and get some intel from the tower. We need to know what's going on inside."

"Agreed. Until then, we need to find a safe place for our new friends. Any suggestions?"

Kurt grunted, the rage at losing his home tamped for now. "How about the prison?"

CHAPTER 42

"Get down!" ordered Jonesy, coming to the fence line of Arundel Castle.

"What's up?" DB didn't have the same angle through the vegetation. All he could see was an emerald wall of evergreen shrubs.

"Strangers on the wall. At least five by my count."

DB squeezed through and looked out at the northern wall. Men paced back and forth, highly agitated by the look of it. The braziers were working overtime, the flames soaring.

"What's going on?" demanded Sam.

"We've got trouble. Wait here while we go check it out."

"No, we're coming with you. If our people are in danger, we want to fight."

He tried to put a brave face on it, but Sam was terrified for his friends and family.

DB held them back, cocking his head. "Wait, can you hear that?"

Jonesy listened over the pounding of his heart. "Talking?"

"More like shouting," said Winston.

"It's coming from over by the river," confirmed DB.

"The canal boat!" Braiden exclaimed.

The five moved unseen through the gloom, utilising cover and shadows where available. They emerged into the open field than ran along the River Arun, and spied the Warthogs immediately. The drivers had angled them to provide some cover to the gangplank of the stranded vessel. Without being able to get the Warthogs too close to the bank in case they collapsed, there were too many openings. Slowly, it was coming under siege from the steady procession of undead leaving the town and castle walls.

"They can't hold them off forever. Let's get moving!"

Holbeck's frustrated answer to an unheard question carried over the brown mud. "We don't have a choice! Open fire!"

Eldridge and Petermann strafed the incoming tide of grey filth with the HMGs, cutting through them like a knife through butter. Harkiss, Dougal, Carpenter, and MacLeod were on one knee atop the Warthogs, picking their shots to clean up the remaining cadavers. It was a no win situation. For each bullet fired, two more zombies came. Their numbers were too great to go hand to hand, and Kurt hovered impotently below the gunners with the others, war pick ready.

"Kurt, it's the boys!" Holbeck shouted over the chatter of fire.

Ignoring the dead, Kurt left cover and sprinted over, pulling all three teenagers into a fierce embrace. "I'm going to kill you, you little bastards!"

"It's good to see you too, Dad," said Braiden, his voice muffled by Kurt's fresh coat. The gore splattered clothing of their earlier endeavours was safely buried nearby.

"Don't cut me. I don't want to be a monk," moaned Winston.

"What's going on?" asked DB.

"Why are you out here?" continued Jonesy.

"Where's Mum?" asked Sam.

Kurt led them quickly back to the temporary safety of the APC position. "The Fowlers have taken over. The fuckers attacked while we were freeing the people at the prison."

"Holy shit," gasped Jonesy.

"What's the plan?" asked DB.

"We don't have one at the moment. We could retake the castle by force, but that might get our people killed. We could sneak in using the escape tunnels, but we've got dozens of weak and dazed people hiding in the boat. We need to get them safe first, or this whole clusterfuck will have been for nothing."

"Ideas?" Holbeck called down from his vantage point.

"Maybe, but I'm not sure Ian will like it," said Jonesy.

"Needs must, brother. We can't stay here," replied DB.

Kurt frowned at the pair. "Who's Ian?"

"A friend. Someone who may be able to shelter us for a bit," said Braiden.

DB agreed enthusiastically. "We can tell you all about it on the way, but you need to get ready to move. It's about four miles away."

"What about Mum?" asked Sam, a child once more.

"She'll be fine. I get the feeling the prisoners are scared of her."

"Really?" asked Jonesy.

"Call it a hunch," replied Kurt.

"Sarge?"

Holbeck looked at Jonesy. "Do it. We're running out of options."

Jason and Sally led the terrified captives back to the vehicles. They kept looking at the castle, and Kurt's heart broke for them. To get so close to a reunion with their daughter, only to have it cruelly snatched away was another blow they didn't deserve. Jason had confided in Kurt that he was relieved in some ways. At least Clarissa was safe inside.

286

Surrounded by villains, yes, but still secure in an impregnable fortress. Their time would come.

Kurt and the others looked one last time at their fallen home. Unfamiliar faces, small and indistinguishable, stared back. Raising a finger, he pointed at each and every one over the approaching dead. It said, *your time is coming.* He couldn't read their reaction, but none of the men responded. Perhaps they just hadn't seen him. He doubted that was the case. They were afraid, and rightly so.

"Roll out!" called Holbeck.

They were on the move again. Forced from their home... again. Kurt clenched his war pick hard enough to hurt.

CHAPTER 43

Captain Haywood looked over the latest logistics reports. Regular food was running low, but the warehouse contained enough MREs to last several years at current personnel levels. Ammunition was dangerously low and he made a mental note to request additional support from Dauntless on the next run. Functional vehicles were, thankfully, in abundance. Qualified drivers were far harder to come by. The Challenger tanks had only one active crew on the barracks. In normal times, it would be a sensible use of resources to train three more. But these weren't normal times. In less than two weeks, a sizeable portion of the London horde would be hitting the front line of the Chiltern fortification. It would crumble in hours.

Haywood turned his face up to the ceiling, picturing the clear sky beyond. "If you're up there and you're listening, please give us some help. Your creations are hanging on by a thread." Letting out a weary sigh, he returned his attention to the written sheets covered in numbers.

Prayer used to bring peace to his troubled mind. He was always cautious about spreading the good word unbidden, however. Keeping faith with God was a private, and deeply personal thing. His appeals to The Almighty seemed to carry weight before the apocalypse. Sending patrols out into the Helmand Province was always fraught with danger. As they rolled out through the gates, he would beg for their safe return. A lack of fatalities during the missions brought him perilously close to hubris. *Pride goeth before destruction, and an haughty spirit before a fall*, he would remind himself in the base chaplain's stern voice. Their safety was in His hands, not Haywood's. Sadly, He seemed to have gone AWOL in the past few weeks. If He was still up there, He wasn't listening any more.

Three knocks came through the office door.

"Come."

Private Morrow entered, eyes cast downward.

The aggravating trait irked Haywood and he snapped at the soldier. "What is it, Private?"

"I've got the latest video for you to look over, sir," he replied, quietly.

Haywood chided himself for the sour tone in his voice; Morrow wasn't responsible for his current malaise. "I'm sorry, Private. I've got a lot on my mind, that's all."

"No need to apologise, sir. Everyone on base is relying on you. Leadership is tough."

Haywood didn't want to explain the command was relatively straightforward. His wavering faith on the other hand? "Thank you, Morrow. I'll check them over once I'm done with these reports."

"Sir, if I may? You might want to look at the footage right away."

Laying the papers aside, he looked up at the pale faced man. "I take it from your expression it isn't good news?"

"Yes and no, sir."

"Could you be any more ambiguous?"

"Probably, sir," Morrow replied, uneasily.

The dread emanating from the private was infectious and Haywood caught himself before offering a prayer. What on earth could be worse than the impending assault?

"Lead on, Private. Let's see what's got your knickers in a twist."

Morrow's face grew a paler shade of white as he turned away. Haywood crossed himself despite his misgivings.

"How's morale holding up?" asked the captain, wishing to take his mind off the chilly encounter.

"There are good days and bad days, sir," Morrow replied. "Baxter is mentioned less each day."

"That's good to know. I was concerned his brutality might have a lasting effect on the barracks."

"You've given us hope, sir. Everyone's jacked to head out and kick some arse."

"You don't seem quite so eager if I may say so, Private."

"Oh, I am, believe me, sir."

Nothing more was mentioned as they made their way down the halls towards the observation suite. Soldiers saluted as they passed and Haywood could see the pent up tension in their faces. Their friends were in danger and they needed a fight. It would provide some catharsis against the repressed guilt they felt. How hard it must have been to watch helplessly from their island as the world died. Forbidden to leave. Forbidden to help. Listening to the screams from the surrounding towns until they faded to utter silence. Morrow's demeanour hinted that the fight to come may be the least of their worries.

"After you, sir," said Morrow, holding the door open for his superior.

"Thank you. Now, let's get to it. What's got you so worried?"

"If you don't mind, sir, I'd like to give you the good news first?"

"By all means, Private," Haywood replied, seating himself before the monitor.

Morrow clicked on the tab bar and pulled up the first drone footage. Once again, Haywood came close to making the sign of the cross as the scene played out. The suburbs to the east of London were awash with the undead. They filled every street, every alley, every garden. Thousands, tens of thousands. No, millions. *We've got to fight that,* thought Haywood. Onwards they shuffled, shoulder to shoulder. Spared the gorier details by the altitude of the Watchkeeper, still the sight of so many zombies chilled him to the bone.

"This is the good news?" asked Haywood incredulously.

"It is, sir," replied Morrow. Seeing the growing scowl on the face of his superior, he quickly continued. "You can't see it, but they've slowed down. I think the winter is actually working in our favour, sir."

"Is that so?" Haywood peered closer, but was unable to differentiate the pace from the last time he had been briefed.

"It is. By my calculations, it gives us at least another eight to ten days before they hit the wall, possibly a fortnight. Provided the temperature stays at freezing or just above."

"Let's hope that it does," Haywood replied, offering a rare smile. "This *is* really good news, Private. It gives us a chance to reach the stranded forces without being rushed. Who knows what troubles we'll run into on the roads north."

"That was my thought, sir," said Morrow, bringing up four individual, smaller tabs.

"What's this?"

"Just a small sample of the survivor groups I've found. Once I extended my grid pattern, they just kept popping up," Morrow explained, smiling at the look on the captain's face.

"That's far more than we ever expected. A hell of a lot more," he replied, counting the tiny fires burning or the heat signatures present in the fortified buildings.

"I think once this gets out it'll fire up the troops like crazy."

"Slow down, Private. This is still on a need to know basis until the admiral says otherwise, understood?"

"Yes, sir," said Morrow, the cheer disappearing from his face.

Haywood quickly stood and held him by the shoulder. "Son, I understand your excitement. I share it too. But we need to be careful. The enemy is millions strong and only growing stronger. We're going to have to make some tough choices in the months to come about who we can reach, and who we would *want* to reach. Knowing what we know, some of those groups aren't going to be the friendly type, if you know what I mean. If word gets out that there are hundreds, if not thousands of survivors out there, what's to stop the soldiers leaving in the hope of finding their loved ones?"

Morrow couldn't hold the words back as they poured out. "Shouldn't they have that choice, sir? Shouldn't *I* have that choice?"

Haywood could see the turmoil on the young man's face at the insubordination. Opting to show patience instead of anger, he replied, "In other circumstances, yes. But not as things stand right now. Those people don't know what's headed their way."

"Isn't that reason enough to try and reach them, though, sir?" Morrow was becoming more aggrieved with each passing second.

"I'll think on that, but all we can do is give them warning. We can't stretch our forces that thin. Think about it," Haywood said, holding him firmly. "If we give them five soldiers each, what good would that do against what's coming?"

"... Nothing," Morrow accepted, glumly.

"However, imagine what can be achieved once we've secured the forces in the mountains and got them home safe. Imagine what we can do to help them once we've retaken Portsmouth and brought our warships home. We'd finally have a real shot at taking back our country."

"I know, sir."

There was no enthusiasm in Morrow. After his previous exuberance, the excitement was gone. "What is it, Private?"

Leaning towards the computer, a shaking hand pulled up the final recording timestamped two hours in the past.

"Dear God," groaned Haywood, slumping into the vacant chair.

The unmistakeable sight of the Channel Tunnel was rendered in ultra-high definition on the screen. Like severed arteries, the twin train lines and shattered service passage bled. Instead of a crimson torrent, a weakly flowing grey ooze poured forth. From a height of ten thousand feet, the Watchkeeper zoomed in on the open mouths below. The full horror of the scene became clear.

"Is that what I think it is?"

Morrow nodded dumbly. "We've got a few visitors from Europe."

Haywood clasped him by the arm. "How many?"

"Just watch, sir," Morrow whispered.

The operator pulled the view back, exposing the wider area of Folkestone. Hundreds of thousands were already through, filling the town with shambling rot. A small compound located on a patch of parkland was already under siege. Suddenly, the video cut away to a view of the open ocean below.

"What happened? Why did it skip?"

"You don't need to see that, sir. They couldn't possibly fight that many..."

"Oh, I see," Haywood replied, sadly. Another hundred enemies were beginning the slow march westward. If enough of them was left to walk.

"This is what waits on the other side of The Channel."

Calais was always a favoured spot for illegal immigrants to wait, hoping for a spot in a lorry or chancing the dangerous lines themselves. Now it was filled with the dead, waiting patiently at the arterial bottleneck of the French tunnels. The drone flew slowly in a south easterly direction towards Paris. It was close to a mile before the tightly pressed throng tapered off, giving way to the arriving stragglers.

"So many..." muttered Haywood.

"And we thought London was going to give us trouble," added Morrow.

"I've got to get on the radio to Dauntless. The Admiral needs updating."

"Can they blow the tunnels?"

"I just don't know, Private," Haywood replied, standing up and heading towards the door. "I want all of your data in a report I can send to the admiral in thirty minutes."

"Aye, sir."

Haywood left the drone operator to his thoughts. As the long corridor stretched out before the captain, he had his own. *Is this a test? Is God really so angry with us He'd wipe out His own creation?* Judging by the millions of gathered zombies eager to traverse the tunnels, it looked likely. Picturing the carefully nurtured view of the bearded benevolent deity, the smile hidden within the white beard disappeared. The warm eyes hardened. Blue skies darkened in the Heavens as God's wrathful nature took hold. It was Noah all over again. Except the rising water was replaced with a flood of flesh-eating corpses.

"We're fucked," whispered Haywood, giving in to despair.

CHAPTER 44

Mike was blind. The hood was thick enough to shut out nearly all light, and was tied firmly at his neck. Infrequent slivers of light carried from the sun through the tight cross stitch. He sucked in great gulps of air, trying to bring fresh oxygen through the itchy burlap covering. The carbon dioxide in his hood was at dangerous levels, and it was all he could do to stay upright as the dizziness took him.

For most of the journey, he'd allowed himself to be led like a small child. At the outset, a fall had rebroken his already headbutt damaged nose, and he didn't want to repeat the accident. Craig had quickly passed the stage of fear, and fought with the Gypsies most of the way. With hands bound, and ankles trussed to allow only small steps, his efforts caused more damage to himself than the gloating men around them. Still, he fought, refusing to be cowed. Each time Mike heard a thump or the crash as his brother was knocked to the ground, his confidence trickled away. They were blood, but Mike felt alien to his brother's insane bravery, as if he was born a different species. On one occasion, he had tried to help Craig, earning a gentle jab to

295

the face. That half-hearted blow to his nose crushed every last drop of resistance as surely as the weak bone and cartilage beneath his bloodied beak.

"Mrs Hampton has got such sights to show you," mocked one of their captors.

The Gypsies roared with laughter.

"What's that from, Lennie?"

"*Hellraiser*, John. Good film."

"I remember that one. It's got the geezer with all the nails in his head."

"Pins," replied the one they called Lennie.

"Yeah, that's what I meant. I wonder if Mrs Hampton will stick pins in their heads?" John gloated.

"It'll be much worse than that," Lennie replied, darkly.

"Fuck you, you dirty cunts!" Craig yelled, launching himself at the voices again. Wherever he had aimed, it was off, and he slammed into the frosty ground. "I'll kill all of you!"

"Get up, you prick," snapped John.

"The killing's only going one way, my son," said Lennie, leading them onwards.

"We didn't do anything to you," said Mike. As the words came out, he detested the whimpering quality in his voice. He coughed to clear the whine. "Let us go. We can be allies."

"All your people are dead, sunshine," growled John. "We don't need a couple of nobodies to help us."

"We aren't nobodies!" cried Craig. Heavy hands stopped the inevitably futile attack.

"We aren't," Mike repeated, the whine returning.

"I suggest you save your energy for Mrs Hampton. You know how she loves entertaining guests," warned Lennie.

"She's saving her best for your friends, Hombre and Matt. Where are they?" asked John.

"Hopefully, they're working on a plan to kill you all," Craig replied.

"Not with his leg all shot up, Matt won't be."

"He won't have gotten far, that's for sure. As for Hombre, one of our scouts will find him."

"Then take your anger out on them! We didn't do anything to your people."

"Mikey, Mikey, Mikey," Lennie chided, rapping on his skull with each word. "Shit rolls uphill, my son. The buck stops with the management, not the poor fuckers on the shop floor."

Mike came close to blurting out a denial of his connection to the leadership. The words died on his lips as he realised the only thing left in the world was his brother. Did he really want to go out completely alone after throwing Craig under the proverbial bus?

No.

"If that's the case, let Craig go. I was the one that ordered the attack on Claire's sons."

"Craig's the top dog, Mikey. We know all about you. Well, not *you*, exactly, we know fuck all about you. I'm talking about Craigy back there. The Big C. King of the Wings. A couple of the boys did short time at Ford and said he was a wanker then. Doesn't look like much has changed."

"I ran the wings from outside," Mike declared, trying to sound convincing. "I'm the only one smart enough to not get banged up. He followed my orders."

"Your brother beat a man to death, and I can respect that. I think you're telling porkies about being the hidden partner, though. It sounds like a case of self-sacrifice to me. What do you think, lads?"

Menacing chuckles agreed with the analysis.

Lennie's arm landed across Mike's shoulders. "And I can respect that too, Mikey. But we are way past deals and talking. *Way* past."

"Then just kill us and get it over with," Mike croaked.

"All in good time, my son. Anyway, we're here."

A shrill whistle pierced the chill afternoon. Following a period of metal rattling against metal, they were forced forward over an uneven, rickety surface. What followed was a hellish trip of shouting, cursing, and unseen blows from adults and children alike. After thirty seconds, Mike collapsed, the combination of pain and lack of oxygen causing him to black out.

———

"Mike. Craig. Thank you for joining me," said a gentle female voice.

Mike tried to sit up, only to find he was secured to something. The individual layers of straps went all the way from ankle to the top of his chest, and both arms were tied securely to the cold steel frame at his side. As the hood was whipped off, he looked left and right at what appeared to be a hospital bed. An intravenous line was already in his arm, making him woozy on top of the recent unconsciousness. Craig was similarly bound to his left, totally unconscious. Another man lay to his right, but the straps only started at his thighs. There were no need for ankle straps as the lower portions of his leg were missing. Spots of fresh blood marred the recently changed dressing.

"I worried that my boy would go hungry through all this," said Mrs Hampton from the shadows. "But it looks like I don't have to concern myself anymore."

Stepping in to the light, she led something by a leash. Something dead. Something that still moved. Something that gnawed gratefully on a severed limb.

Everything started to go dark. The last thing his mind registered was the insane grin and trail of spittle on the crazed face of his amputee bed fellow. Mike fainted again, but the welcoming void only provided a temporary surcease from the hideous fate that awaited.

THE END

CHECK OUT THE OMP WEBSITE FOR
A COMPLETE LIST OF OUR TITLES

WWW.OPTIMUSMAXIMUSPUBLISHING.COM

BOOKS ARE AVAILABLE IN BOTH PRINT
AND ELECTRONIC FORMATS

BALLYMOOR, IRELAND, 1891

Patrick Conroy, a young American student of medicine in Dublin, decides to take a break from the hustle and bustle of the big city and spend a month in the quietude of the wild and beautiful Glencree valley, County Wicklow. However, surrounded by local legends and myths, he is soon dragged into an ancient mystery that has haunted the village of Ballymoor for centuries. Set on the background of the tumultuous years preceding the War of Independence, and colored by Irish folklore, the Haunter of the Moor is a ghost story written in the style of Victorian Gothic novels.

A modern dark urban fantasy, telling of two powerful families who uphold a secret duty to protect humanity from a threat it doesn't know exists.

Though sharing a common enemy, the two families form a long-standing rivalry due to their methods and ultimate goals.

Forces are coalescing in a prominent Central European city criminal sex-trafficking, a serial murderer with a savage bent, and other, less tangible influences.

Within a prestigious, private university, Lilja, a young librarian charged with protecting a very special book, finds herself suddenly ensconced in this dark, strange world. Originally from Finland, she has her own reason for why she left her home, but she finds the city to be anything but a haven from dangers and secrets.

Book One in a planned series.

Two hunters pursue the same prey.

Fate has forged the slayer, Trey Thomas and the Sandrian vampire, Adalius, two natural enemies, into an uneasy alliance against an evil more powerful than either have ever faced. Only together do they stand a chance of defeating Anna; if they don't destroy each other first.

As they pursue Anna, the apprehensive Lycan watch as a confrontation looms on the horizon between vampires, the New Bloods and the Old Guard, which threatens to plunge the vampire world into civil war and trigger an all-out supernatural conflict which in the end could destroy them all.

Killing is the sole province of the religious fanatics, an axiom as true today as it was some five hundred years ago; and no nation, region or person is immune.

Europe had clawed its way out of the Middle Ages with the dawning of the renaissance, only to be plunged once more into darkness, as the dogs of war circled to destroy its resurgence during the 16th century. The Islamic successor to the Roman Byzantines, the Ottoman Caliphate, flexed its muscles to conquer much of Western Asia, North Africa and South-Eastern Europe. Christian Europe shuddered when the once invincible bastion of the Knight's at Rhodes were defeated; and now trembled as the Ottoman army rattled the very gates of Vienna. No Christian army, it seemed, could withstand the ferocity of the Azabs, the Akıncı, the Sipahis, the Janissaries, and ruthless Iayalar's of the all-conquering Islamic hordes.

This then is the cauldron into which Gideon de Boyne is unwittingly thrust with his small army of dedicated Christian warriors. On the hostile island of Crete, at the doorstep of the Ottoman Empire, Gideon must face not only the overwhelming force of Muslim warriors but his own inner conflicts of the futility of war and his very Christian beliefs.

Will he succeed and come out of it unscathed?

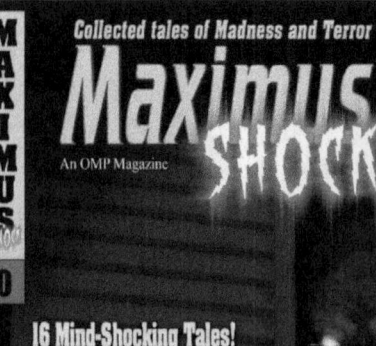